MICHAEL DOWNING'S

A Narrow Time

"I see now that the surest means of securing one's own happiness is to avoid introspection. Knowing myself has produced little in the way of comfort and joy for me or for those few people who, by reason of relation, had reason to believe in me. By way of defense, let me say that I did not set out to expose myself to anyone. But accidents do happen."

A
NARROW
TIME

A
NARROW
TIME

Michael Downing

Vintage Contemporaries

VINTAGE BOOKS · A DIVISION OF RANDOM HOUSE · NEW YORK

A Vintage Contemporaries Original, November 1987
First Edition

LIBRARY OF CONGRESS CATALOGING-IN-PUBLICATION DATA
Downing, Michael.
A narrow time.
(Vintage contemporaries)
I. Title.
PS3554.O9346N3 1987   813'.54   87-40073
ISBN 0-394-75568-5 (pbk.)

Author photograph © 1987 by Peter Bryant

Designed by Ann Gold

Manufactured in the United States of America
10 9 8 7 6 5 4 3 2 1

To Mary Ann Matthews,
for seeing through

We waited while She passed—
It was a narrow time—
Too jostled were Our Souls to speak
At length the notice came.

—Emily Dickinson

A
NARROW
TIME

AN
ARTICLE
OF FAITH

I SEE NOW THAT the surest means of securing one's own happiness is to avoid introspection. Knowing myself has produced little in the way of comfort and joy for me or for those few people who, by reason of relation, had cause to believe in me. By way of defense, let me say that I did not set out to expose myself to anyone. But accidents do happen.

DOCUMENTATION

| I |

I AM ONE OF those people who have no sense of direction. After more than ten years of driving the well-marked streets of Fairfield County in Connecticut, I rely on memorized routes to the supermarket, the bank, the school, friends' homes. The few long trips I've made without my husband, Ted, required maps and diagrams and detailed notes describing the point at which a right or left turn or a highway exit or entrance has to be negotiated. And, of course, landmarks or signs that prove I've overshot my mark or overlooked a relevant fork in the road.

The route to my parents' home in Braintree, Massachusetts, should have been an exception. During the year before I married Ted Fossicker I made no less than two dozen trips from the old house that was still my home to the modern, split-level Ted had built for himself on a hill in Fairfield County. But I was always on a bus, frequently pretending that I was aboard a huge ship bound for England. There I would meet Ted before he married the beautiful, rich woman who left him exactly one year after their wedding. Or I was speeding through the desolate

4

outback of Australia to rescue Ted from the lonely wood-frame house in which he sat alone after receiving the news that both his missionary parents had been killed when their milk-truck chapel veered off a small cliff. (This scenario would allow me to interrupt Ted's life in advance of his education in England and his ill-fated first marriage.)

Even as we made what I figured would be our last family trip to Braintree, I made no attempt to keep abreast of our progress. Ted had guaranteed that I'd arrive in time to spend a few hours with my parents before they set off for retirement in Phoenix, Arizona. He'd roused the entire family at five-thirty, yelling "Happy Fourth of July" several times, prodded me into making a Thermos of coffee, and cajoled Paul and Patricia with a box of chocolate doughnuts. Sarah, as always, needed nothing more than her doll that shed realistic tears and a promise of being let alone in the backseat of the station wagon.

The early hour left Ted and me in a sort of stunned silence, though we were also eavesdropping on our children. Patricia seized these hours with her captive younger brother to explain the social demands on a seventh-grader whose sister was a freshman in high school. "You know how we walk together after school? That's gonna change in the fall, okay? Or like when there's a game at the Boys' Club and Mom says we can go?"

"I know already." Paul had caught on after a few dozen examples. "I go with my own friends in the fall."

Seriously, even gravely, Patricia added, "If you're allowed to go. I'm talking about high school games."

Finally Ted interrupted Patricia's discourse. "We're really early. What time did you tell them we'd get there, Anne?"

"I told them nine-thirty, but we can be early. It's after eight. They'll be up. Where are we?"

Patricia stuck her head between the front seats. "You said we could go see the building. Dad? Remember?"

"Why do you think we got off the turnpike already? That's where we're headed. Promise." Ted did not turn and explain this to me, even after what I considered a long pause.

"Ted? Could you let me in on this little side trip? Where are we, anyway? Let's just get to Braintree for now." I could see my parents waiting impatiently in the house, deciding to give the Fossickers ten more minutes before they left. "Are we even in Massachusetts?"

Ted laughed. "Where have you been? We're about ten miles from your house. We could walk and still make it."

"I'd rather just drive."

Patricia's head re-emerged between us. "You promised."

Ted was as amused by Patricia's insistence as he was by my annoyance.

Still smiling, he looked at me. "You absolutely refuse to ask now, right? About the side trip. You're betting that if you just sit there I'm going to forget the whole—"

Classic Ted. Reading me aloud. Despite myself, I smiled. "You win. I'm reduced. Where is it you were hoping to take us instead of just getting us to Braintree three and a half minutes ahead of schedule? Maybe we could take in a movie or our first trip to the beach for 1984. Really. I'm absolutely open to suggestions."

"Patricia wanted to see the office building I put up."

Patricia added, "Where you met." As if I might not make the connection.

Confused, but anxious for any sort of diversion, Paul said, "You met Dad at an office? I thought you guys met at a restaurant."

Knowingly, Patricia corrected her brother. "It was a bar."

Virtually lost, Paul said, "You're taking us to a bar?"

Family history. I intervened on Paul's behalf. "I met your dad at a restaurant. With some friends of mine. We were going to have dinner."

Ted said, "They were all in the bar. I dragged your mother away to have dinner with me—"

"No, but where are we going now?" Paul was having a truly rough morning. "Where are we going is all I asked."

I burst into laughter. "The office building is where. Paul,

listen. I met your dad while he was overseeing this project in Quincy. It was his company's first project outside Connecticut. He built this office building. One night he was out having dinner and he asked me to join him."

Perfectly serious, Paul asked, "So why are we going to the office building now?"

"Oh, Paul." Patricia could see that she had much to teach her brother. "Can't you see? It's a landmark."

| II |

The Midtown Pediatric Professional Building was an unassuming landmark. Ted directed the car into the empty parking lot, but none of us was moved to get out and make a closer inspection. The concrete-and-glass structure was plain, its lack of ornament its principal strength.

Proudly, Paul said, "It's the best building around here."

Ted smiled appreciatively.

In fact, it was the best building in sight. It even seemed elegant compared to the squat glass cubes and oddly asymmetrical complexes that formed the adjacent office space. "Do you still like it, Ted?"

"Only for sentimental reasons. I can't even see the building, really. I just remember coming back to the foundation the morning after we met and knowing I was in love and feeling stupid and really happy. Really happy."

This display mesmerized Paul and Patricia. To add to their astonishment, I put one arm on his shoulder, leaned over, and kissed him. "You're the greatest. No kidding."

Paul was exasperated. "So that's why they stopped here."

| III |

As we pulled out of the parking lot, Paul said, "I think Sarah is awake, Mom."

"Let her be for now, Paul." Ted looked at his watch and turned to me. "Right on time."

"I truly haven't let myself think about what this is going to be like. I mean, them leaving. Carol taking over the house. Taking on the house? Whatever. I can't imagine how she can afford to run a house on a teacher's salary. Not to say why that house, of all houses." I stopped talking in the hope that Ted would offer some advice or strategy for the event. But he seemed to be interested only in listening to me. "I never get an answer from anyone about why they're going to Phoenix. Florida is one thing."

"Well, I suppose Phoenix is another."

This was a cue from Ted; he was not even listening, really. He was letting me be, letting me go at it with myself. It was a familiar pose. He laid no claim on the Johnson family, my clan.

From the first, Ted declined admission to that life. He would listen to me rant and rave about their objections to his status as a divorcé, their misgivings about his odd, zealous missionary parents. But he never attacked them or their ridiculous judgments of him. Only on two occasions did he even have a memorable reaction. The first was when I informed him during one of my covert visits to Connecticut that my mother had warned me about "fooling around with that playboy." He was absolutely thrilled to have assumed such unlikely proportions. And for a few weeks he signed the notes he sent, SCANDALOUSLY YOURS. The other instance came much later, after I'd told my parents that I was going to marry Ted in a Unitarian chapel in Connecticut without the assistance of a Catholic priest. I tearfully related to him that neither of my parents was going to come to my wedding, which also ruled out the possibility that my brother Richard and my sisters Carol and Theresa would attend.

"I wouldn't say this if I wasn't so sure. I mean, I know this. A fact. I know this is a fact. If you show up to marry me, so will your parents. I guarantee it. Not that they'll cry and smile

and think I'm swell. They'll come. Not coming would be surrendering."

I not only didn't believe him, I actually resented his thinking
that he could outguess them all. But I also used his prediction
as a kind of crowbar to leverage myself out of Braintree, to pry
myself free from the threat of being abandoned by my family.
And, three days before the wedding, my mother said, "We love
you too much not to at least stand by you."

Almost fifteen years later, when my parents told me they
were leaving home, I had to strangle my urge to beg them not
to go. Because I loved them? I only knew that for better and
for worse they belonged in Braintree, at home.

| IV |

My parents greeted us on their front porch. They'd been keeping
watch over their car and the little trailer attached to it. Their
embraces, the few words they uttered, even the way my mother
held the screen door open and let everyone pass by her, seemed
intentional, planned. I helped Sarah, who was still not fully
awake, by leading her into the living room.

From behind us, my mother said, "Maybe the children would
like some juice and doughnuts. They could have a little breakfast
in here."

Which explained the small china plates and the napkins carefully folded on the low coffee table. But it did not quite explain
the weirdly placid atmosphere. It was evident from just passing
through the living room that the house had been meticulously
cleaned, painstakingly arranged. There seemed to be an abun-
dance of framed pictures, porcelain statues, neat stacks of magazines and books.

Uncomfortable, my children sat in oversized chairs, retreating
from the oddity of this event.

As if she were speaking to perfect strangers, my mother said,
"I'll give some food to your father for you." I followed her to
the kitchen. "Theresa and the children were here Saturday, and

for dinner last night. But the boys had a baseball game today. Too bad."

"Is Richard coming?" I hoped that an untimely disaster in Richard's life might account for the almost mournful atmosphere.

"Richard was here for dinner too. Last night. We said goodbye then. He is still out of work. God bless him, he does have a knack for losing jobs."

When I made it to the kitchen, my sister Carol said, "Speak of the devil," pushed her way by Ted, hugged me. "Nice to see you, stranger. You're looking well. You must not be working too hard editing all that high-tech hooha."

Reflexively I registered that Carol had put on her blue jeans and one of her oldest sweatshirts to mark the auspicious occasion. "I hope you didn't get dressed up just for us." I smiled. "How are you?"

"I've almost got this running." She returned to the dishwasher she was installing next to the sink. She looked at me blankly, as if to call for peace. "Without Mom here I'll have to deal with the dishes."

Preferring to fuel the tension, my mother said, "It's about time. Ted? This is for the children." In one breath. Then she added, "I told you they'd all get here on time this time, Carol." For good measure?

Carol turned back to her task under the sink. Only then did I notice that my father was leaning against the refrigerator, staring at a beer in his hand, looking confused about how it had got there. Ted left for the living room with a tray of pastries and juice. As if on cue, my father snapped open his beer.

Looking at me as she sat at the kitchen table, my mother said, "It is not even ten o'clock. Not even."

Sucking at the foam on the top of the can, my father walked past me. "Oh, Eleanor, it's a holiday."

After we heard him close the screen door, my mother said, "Every day is a holiday since he retired."

I took the chair opposite hers. Carol whispered, "For God's sake, it's just a beer."

Before my mother could respond, we all heard Paul yell, "I don't mean that, Dad. But it's like a museum in here."

I stood and went to the electric percolator, as if I might die if I didn't immediately have a cup of coffee. I couldn't look at my mother or my sister. "I thought the house would be empty. I guess I imagined you would be taking the furniture. I mean, not that you should. I know the place in Phoenix is furnished, right? I guess it must be a joy, really, to have it all be new. How far are you hoping to drive today?" I forced myself to sip hot coffee, to shut myself up.

"We're in no particular rush. We have some options, depending on how we feel."

My mother sounded ancient, spent. I offered to pour her coffee, to get her some juice. I wanted to hand her something solid, a prop, to make her seem less ghostly.

"I imagine it will be nice to see some of the country anyway. We've never spent any time driving outside of New England. Mostly to the Cape or to your house. Of course, the car doesn't have air conditioning." My mother was still thinking about that museum crack.

I joined her at the table. "Come on, you must be excited. I mean, the whole thing is kind of an adventure."

"It's just two people retiring. It happens all the time. I mean, if Carol quit her job to run off with a young man or if you found yourself all alone, somewhere new, that would be an adventure." My mother said so as if she believed it.

"Those are disasters you're describing." Carol loves to teach math. I love Ted. How many times do we have to tell you? "I don't know about you, Carol. But I don't have any last-minute announcements."

But Carol was too angry to answer. "I'm going out to see if Dad needs any help with the trailer."

"She has her friends coming over to dinner tonight." This constituted a desecration.

More for pity's sake than out of loyalty to Carol, I said, "Good for her." I did not want to exchange terrible truths about Carol with my mother.

Ignoring my cue, my mother continued. "I think Carol gets defensive about you not visiting more often, especially since you knew we were leaving. For good, I mean."

"Yeah, well, Carol doesn't have a family." It was a simple concession to my mother, like paying homage.

My mother yawned. "I haven't even been drinking." She looked at me, expectantly.

Was I supposed to say something about my father's drinking? Confused, I smiled.

Impatient with my dullness, she looked at her watch. "I don't know what made me think we should wait until noon to leave. You know, you get a plan into your head and it sticks. I mean, what's to wait for now?"

I'm here. I came here, as arranged, right?

She stood. "I guess we just always like to delay the inevitable. That's what I felt like all week. I kept getting this or that in order, as if it mattered how we left things. That's what none of you understands. We were always holding on to everything, your father and I. Holding on to it all so you could all enjoy it. You have no idea what it was like for us when that ridiculous hospital tried to bully us out of this house. Do you have any idea how it was for your father? They were offering twice the market value. Twice. One by one we watched the neighbors cave in. You have no idea. After all we'd done to get here they were just going to throw us out? That was an adventure. You don't remember it, but that was an adventure for you, I'll tell you that." She was pacing now, moving out of my range. "Not only that, but the lies. The Higgins family? The Belcores? They promised not to sell. A week later we are the only ones with the guts to stay. Do you understand that they literally tore down a whole neighborhood? To build a parking lot? For a hospital that to this very day has never needed half the parking spaces?"

I recall perfectly the horror of my parents' refusal, Carol and I crying as my father responded to our begging with a single phrase: "I will not be moved." And I could still see my mother carrying the hundreds of pickets delivered by the hospital so that we could have a fence and at least the semblance of privacy. One by one she took the pointed white boards from the pile on our grass border of a yard, carried each one to the center of the parking lot, and threw it so the echo of it scraping could be heard as she returned for the next. Astonished, Carol and I huddled in the kitchen, vowing never to return to school, knowing that we would not be allowed to hide. We were not even allowed the dignity of a fence. As my mother said that night, when she told my father what she had done, "Do they think we're peasants? That they can just pretend they didn't destroy our property?"

My mother was staring out the window over the sink. "Come here. Come on, take a look. There are, what? Two dozen cars? With space for two thousand."

I couldn't bear to join her at the window. Me, of all people. The first deserter. Richard's short marriage had never kept him away from the old house for more than a few days at a time. Once Theresa's husband left for his death in Vietnam she became a daily visitor. And Carol had outdone them both. She'd vowed to go down with the ship. As if that might make sense of the Johnsons' refusal to be moved.

"I can't tell you what it was like for me after all that, sweetheart." My mother looked at me as she said so. The fact that I had lived through this same episode did not register. Perhaps it never had. "I don't know if all that makes it harder or easier to leave now. I really and truly don't know which it is. Maybe I'll never know." She headed for the back door, leaving me without another word.

| V |

Within fifteen minutes, Ted and I and the children were standing on the porch with Carol. My mother and father were seatbelted into their beige sedan. Sarah was already waving, sensing that it was called for. Seeing Sarah wave goodbye reminded me that I had not given my mother the letter I'd written over the course of two months of fitful starts and endless dissatisfaction.

"Wait. Hold it!" I ran to their car with my purse.

My mother looked at me as if she were annoyed that I'd interrupted the parade. Then she smiled. "We didn't forget something, did we?"

I couldn't make myself give her the letter. It was as simple as that. I was standing in the middle of a parking lot, the yard of the home that I had been forbidden to abandon for a divorced playboy. This was the end of the story? They get to leave feeling noble, but the price of my leaving is unchanged? They get to leave, and Carol gets marooned in this ridiculous island of a house?

My mother laughed, uncomfortable under my silent scrutiny. "Are you coming with us?"

I looked at the envelope, pulled the letter out, and stuffed it into the bottom of my purse. I handed her the envelope and the check I'd enclosed. "I forgot to give you this."

Gracelessly, my mother pulled the check from the envelope, then folded it and put it in the glove compartment. "You shouldn't have done that. You're always too quick with your money. We don't need your money, Anne."

"It's just a gift. One for the road." I blew a kiss and backed up to the porch stairs.

They drove past us, slowly made their way out of sight, as if they were just any two people in the world in a car heading west. They were gone, implausible as that seemed.

After several awkward silent minutes passed, it was obvious that no one could make sense of their leaving. Carol and I exchanged vows to stay in touch. She wrapped the uneaten pastries for the kids. I kept glancing at the point in the road where I'd lost sight of the puny caravan. For a sign? Or still convinced that they were bound to come back home?

| VI |

Hours after all three children were again asleep at home I told Ted about not delivering the letter. I actually confessed this sin of omission.

"The letter that took you a month to write?" Ted had been all but asleep before I sat next to him on our bed. "On purpose didn't give it to them?"

"I couldn't." I handed him the letter, watched him quickly read it.

Dear Mom and Dad—

How your love does shine on me. How time past and present comes together now. I remember your tears when I started college, your advice and guidance as I prepared to marry Ted, and now I am just grateful I have this opportunity to cheer you both on as you move together into the future you've both earned.

Dad, you always told me not to be too sentimental. Mom, you always told me to believe in my dreams. Well, here's to you, Dad. You don't need the details of my love and respect for you. You know I treasure being the daughter of you, My Man. And, Mom, you're on the right road. Again. You'll have a whole pack of new friends within a week and you'll always have a home here in the Connecticut wilderness—in a house run according to your own rules and wisdom, I hope!

I won't wish you happiness and peace. I'll just thank you for sharing those gifts with me so I have something of real value to give to my own children. I'll always need you both and love the life you gave me.

Happy trails!
Anne

Ted looked at me, trying to get a fix on what I expected him to say. "In my opinion? They would love to get this letter. It's a letter they would like to think of you writing."

"Nothing in it strikes you as sort of funny?"

Ted handed me the letter. "See, I didn't hear you explain the rules here, Anne. I'm supposed to guess what exactly?"

"For God's sake, Ted. It's a complete lie. What is this?" I wagged the letter, disowning it. "Happiness? My father? Peace? The only peaceful minutes in Mother's life were when she got some condition so that she had to go to the Lahey Clinic. What is this?"

"It's overstated, fine. Or is it understated? The wedding business, for instance. So why did you write it, then?" Ted's interest in the answer to this question was tenuous, at best.

I folded the letter. "To prove I could, I suppose."

He shook his head. "Like committing the perfect crime." He smiled. "Did I pass? Can I sleep for a while before the next round of questions?"

"Good night, Ted. Go to sleep."

"Thank you, Anne."

Though I could not imagine ever mailing the letter, I suspected my reaction to it was out of proportion. Characteristically, I compromised between the extremes of destroying it and sending it. I put it in a linen closet, under a pile of sheets. I figured I would think about it later.

UNVEILINGS

| I |

THE FOSSICKER family was at its most impressive throughout the middle and late summer. Each member gave him or herself over to a personal endeavor with energy that mimicked professionalism of the highest order. Of course Ted was a bona fide professional, available to his several project managers spread out across New England at the height of the construction season. He traveled almost daily from one site to another, communicating with me solely by telephone for a month. Patricia had won early promotion at Camp Whitawet and was serving a stint on the Connecticut seashore as a junior counselor in training. She was still subject to the rules governing campers, which restricted telephone calls to the weekends—a policy designed to guarantee that sponsoring parents got their money's worth for their children's overnight camping experience. Paul, only eleven, had earned a spot at the state university's sports camp for children. He caught a bus just before eight in the morning and returned at six, six days a week; quite uncharacteristically, he allowed his fantasy life to spill over into dinner conversations during the four weeks of training. He uttered complaints about the disadvantage of playing on the road so often and repeatedly offered his autograph to his younger sister and her friends.

I was gearing up for the fall. Having completed one year of part-time staff work at *Aerohead* magazine, the company monthly for a local aeronautics research and development laboratory, I accepted a promotion. I worked almost fifty hours a week. It had been prearranged that I would be on vacation for the month of August and begin as a full-time copyeditor on the very day that my youngest child, Sarah, entered first grade at St. Cecilia's.

Still, it was Sarah, not yet six years old, who outshone the other Fossickers. Before her taxing schedule of kindergarten and day care had run its course in June, she announced her intention to join the Girl Scouts as a Brownie. She sat me down at our kitchen table and spread before us the packet of information provided by Sister Clare, the able kindergarten teacher and brave volunteer leader of the local Brownie troop. The pitch of Sarah's earnestness reached its height when she turned to the uniform requirements, detailed in full-color photographs. "They make them in all kids' sizes, even the caps. And you sell things, like maybe some cookies, say, but you don't keep the money. You give the money away to somebody who needs it, say. They make you memorize and pray, I think. And you have to wear the clothes, even to school instead of the school uniforms on some days when Sister Clare sends a note home. Even the caps, you wear them in the school building. It starts in the summer but Sister says I could skip some meetings for going to Maine. Sister says in Maine there are even Brownies. Same clothes. And caps." All the while Sarah kept her thin blonde hair gathered in her hand at the back of her head, as if to demonstrate her fitness for the brown cap in the photograph.

I was appalled. I had reared a throwback. Like the reintroduction of ROTC on college campuses and the invention of the Moral Majority, the re-emergence of such sexist training grounds as the Brownies and Camp Fire Girls in schools seemed to me atavistic. Not ten years earlier, my eldest daughter, Patricia, had scorned such activities. She would play soccer, thank you, and run for student-body vice president. Onto the template of Patricia's raised consciousness I laid my postadolescent history of rebellion, sisterhood, and cynicism. Even at St. Cecilia's, the midseventies had given rise to classroom debates about the legitimacy of public funding for abortions. And Patricia was susceptible enough to my tirades, my coaching, to acquire at least a modicum of the feminism that—in theory, though hardly in practice—I fought to maintain.

It was sobering that this second daughter—whose face and mind and verbal agility and willfulness resembled my own to a degree not approached in the demeanor of her sister—had abandoned the cause before rational debate was even possible. And her mind was not for bending. Sarah loved regimentation, a feature of family life that was absent by design in the Fossicker household. Despite my discouragement, she was naturally inclined toward the cheapest form of glamour and glitz as presented in the plastic bodies of teenage dolls or overdressed women in church. Unlike her sister, Sarah expressed no interest whatsoever in the workings of her own body or in its apparent dissimilarity to the bodies of her father and brother; instead, she simply desired to "get a baby if a kid can get a baby."

All of this provided an endless source of amusement, and not least of all for Ted, who considered Sarah's girlish longings to be a sort of judgment on me. She was funny, in fact, often absolutely hilarious, as is any child with particular longings that circumvent both instinct and impulse and manifest themselves as palpable desires.

An impulse to join a Brownie troop can be dissuaded or subverted. But what lengths are justified in the disruption of a pure and almost holy desire to don a brown cap and learn to tie knots? This was Sarah's unwitting strength, of course. In a child, such a disproportion between desire and object is, at best, endearing; even at its worst, it is endurable. But from an adult, a violent and sustained attack on the Brownies is always ridiculous, ineluctably cruel, inevitably impossible.

| II |

Looking like a soldier of fortune, Sarah was slow to leave the house these summer mornings. Almost daily she invested me with the responsibility of attaching a ribbon or badge to her uniform sash, each earned by a display of virtue or skill. Her last act of the lengthy dressing ritual was inspection, which she performed in front of a full-length mirror conveniently adjacent to the front door; generally, her cap merited repositioning. Reassuringly she would look up at me and say, "I'll be back. Don't worry." It was not for me to respond; in an ancient midlength nightgown, my hair in a makeshift ponytail, I would wave, the good woman on the home front, already sure to be late to work.

One particularly frenetic morning found me still at home at nine-thirty. I called the *Aerohead* office and no one answered the phone; this prompted me to relax. Even if I did not arrive until ten-thirty my tardiness would not seem too egregious, relatively speaking.

These details recall themselves to me only because of the extraordinarily odd experience that followed. I moved to the living room in the front of the house with my coffee, coddling myself in the breeze through the open windows. Uninterestedly at first, I watched the progress of four men along the street. A small truck seemed to follow as they stopped at the end of each driveway for a few minutes, then passed on to the next.

As Ted built this house on a corner and on a small hill, I was able to witness the team of men and their progress from more than a quarter mile's distance. It was not clear what service they were providing or what aspect of the neighborhood property they were inspecting. Remembering the struggle with Paul the night before, which finally resulted in his placing two of his worn-out bicycles alongside the garbage cans, I wondered if perhaps a new private sanitation service had been contracted to collect on our street. Hoping that this would not mean that I could no longer rely on the twice-weekly collections, I wandered upstairs and began to dress. When I saw that the men had wended their way to our driveway, I watched with renewed excitement as they seized on the two bicycles and waved the truck closer. The two men loaded the bikes into the nearly full pickup. Two others carefully picked through our pails, occasionally evaluating a bottle or can. When one of the men looked toward the house, I jumped away from the window, pulled the blinds closed. To respect their privacy? To protect myself?

The following Thursday and Tuesday I posted myself in my bedroom just after Sarah left the house and followed the progress of the band of middle-aged men from one neighbor's garbage to the next. A station wagon had been added to the pickup, both vehicles drive by women. Wives? I had intentionally arranged our pails several yards from the curb. I wanted to see how far onto private property they would venture. Undeterred, the men walked across my lawn, scavenged, impecuniously rearranged the refuse and the containers, climbed into the truck and car, and drove away.

Initially I was fascinated. Though somewhat put off by the presence of female accomplices, I felt as if by watching I was involved in a dangerous flirtation with desperate, grabby men. But I also worried that I was ritually throwing away articles of value.

Ted was unimpressed by my descriptions of this new routine and attempted to convince me that the men had been contracted to provide a particular service—perhaps they were scrap-metal salvagers. I had assembled an inventory of the stolen goods, however, which dismissed this possibility. I demurred at his suggestion of speaking to neighbors; though I knew perfectly well that others were aware of the plundering, I also sensed that we had all adopted a pact of silence. If I went public with my story, wouldn't I risk attracting more scavengers?

After two weeks of intermittent reports, Ted made it clear that he was humiliated that grown men wanted his refuse. He took it as an indictment.

I was less willing to accept this obvious, material interpretation. I once laced my garbage with small items of enduring utility: a can opener, an extension cord, two children's books, a serving spoon. These items were removed by the men from the bottoms of brown paper bags filled with coffee grounds, wasted food, and newspapers. I was surprised and disappointed that these buried treasures, relatively speaking, were no more exultantly received than were old cereal boxes and odd bits of paper.

Finally, I stopped baiting and observing the men. In my memory, they are more prominent, more suggestive than they were even in my imaginative landscape of that summer. But I did not forget that they had been here. Weeks later I would think of the strange band. If I accidentally left the garage door open, would they plunder that stash? Would my presence in the yard have dissuaded them from trespassing? Seeing me, would they have given up on my neighborhood entirely? Would such men rob a house? Kidnap a child?

The questions ceased to interest me. As a sort of finale, before we left for vacation I waited for the men on a Thursday morning, but they did not appear. Ted was at home, having finished his Grand Tour of the Northeast. When I told him that the ritual was apparently ended, he asked, ever the good sport, if I had figured out what the men had been after.

"I tried," I said, filling my briefcase for work.

Ted laughed. "That's your way of saying you failed."

| III |

The first Saturday of August, a few hours before we began our annual trek north to Maine's Boothbay Harbor, I reluctantly opened the manila envelope addressed to me from my sister Carol. I knew from my weekly five-minute conversations with my mother that Carol had spent a week in the Phoenix suburb where my parents now resided, and I accurately guessed that the contents of Carol's missive would detail my parents' existence.

Naturally, the letter was a photocopy of an original sent out to cousins, aunts, and a few old friends. Carol was intent on assuming the role of the family archivist. Accompanying the letter, and numerically keyed to pertinent sentences, were some color photographs.

I would rather have lived with my imagination. The details provided by Carol fell short of the circumstance I had ascribed to my parents' retirement.

On the third floor of one of several white stucco buildings was the two-bedroom apartment in which Carol visited Mr. and Mrs. Johnson. Carol did not stay in the apartment because, as my mother had pointed out, sleeping on the couch would afford her little privacy. This was brought into sharp (intentional?) focus by Carol's pictures of the two bedrooms, referred to in the text as "Dad's room" and "Mother's room." The building was a multipurpose dwelling, with a large grocery store, laundromat, video shop, bookstore, and a small coffee shop. In its entirety, it was known as the Panamerican Complex. Though undetailed in Carol's letter, it appeared that the apartments had been the afterthought of an overzealous developer who had constructed six four-story white crescents on an isolated stretch of parched land. An official Panamerican postcard showed the complex in its fullness, all but my parents' building adorned with neon signs for commercial enterprises ranging from attorneys-at-law to a fitness spa.

Carol's only real news was announcing that my mother had been offered a job in the registration office of the Panamerican Complex, where she would screen the applications of retirees. Though it seemed she would be needed only a few days a week, a great many sentences were expended to detail the prominence into which this job would thrust our mother.

Seeking out the first available job after years of determined unemployment—only a few weeks after her husband had retired—raised questions about my mother's motives. I tried to ignore the implications. Carol reported that my father was looking forward to finding a partner for golf or tennis. Wittingly or no, Carol was simply transmitting my mother's lie. I knew that my father had never so much as held a golf club and that he considered tennis a game for sissies; Ted's love of tennis was a matter for distrust.

Before I stuffed the contents back into the envelope, I stared at the picture of the living room, trying to locate my father on the new sofa with its foamy floral cushions; I wondered if he ever snapped open a beer and mindlessly let drip a little foam on the wall-to-wall carpeting. I could only manage to place him at the large living-room window, staring out over the new air conditioner, surveying the flat, treeless desert beyond the parking lot, calmly trying to figure out exactly where in hell he was.

| IV |

Whenever Ted was asked to describe the house he'd built in Maine he would explain that it was "an impertinent hybrid, NASA rustic." In fact, it did look like a sci-fi space colony rendered in stone. The central stucco structure was a half circle; the arc was a wall of glass fronted by a large and uneven brick patio and faced the sea. The main room was huge—thirty by thirty—and housed a counter kitchen that could be closed off like a big closet and five old sofas of varying dimensions, each purchased at a local yard sale. A sofa per person was the great luxury of the vacation house. Like antennae, three protrusions from the backside of the living room formed the bedrooms. Each bedroom was essentially a large cube with windows, reached by walking through a ten-foot hallway, both sides of which were lined with closet space. Two large bathrooms were nestled between the center and the two outer bedrooms.

This house was Ted's proudest achievement. Characteristically, he was aware of its shortcomings and the objections that could be raised against it with impunity.

The house was designed without compromise, a feat Ted knew to be inappropriate in the real world. It was his testament to function over everything. His dubious triumph was unmistakable. Of course, Ted knew he had produced something so queer and pure as to provoke adulation or disgust from visitors, not to mention neighbors. He made a point of remembering people's initial reactions to the building. Often, to my shame, he would repeat my own, as a way of reassuring a newcomer that offense would not be taken. I had said: "Frankly, it is hideous. It doesn't move, for God's sake, does it?"

| V |

Like a child to a parent, I posed to myself one question every summer, without fail: Why can't we live like this forever? What few pat answers I invented were reliably sensible and never convincing.

As it did every year, our vacation officially began after we'd hastily unpacked suitcases, opened every door and window, assembled on the patio with the remains of the lunch and snacks packed into the car for distraction during the long ride north, and Ted had said, "This is living." Surreptitiously, each of us would pry off shoes or sandals. Ted lifting his arm to a button on his shirt was the signal to prepare to sprint. After much hesitation he yelled, "Last one in the water is a rotten egg." Stripping off clothes selected with this race in mind, trailing them behind us like debris along the steep path of soft sand until only bathing suits remained, we ran, screaming and laughing. Always, the water was cold beyond remembering. The long since arbitrated official rules required complete immersion of the body, which prevented the fastest from claiming victory. This was a test of mettle.

As the rotten egg, Patricia was responsible for retrieving the strewn clothing and returning to our private cove of a beach (appropriated, not legally demarcated) with towels for the braver contestants. The major disgrace this year, however, was losing to me, who, after two straight years of cowardice, had become the odds-on favorite to keep the title.

A number of arrival-day rituals had to be carried out before the long-awaited lapse into irresponsibility could begin. Ted and the two older children drove the three-quarters of a mile into town—an aggrandizement, really. At the confluence of three two-lane streets was the archetypal service station, post office, and general store. This was not merely an acquisitive adventure, however. At this point, the car was turned over to Nate Hellmond for its annual tune-up, after which it was stored until we undertook our return to civilization. This became a tradition as the result of a dare issued by Ted and had proved to be of service to our individual senses of remove. For Ted, it necessitated a daily walk of almost two miles to the sole public tennis court, where partners met season after season for endless matches and unsolicited criticism. Patricia and Paul had long since learned backwoods routes to homes of friends and the two local camps; they understood that requests for transportation were verboten and gladly acquiesced in light of the privilege they won in return. In Maine, their evening excursions were not cut short by preset limits but instead were governed by the length of the event they were attending. Almost without fail, an evening at a movie at one of the camps returned them sweating and exhausted; frightening each other with shadows and the distant rambling of an insomniac squirrel, they charged at full speed until within sight of the light of home. For Sarah and me, the absence of the automobile simply reinforced our pleasure at being away, unnoticed, unattached. Gregarious to a fault at school and in day care, Sarah was a determined loner on the beach, not above literally ignoring the greetings offered by adventurous children from the other houses in the hills above the water. Despite my empathy for her will to be alone, I had taken to questioning her motives. She offered little in the way of explanation and certainly did not feel compelled to excuse herself. Less intrepid than Ted or the other children, I realized that I provided a role model for her peaceful isolation. Until Ted joined me on the beach with his personal beach chair (the outdoor corollary to our old sofas; we each had a reserved seat on the beach), I was alone with the water and the sun and a book, mindful occasionally of Sarah's stillness at the water's edge, her feet slowly covered by sand brought in with the waves.

In fact, I did read a lot, but I probably spent as many hours watching Sarah, hoping not to interrupt whatever it was that held her there. Oh God, I do not hope even to approach an explanation for the complex of emotions and ideals she inspired in me with that odd, unknowing peace she contacted in the world. Her world.

I have yet to meet the mother who is more alert to the speciousness of a parent's praise of a child than am I. And yet— maybe like every mother—I ask you to believe that my daughter, this Sarah with her back to me on the beach, her solid body and limbs lit by the sun and reflected light from the endless water over which she kept watch, day in and day out, was in possession of an extraordinary sensibility. It was not her personality, it was something that was incomplete and unexercised for stretches of months at a time. It was not her way or her manner—nothing like the qualities by which all of us recognize each child as a unique, remarkable presence. Here it is, a bald and easily explained or dismissed assertion: I could see through Sarah. Not regardless of her; with her I could see what she saw. I never thought to quantify the experience of catching her in relaxed concentration and being drawn into the peace she had solicited in the water and the light. I still don't think of it as a mystery or a miracle that exists outside of nature. It is a facet of Sarah, a fact about a child.

| VI |

From a remove, it is obvious that a few simple routines sustained us in Maine. After Sarah went to bed and plans were made for a visit to one of the camps or a night of Monopoly or Scrabble, I would either roast a chicken or mix tuna fish for the next day's lunch. In the morning, the children were free to pour cereal, adorn it with any of the available berries, wash their dishes, and leave a note as to their expected whereabouts if Ted was already gone to town and I was not awake. Ted retrieved lunch from the refrigerator on his way back from town. Dinner was reliably composed of steak or fish and fresh corn and a salad. Once a week Ted sprang for lobsters, which the general store would secure from local fishermen at a price one might read with shock on a menu in Venice or Moscow. Ted cooked dinners on a rusty old little grill. It was but one of the patent romances that we observed, the one about men being more adept over a charcoal fire than women.

I was going to object, perhaps?

Rainy days were not exceptional. Ted fiddled with a window or a floorboard, rather slowly and casually. I often convinced Sarah to join me on the beach for kite-flying, usually a total failure. Paul and Patricia more often than not played cards, the radio tuned to as modern a station as was within reach on a cloudy day in Maine.

The radio was another romance to which we clung. I'd ruled out television and telephone from the start. As a result, Ted relied on his tennis partner's phone. He knew that installing one would defeat my purest resolves. The radio was admitted as an artifact, a reminder of a simpler, less-ferocious past. In truth, both Ted and I were too young to attach any personal sentiment to the television's nonphosphorescent precursor. Still, in light of its progeny, the radio seemed harmless and rather likable.

| VII |

Perhaps we were under the influence of the house's satellite design; Ted and I agreed that we felt elatedly alone every night. In celebration of this feeling, I guess, we never wore clothing in bed.

If such a thing as a sex life exists, the one Ted and I cultivated year-round surpassed whatever ideals I had conjured in my youth. This quality (even the quantity, frankly) was not altered by proximity to the sea. But I relished the chance to hang on to Ted, to move with him for hours, and then to walk to cool bricks on the patio, to be caught with him in a darkness that was permanently dispelled by the modern world at home. He would hold my back to his chest and we'd speculate on the proper names of star clusters or the status of the tides.

I know full well that I am an able cynic. I can identify the obverse, impure motive for the happiest of stories repeated by a friend or relative. I distrust children with dispositions of the variety hailed by teachers. But I am not an idiot. Held against the warm body of a strong man who loves me, distracted from a confused scan of the stars by the breathing of a man who wants nothing more than to hold me in the half-light of a night sky, I am guileless, faithful, a distillate of Anne, a child.

| VIII |

Remedies and wives' tales; I have passed them on with randomly selected physical traits and emotional propensities, hopefully, sacredly, thoughtlessly. As an antidote to feelings of loss, administer optimistic anticipation; I prescribed this remedy to my family as we prepared to leave Maine. I forced myself to swallow a few large dollops of the same bad medicine. Bravado or hope?

Comfort came as sloth. The Fossickers did not have to clean or wash anything left behind. A real estate agent who had rented the house to a local teacher for the off-season would ready the home for occupation and pester the tenant throughout the year to guarantee that the house was turned over to the owners in a condition so pristine that it should have been a source of humiliation to said owners. It was not. The proximity of godliness to cleanliness was one of the prescriptions that I did not pass on to my children. Where was the virtue in exacting labor from family members when an otherwise necessary partner (the agent) would provide the labor at no additional charge? I actually constructed such propositions during the first few years of my married life, thinking to make of each behavioral lesson a conscious choice. I gave up the formulations later, not surrendering the whole affair to chance, exactly, but trusting my own instincts, which I considered rational. Rational instincts: I trounced on hundreds of homespun truths to achieve this perfect oxymoron.

I think I hit a low point of self-respect when I cajoled Sarah— she was only about half an hour shy of hysteria when we were all finally in the car—by expounding on the adventures she would encounter as a first-grader Brownie. I knew the ineffable question that taunted her, and for which I had no adequate response: Why can't we live like this forever?

| IX |

School for the children and full-time employment for me began on the first Wednesday after Labor Day. The only real trauma for the Fossickers in the start of the new fiscal year focused on Sarah's attempts to memorize her schedule, which changed daily. Mondays and Wednesdays she would take the school bus home, where Patricia would act as paid babysitter. Tuesdays and Thursdays she would be bused to the Girls' Club for three hours of day care with eleven other first- and second-graders. Fridays, the St. Cecilia Brownie troop met and performed various heroic deeds. At last, I found an unused datebook and created a written agenda that Sarah could carry in her backpack, eliminating the doubt she harbored about her capacity to select the correct bus on a given day.

Ted balked at the idea of his youngest daughter armed with a daily planner. After she and Paul and Patricia left to catch their respective buses on Wednesday morning, he tried to reopen discussion of my job and its implications.

I was annoyed and sympathetic, almost simultaneously. "Not my decision, Ted. It was both of us who decided. You agreed. I mean, I know I instigated it. But what did you expect? That I would wait around until you suggested I do something with my life? Would you feel better if I hadn't given her the calendar?"

"I'd feel better if she didn't have to worry about flextime at six years old."

"So would I. I would also feel better if you anesthetized me."

Ted opened his briefcase and rearranged the contents. I knew this routine well. He was stalling, hoping I would resume the conversation without forcing him to respond to my ill-timed joke.

I obliged. "We didn't go into this blind. If it doesn't work out, I can quit, I guess. Or we can try something else."

Ted was still reluctant to speak. "Like what?"

I began to load the dishwasher. "I'll get her a personal computer. Or a dog or something. Are you trying to make me feel responsible? It's working. I knew it wouldn't be simple, getting used to a new routine. But I am not abandoning her. Only two of those days are in day care."

"No. It's as much my fault. Responsibility, I mean. It's just that she doesn't get to come home and have a snack and tell you about her day. Am I being ridiculous?"

"Yes. No. I guess not. But neither Paul nor Patricia ever came rushing home to see what Betty Crocker had whipped up for them. Maybe we should get a microwave?"

Ted laughed. "Now she'll resort to technology?"

"If I were a better woman, I would stay at home and adopt boat children or Ethiopians and invent new Jell-O desserts."

Ted stood. "You're right. This is pointless. And it is my fault. I know you want to work. You're a great editor. Sarah will be happier than most kids who come home and find their mothers with the soaps on TV and a roast in the convection oven. I know all that."

Ted had finished his mantra and kissed me goodbye. I wanted to tie myself to a chair, or plead insanity, or abandon home life altogether. Who the hell invented the Working Mother?

| X |

My daydream as I drove to work: I am selected as a finalist on a game show. (Yes, I've done it all—watched midmorning game shows as warm-ups for the afternoon soaps, switching from one channel to another to witness winners and losers as the actual retail price or the big deal of the day is revealed.) I am given a choice of three doors. Door Number One conceals domestic bliss. Door Number Two conceals professional success. For some reason I know this much in advance. Naturally, I cannot resist the allure of uncertainty and I choose Door Number Three. After much applause and screaming, the door slides open. Inside, are both Door Number One and Door Number Two, both permanently secured with comically outsized padlocks.

| XI |

Friday afternoon, just before four o'clock, I was paged on the office intercom. Rather than picking up the phone in the office of the art director, where I had just finished complaining about the layout of the upcoming issue, I walked the fifty feet back to my office. Before I reached my telephone, the intercom buzzed and the receptionist yelled, "Anne Fossicker! Anne Fossicker, your daughter needs you!" I shut my office door, humiliated.

Patricia was hysterical, apparently talking to someone while she waited for me to answer. When I finally caught her attention, she was irate. "Where have you been? Sister Clare is really hurt. She had to break a window to get into the house. What? She says she's okay but I didn't mean to tie up the phone. Honest, Mom."

Before I could interrupt to ask a question or calm Patricia, Sister Clare spoke to me, apparently having given up hope that Patricia would convey the essential, still mysterious message. "Get home, Anne. This is Clare Messina. I have to see you immediately."

"You're hurt?" I was beginning to invent a physical fight that had just ended between my daughter and this nun.

"Get home. Something is very wrong. Sarah didn't call you, did she?"

"What is today? Friday? She's at Brownies. Why aren't you there? What the hell is going on at my house?"

"Get home. I will call your husband. Patricia, do you have the number? She does. Drive safely. Hurry."

Uncertain when Clare was speaking to me and when she was speaking to my daughter, I failed to register the fact that she had cut our connection. When I finally did, I dialed my home telephone, was relieved, I think, to hear a busy signal. Clare was calling Ted. That much was easy to comprehend. I collected my bag and coat and headed for home, convinced that Patricia had been besieged at home because of involvement with drugs or a boy; in advance I decided that Clare had overreacted. I prepared to castigate her for abandoning the Brownies, regardless of the severity of Patricia's alleged crime. Why couldn't one of the high school teachers have chased her down?

It is a fact, or nearly a fact, that all mothers have compulsive imaginations where their children are involved. As I pulled into our driveway, already able to see the shattered glass of the front door, I calmed myself by imagining how frightened Patricia would be after being caught doing something she was not licensed to do, and under such dramatic circumstances.

Sister Clare greeted me at the door, a makeshift gauze bandage wrapped around her left hand. Her usually calm, sallow face was sweaty, her dark curly hair matted against her head. Her white blouse and pleated blue skirt showed small stains from dripping blood. The sight of her unnerved me completely.

I screamed. "What the hell is happening here? Why the hell did you break down the door? What are you trying to prove here? What is the matter with you?"

This brought Patricia to Clare's side. She had clearly maintained the hysterical pitch she'd achieved during our abortive conversation. "I was on the phone. I couldn't hear anything cause the radio was on. Loud. Maybe it's not too late. Hurry up. Sarah is missing."

Oddly, I can describe what I felt on receiving the news. My heart performed an unprecedented function. It ceased pumping and simply sucked blood from my head and the rest of my body. It expanded, and I experienced its stress as chest cramps. I turned my head to the base of the house, feeling that I was about to vomit. Clare ran to my side, anticipating this. Of course, I only heaved violently and unsuccessfully; my bloated heart muscle was too large to be forced through my throat. Clare put her arm over my shoulders and roughly escorted me into the house, impatient with my weakness. Patricia began to speak to me and I closed my eyes, hoping that she and Clare and the shattered glass might disappear. Clare seized the moments of my recovery as the time to call the police. Once that was done she would not tolerate inaction. Ted arrived within fifteen minutes and, finally, the few facts available to us were organized and examined.

THE
FACE OF
GOD

| I |

CLARE WAITED for the young policeman, who arrived just after Ted. Officer Tim Hall introduced himself and meekly accepted as protocol Clare's instructions to sit and join the family in witnessing her testimony. A false calm held us all. I could see that Ted and the others shared my instinct; each of us believed that upon hearing the salient details of Sarah's whereabouts we would be able to dissemble the hidden key to the alleged mystery.

Looking rather heroic with her slightly bloodied bandage held at her side, Clare stood and recited. "Sarah was meant to arrive for our first Brownie meeting—I am the leader for the St. Cecilia troop—at three-fifteen. I waited until three-thirty, thinking that several of the children would straggle in late, though I don't allow tardiness to go on later in the year. Four of the children who'd signed up in June were absent, including Sarah. For your purposes, Officer Hall, she is average size with short blonde hair and blue eyes. I am sure Mrs. Fossicker can provide you with a recent photo. I asked the children if anyone knew why the other four were not present. Three of the girls had been absent from school, a fact I checked with the register from the first-grade teacher, Mrs. Shaw, Sarah's teacher. Sarah was marked absent, too, but Tracy Meagher spoke up when Sarah's name was mentioned. Tracy said Sarah had been on the bus this morning. I asked if she had been in Mrs. Shaw's class and Tracy said Sarah—who is her best friend, in fact—had told her that she felt sick when they got off the bus. Tracy did see Sarah go into the school building, but Sarah entered by the side door, rather than the front door with the other children. Tracy did not know why, but seemed to think it had to do with Sarah going to the nurse's office. I questioned Tracy about this, since the nurse's office is near the front of the building, but Tracy had no explanation. It was then that a second child, Karen Flynn, spoke up and said that she'd come to school late and had passed Sarah in the hall. Sarah was walking toward the front door. Karen did not speak to Sarah, which makes sense if you realize that Karen had not been with us for kindergarten and only knew Sarah because they had assigned seats in Mrs. Shaw's classroom by last names—the two girls sat near each other. Apparently Mrs. Shaw just heard Tracy say that Sarah was sick, and checked her off as absent. I think from what Tracy said— the friend on the bus—Mrs. Shaw figured that Sarah was at home. Oh, and when I pressed Karen to remember something else, she began to cry and then said that Sarah was crying when she passed her in the hall. I don't know if Karen was making this up or if she just sensed danger when she remembered seeing Sarah but it was that—that's what tipped me off that something was really wrong. I paged Sister Jean Bromar to cover the Brownie meeting. After five minutes of busy signals on the phone I drove here as fast as I could—panicking, obviously. When I got to the house and I couldn't get a response I, I don't know why, without any cause, really, I thought Sarah was in the house. I know it sounds ridiculous, but that's what made me put my hand through the glass in the front door. A reflex of some kind. Patricia came screaming down from the bedroom. That's when we called you, Anne. My God, she's already been gone for eight hours. Where would she go? Why would she do this?"

Officer Hall interrupted Clare and forced her to sit in a chair.

He was a notably short man—a few inches shorter than me—and handsome in an ordinary way with dark hair. Black Irish? He spoke softly, staring at me. "I'll need two or three recent pictures. I have several questions for each of you. I want you, Sister, to have your hand looked at by a doctor, immediately. I am going to call the station and set up an evening scan of the area and put out an APB—with children we don't wait the usual twenty-four hours, regulations or no. Anything about her schedule or friends' names and the like that might help in any way—don't be choosy, be exhaustive. Write everything down now. In fifteen minutes I want to mobilize. Acting quickly and being prepared are the only chance we have. Relatives. Names of relatives in the area who might have contacted the child in any way recently. Does she know her home telephone number and address?"

I could see that Tim Hall was losing his focus. Questions were running ahead of procedure. "Yes. She knows everything a six-year-old knows. She could have been run over by a car or fallen down somewhere." I thought I was being brave. "There is no reason to panic, of course. She's probably just wandered off somewhere. Right? Or something might have happened. Why would someone kidnap her?"

Ted pulled me into his embrace. "You get the pictures. I will start a list. Patricia, make a list of her friends, as best you can, and put down the names and addresses of your aunts and uncles and your grandparents. Officer Hall? Don't you want to call the station? Clare, call a cab and get to the hospital." Ted handed Clare a twenty-dollar bill. "Come back here if you can when you are sure you're okay. Someone will be here or there will be a note about where we are." With conviction bordering on anger he said, "I do not intend to lose my daughter."

Ted successfully stirred us into action. I drew the photo album from its nest of clippings of Paul's basketball achievements and brochures for Ted's contracting services. I pulled dozens of pictures of Sarah from plastic pouches. It was a picture of Sarah on the beach in Maine that defeated me. She was alone on the sand, balanced on one knee, both her hands on her head. I kissed the picture, pressed it to my breast, then kissed it again and again. As if I had been trained in the procedure, I began to lick the photograph, pausing occasionally to administer a long breath to Sarah. I honestly hoped to animate the child in the sand, to bring her to life. I worked furiously, knowing it was my only hope.

| II |

Before it all began—hours with strange, officious men in uniform refusing to offer reassurances; photocopies of Sarah's image delivered through the mails and by hand at major traffic intersections; neighborhood and even city-wide search parties; graceful, disturbing hints of negligence or oversight delivered by my mother and my sisters—before Sarah's absence registered as anything more permanent than a terrible fright, I revived my memory of watching Sarah at three years old as she repeatedly dunked her head beneath the freezing waters of Boothbay Harbor.

She was sucking air as she bobbed, her hands wagging uselessly but ecstatically just above the water. Finally, as she lifted her head to draw another breath she stopped, and holding her hands together under her mouth, she parted her lips and salt water flowed out into the tiny cup of her two palms. She tried to examine the water before it slipped through the webbing of her fingers, as if to understand how it had got inside her mouth. Rather scientifically, she dropped the cupped hands into the water and filled her mouth with the sea. This solution she rejected immediately. Tentatively, then, she dunked her head into the water, raised it, and repeated the procedure. Recupping her hands, she opened her mouth above them, apparently to ascertain what might have entered her mouth this time. When she saw that no water had seeped into her closed mouth, she shook her head, ostensibly confirming her suspicion. She then came to shore, took up a sentinel-like post next to my chair in the sand, stood watch over the slight waves.

After several minutes I asked, as casually as I could manage, if she thought she would rather live underwater.

She didn't move. "I want to taste air."

| III |

It was moving out of the house that stirred panic. Four cars and an idling taxi were haphazardly crowded into the driveway. Several of the front porches of neighboring houses were filled with small crowds, mothers and children who'd survived this unanticipated, unobserved Passover. The coolness of the late afternoon air set off an involuntary hope that Sarah was inside. But wouldn't she be found more easily if she were outside? I thought it best if she was inside, staring out through a huge plate-glass window, perhaps in a drugstore or a beauty salon.

My next impulse, completely without personal precedent, was to communicate with my daughter via some mystical current, or across a speculative fifth dimension. I thought to establish contact with Sarah by using ESP. I conjured images of her, I repeated her name, I even held my hands against my head to produce pressure. For additional wattage?

Unsatisfied, I retreated to that most ancient and universal of prayers: Why me, God?

Ted ushered me into the car, tipping me off to the fact that I had been outside of my home for something less than a full minute and had already exhausted several sources of hope or solace. Only after much commotion did I realize that Ted was pulling me out of the car into which he had just escorted me.

Ted was yelling. "Where is he, Anne? For God's sake— where is Paul?"

Patricia was crying, holding on to her father's arm. Officer Hall had come to join the inquisition. For a moment I felt giddy, irresponsible. To myself I said, "Two down, one to go." The crowd seemed to press closer, as if to physically extract an answer from me. In that moment I realized that my husband, my daughter, and the police officer on the scene had gathered around me as a sort of reflex accusation. And it was my instinct to accept center ground in the developing tragedy.

Ingeniously, though quite unintentionally, I spoke the very words that I was formulating to ground my own ascending panic. I spoke aloud, to defy the confusion that marks the onset of an unmanageable sadness. "Paul, as you well know, Patricia, was playing basketball with Bobby Ameron and is sleeping over at his house. You knew that too, Ted. That was a fact you could have used. We have to use facts from now on. Patricia, go call your brother and tell him to meet you here at the house. Do not tell him what has happened until he gets home. Tell him to take a taxi home. Isn't that the best thing to do? Yes. Ted? Give Patricia money for Paul's taxi ride. Now, Ted. Patricia, you wait here for Sister Clare to come back. Dad and I might be back before her. We'll see. Now, any more questions? We're just wasting time now, aren't we? Until we get the reports filled out, Officer Hall?"

Officer Hall nodded and led Ted and I to the station. Just before we followed him into the nearly dark headquarters, Ted embraced me and detained me in front of the large glass doors. "You don't think she's coming back tonight, do you?"

I was on a temporary high of rationality. "If a child can be lost for eight minutes or eight hours, why not eight days or eight years?"

Ted would not let me go. "That's not good enough for me, Anne."

I did not want to be forced to think about Sarah lost, Sarah gone. "The only thing I know is that I don't want to pretend and I don't want to invent. Use facts."

Ted pulled me tight against him. "How many facts does it take to make a miracle? Tell me. Eight? Ten?"

| IV |

Facts gave way to countervailing truths and contradictory tenets. Officer Hall's assurances notwithstanding, we were told by a desk sergeant that an APB, by dint of regulation, could not be issued until twenty-four hours had elapsed. Sarah was variously recorded as a Missing Child, a Potential Kidnap Victim, and a Juvenile (not a delinquent, though the term did apply literally). Our chances of recovering our child were excellent, impossible to evaluate, better in the morning, better in autumn than in winter. The police department relied on standard procedures in searching for missing children; the department followed a recently adopted county-wide policy on missing children; there existed no formal procedure for conduct of an investigation before proper classification of the child's status. Family members could not accompany officers in squad cars; family members were encouraged to conduct personal searches; family members should stay at home in case the child tries to contact the home; family members should cooperate by leading officers to likely hiding places or the child's favorite sites; officers generally have a good idea where a child would hide. Depending on the classification system you find most helpful, twenty-seven, thirteen, or six children were reported as missing in Fairfield County in the first nine months of 1984.

"Hello, Officer, my name is Anne Fossicker. I wonder if you can help me locate the silent tornado that engulfed my youngest daughter."

HALF-SEEN
OR LOST?

| I |

I KNEW EXACTLY where Sarah was when Officer Hall asked. She was at the minimall three blocks north of her school. I knew she would head for the safety of the small stores and half-familiar sales clerks. When he asked if I could think of other places Sarah might hide, I knew she'd gone to the library, only a few blocks from the mall. I also knew she would be in the bathroom at the new gas station—a public service that fascinated her for no known reason—that was across from the movie theater. Without a doubt, though, I figured she would be stopping at the water bubbler on the side of the library. If she hadn't stopped at the mall.

Officer Hall doubted my certainty. He thought it would be best if I went home and Ted rode with him to search the obvious, public places. Embarrassed by his inability to issue the promised APB, he was devoting overtime duty to the search. I knew this was retributive justice and that his enthusiasm would soon flag. He was young enough himself to have a child of Sarah's age, to whom he would feel more bound. If he had no children of his own, how long could I expect him to stretch his imagination and maintain any sort of empathy with my plight? Worse, two hours in the station—issuing bulletins, placing calls to relatives, repeating addresses and ages and descriptions—had failed to raise more than cursory interest from any of the several officers involved. They'd heard it all before, seen the panic, heard the inflated claims about a young child's sense of responsibility and unusually sound upbringing. No one said so, but I heard each man's response to this fetus of a tragedy: "She's a goner."

| II |

Before protesting aloud about Officer Hall's choice of Ted over me as his temporary partner, I repeated a command over and over to myself: "Make sense." From what I recall of the following half hour, I failed utterly to observe this, my own advice.

"Why Ted?" I looked at Ted as I spoke. He and I and Officer Hall were seated on three old folding metal chairs in an un-trafficked corner of the station lobby. "You see my point, don't you?" No confirmation. Looks of concern from the two men. "I know Sarah in the way a mother knows a daughter. Let's face it. How many times have I walked around these streets with her? You pick up a lot of tips. Useful information." Officer Hall smiled. Appeasingly? "I know it's not a competition. I'm just being reasonable." Querulous smiles fade, simultaneously, to doubt. "Oh, look at the two of you." I tried and failed to sound ironic; crying betrayed me. I would go home, hopeless again. "You don't even think there is a chance of finding her. Do you? Either of you?"

Ted took my hands. "She isn't lost forever. I'll find her."

Officer Hall stood. "We should start off, Ted."

"You're lying, Ted. To me, anyway. I hope you at least have the decency to lie to yourself, too. As long as you're lying to me, I mean. Find her, Ted. Tonight."

I resisted the offer to be driven home. I had already fixated on the outlines of a plan of my own—a route home that would encompass several of the sites I suspected of being among Sarah's favorites. As nonchalantly as I could, I asked Ted and Officer Hall for permission to stop at the minimall and the library.

Ted deferred to Officer Hall, who was annoyed by this time. "It's a bad idea, Mrs. Fossicker. The whole objective is to divide and conquer. There's a good chance that your daughter will try to contact the home."

"I just have a sense that I could do this part better. I mean, since I know the help at the mall stores. You see?" I was humiliated at having put myself in a position to ask permission. Women are the perfect prisoners as a result of this sort of behavior. We resort to humbling ourselves every time we ask, as individuals or a community, for permission to exercise our freedoms. Our obsessive obedience signals our goodwill, our eagerness to accept the completely apocryphal doctrine of fair play. "You think I should skip the mall?"

Officer Hall had run out of patience. "Yes. Go home. For everyone's sake. Honestly, this is not a game for me and your husband, Mrs. Fossicker."

I yelled. "No kidding? I knew that, thank you very much. Games have rules."

Ted's embrace was as much a threat as a comfort. A police officer was assigned the duty of driving me home.

| III |

In a fit of energy and misplaced enthusiasm, I tried to explain to Officer Jack Callanan, my chauffeur, what I felt like at the moment. After all, he had asked, if absentmindedly. Within minutes I had reduced Sarah to fit a host of banal analogies. Sarah was an amputated limb, a lost car key, a name one can't quite remember. Jack Callanan finally said, "I guess there really is nothing like losing a child." He was right, of course. He knew that she was nothing but Sarah and she was nothing other than gone. Seeing that he had deflated me with his literal-mindedness, Officer Callanan innocently (I believe) asked the question that I had anticipated since first learning of Sarah's disappearance.

"Do you work, Mrs. Fossicker? I mean at a job, at an office?"

Defensive, guilty, and relieved, I said, "Yes. So does my husband."

Like a conqueror's flag over my native territory, the banner Working Mother was hoisted above me. Working Mother: contradiction in terms or redundancy? In either case, it was the indictment I sought. Having for years satiated myself and mollified Ted by reining in my editorial ambitions and maintaining only a part-time career, I could hardly escape the significance of the coincidence of Sarah's disappearance and my opting for a full-time position. I was susceptible not to the logic of the coincidence (if any) but to the mere fact of it.

Knowing that others would raise the accusation or, at the very least, that I would extract it as an implication from future questions and facial expressions, I wanted to know what sin I could charge myself with successfully. Not the lazy, generational wisdom; not the biological blasphemy; I wanted to know what had restrained me for so long, what could be salvaged of my reticence to leave home for most of the day.

Questions and doubts about the quality of nurture, the fulfillment of a child's psychological and physical needs, did not interest me. I knew by experience (one of the few morsels of knowledge gleaned from experience that is truly universal, tragically enough) that childhood is a series of thwarted, ignored, punished, altered, and eventually repressed needs and desires. My sin was simpler. Choosing to become a Working Mother, I alerted my children to the fact that I was no longer readily available as a witness. That was it—I had cut off the only source of my children's ongoing sense of certainty.

It is a matter of proof. Women traditionally served their children by witnessing their youths. They could be called upon to attest to its peculiarities and even its mere existence at appropriate moments in their children's adult lives. The wonder and torment of change, of fleetingness—women accumulated this knowledge and did actually hold it in their hearts. (I would have dismissed this as sentimentality if I had not come to know it as a fact, albeit a fact with mythic implications.) Adults seem to require proof of a prior existence. Not photographic evidence, not public record; adults must know that at every possible juncture during their existence on the earth they were beheld by someone who loved them.

And here was Sarah before me, displaced from geography, her daily planner in her hand, her pack heavy on her back. How recklessly I delivered my child. How willing I was to hasten her into the world. Prepared for what? To be a sturdy, resilient victim? I issued prayers of supplication, vows of sacrifice and repentance aimed at leveraging my child back from the hands of the angry God whose existence I doubted.

Officer Callanan jumped out of my car and headed for the cruiser that had followed us to my home. Jolly to the last, he yelled, "Good luck!" I watched him and his partner disappear down the street and accepted his friendly blessing. I tried to make myself believe in a random universe in which luck would play a determining role.

| IV |

The window glass that Sister Clare had shattered with her bare hand was cleared away and replaced with a blank piece of brown cardboard attached to the door frame with masking tape. It reminded me of the humble appearance of summer cottages at Boothbay Harbor after they'd been closed for the winter. Clare was seated in my living room with my two remaining children, all of them eyeing me suspiciously as I attempted to appear calm.

Patricia said it first. She did not look at me. "Where's Sarah?"

The question still registered as a shock. I was terrorized again by my inability to account for the whereabouts of my youngest daughter. Reflexively, but hopelessly, I answered with a question: "She's not here?"

Paul, who had joined the tragedy midstream and seemed to take offense at any failure of common sense, said, "Of course she's not here, Mom. That's what it means to be lost. What?

Did you think she would come back by herself maybe? Where's Dad?"

"With Officer Hall. Searching for her. For Sarah. They can't do anything on a larger scale until tomorrow." I could not make myself sit down, tired as I was. "Thanks for repairing the window, Clare. Oh, God, your hand." I was staring at a bulky bandage that half-concealed a metal brace.

Clare balanced the hand on her lap. "It's more impressive looking than it really is. They were afraid I'd done something to my wrist. This thing—the metal thing—is a splint."

I still couldn't move. I believed this was obvious to the others in the room. "It hurts?"

"Not at all. Strange, for looking so bad, huh?" Clare came to my side. "I made a little soup. For dinner. Why don't you come into the kitchen, Anne. There is nothing to do, really, until Ted comes back. Is there?"

That was what had cemented me to the floor. Once inside the house, there was nothing to do. Short of Sarah wandering in through the front door in need of food or a bath, we were assigned the unbearable task of waiting. For what? The idea of moving to the kitchen, the four of us eating a hot meal prepared by someone from the world outside the family—this had the appeal of seeming preparation. I adopted it as a temporary reprieve from the waiting. "We will all eat. Your dad will have news or something for us to do soon and we should be ready."

Paul, designating himself man of the house, said, "I bet they already found her, or are about to."

I intentionally turned away from him. What was the point of dashing the hopes of the one among us not yet beaten? But I saw Patricia's face react against her younger brother: scorn and contempt for such naiveté colored her old.

| V |

The four of us ate slowly, as if believing that the source of our next meal was unknown. Politeness was optimal: in fact, the only words exchanged were direct requests for a bit more soup, some butter, an offer of milk or water. I knew I was responsible for the extremity of this atmosphere, that I somehow had led myself and my children to believe this day was a permanent state of affairs. But I could not dismiss my certainty that Sarah was gone forever. The silence around me seemed unalterable. Occasional timid spoken requests and the irregular chink of silverware against glass bowls did nothing to dispel the pall. I waited to hear Sarah's voice, Sarah's noise.

| VI |

After a full five minutes of utter silence, Clare announced that she'd forgotten to show me something about the window she'd broken and led me out of the kitchen after she had urged Paul and Patricia to clear the table. By the front door, she pointed to bloodstains on the carpet and promised to try to remove them.

I was still engulfed in silence.

"Anne, I am staying as long as you want me here. You only have to nod if you want me to leave. If it would be easier. You understand that, right? But you have to talk, tell me what I can do. The kids, too. I called the school and the janitors have searched the building and the playgrounds. They have no sign of anything. I called the parents of the two girls who saw Sarah this morning. They also spoke to the police and want you to know they'll do anything you ask. You have to start asking, Anne. This is the important time. We can't rely on the police. We have to find her. I know it must seem hopeless, but my God, there is the chance. What are we going to do? Give up?"

I felt betrayed momentarily by this covert optimism. "Maybe we can get together a posse?"

"Why not? Are we going to wait until tomorrow morning to try to get some people to cover the city? I can get hold of lists. The nuns at the convent can start making calls. This is the sort of thing that ought to be publicized. If it turns out that she's not really lost, all we do is call it off."

There was nothing for me to refute. Who was I to give up hope so readily? Grateful, and suddenly impressed by Clare (her wound now seemed some kind of symbol of her commitment to the cause), I deliberately set about to manufacture hope.

| VII |

Patricia and Paul, no less than Clare and I, were responsive to the sense of mission as I described it. Every extant photograph of Sarah was assembled. Lists were to be made of every place she had ever been, every child and adult she knew. Clare took on the massive task of setting in motion a search party. She and several of her fellow teachers divided the registration lists and began to make telephone calls to homes, inviting adults and children over the age of twelve to assemble at eight-thirty at the school; younger children would be cared for in ad hoc day care administered by elderly nuns. Enthusiasm led to innovation.

Clare left after about an hour, not wanting to tie up our telephone with calls that could be made from the school. She also seemed eager to be at the center of activity, which was quickly shifting from the home front to the public arena. She took with her a few large photographs of Sarah, which she vowed to photocopy "until the machine won't run anymore." It was her idea to hand photocopies, along with pertinent details about Sarah, to each volunteer, and to have thousands of extra copies made for distribution at major traffic intersections, churches, schools, area stores, the train and bus depots and, if necessary, for mailing. She figured the younger children, left in the school during the search, could be enlisted to stuff envelopes.

Seeing that Patricia and Paul had nearly exhausted their imaginations with list-making, Clare instructed them to assemble posters, for display in stores and restaurants, with one of the many photographs of Sarah prominently mounted on each. Confronted with the practical problem of a base material, she correctly guessed that I had a few rolls of plain white shelving paper. Before I thought to offer her a ride to the convent, she spotted the station wagon that had been called to retrieve her. Her only words as she left were, "Get some sleep. Everybody has to have their wits about them."

For the next forty-five minutes our attention was focused entirely on practical exigencies, and speculation about the number of parents and schoolmates from the grammar and high schools who'd join the search. Difficulties and doubts were easily dismissed in this atmosphere.

Unsuspecting, Ted and Officer Hall somberly entered the house just before ten o'clock. With them, reality threatened to overtake ingenuity. After their initial boasts and enthusiastic predictions about Clare's plans met with barely masked reproach, Patricia and Paul volunteered to continue their work in their bedrooms, promising to set their alarms. This detail so impressed Officer Hall that I figured he must have children of his own.

Ted embraced me, held me for a full minute at least. Officer Hall grew impatient, finally seated himself on the sofa. I was still generating false hope: "Nothing yet? It's impossible at night, I guess. I'm sure someone has taken her inside."

Ted said nothing. He sat in a chair opposite Officer Hall. They both refused offers of coffee and supper.

As nonchalantly as possible I said, "Will someone from the police want to be involved in the search, Officer Hall?"

He was staring at his hands, looking for all the world like a movie cowboy. "There will be no public search party, Mrs. Fossicker. Perhaps in a few days a project to involve the child's friends can be put together. There simply is no way to utilize a lot of laypeople effectively. Think of the problems that could create."

Ted seemed not present.

I agreed with the logic I presumed was lurking behind Officer Hall's tired proclamation. And it was fear of that logic—which could only lead me to tolerance of a world in which young children disappear without cause and without explanation—that overcame common sense. "I am not being very clear, I'm afraid.

And I am sure you are tired and have a family to get back to. But there will be hundreds of people at St. Cecilia's tomorrow morning around eight o'clock. The police department can ignore that fact or help us do something effective."

Ted stood, which I took as a signal of his intent to intercede. But before I could object, he extended his hand to the young policeman. "I cannot hope to repay your kindness, Tim. Bless you for tonight. And I have to tell you that you can do everything you want or need to to put an end to the gathering tomorrow. But I will pay for radio time and television time to keep the crowds coming. We need help. I won't lose her. There isn't a procedure in any book that will guarantee results in this sort of case, is there? Please don't make us fight just to accept the help of ready volunteers. Please." Officer Hall stood as Ted did. They shook hands. "I want to see my children. You can discuss any necessary details with Anne." Ted left without another word.

Officer Hall looked completely daunted by the fixity of Ted's emotions. "I'll have some men there. It's just that numbers always tend to slow things down."

"Delegate to me, to Sister Clare. We all don't need to be out in the streets—"

"I'll see you at eight. See that there is plenty of coffee. Call that doughnut store on West Main, use my name. Tell them how many people you expect. They provide them—as a service." For the first time Tim Hall engaged my stare. "I'll have some other names for you tomorrow—agencies and lawyers who are involved in this . . . with this issue. Maybe it won't be necessary at all. But it is the sort of information you can always save and pass on to someone . . . should you know about someone . . . I hope it isn't necessary. I hope that very much, Mrs. Fossicker. Good night."

| VIII |

I cleaned the kitchen and the living room before heading upstairs, moving familiarly, calmly through my routine, as if I had entered the eye of the storm. When I finally joined the team in Patricia's bedroom, I found them all asleep on Patricia's double bed. Unlikely and impractical as was the arrangement of their bodies, I could not bring myself to rouse them. Intentionally or not, this is the end Ted had sought when he opted out of the discussion with Tim Hall. I knew that if I attempted to join them I would only disrupt their rest. I did not believe I could achieve sleep, even tangled with my family. I covered as many limbs as possible with a quilt from Paul's bed and left them in darkness.

Resignedly, as if on command, I gathered a few pictures of Sarah, my coat and purse, the car keys, and headed out into the night. I reached the movie theater as its final show ended and sat in my car to check the faces in the crowd. I yelled her name, fixing my gaze at the middle of the men and women, pretending to have spotted her. No one seemed to notice me. When only a man with a broom remained, I drove into the gas station across the street and showed a picture to the teenager on duty. He said he'd never seen the little girl, agreed to let me use the bathroom where, by now, I fully expected to find my daughter. It was empty. I checked the window, which was locked. In case she had escaped as I entered? I left a picture with the boy, who was regarding me warily, glancing down at my hands every few seconds. I drove to the library, parked the car, and walked to the water bubbler at the building's side. There, hidden from the lit street, I yelled her name several times, letting a few quiet seconds pass between each shout, straining to hear movement or a voice raised in response.

It was only seconds after I drank from the bubbler mounted on a cement stem that I had the first visitation. Sarah, as she had looked in her uniform on Friday morning, appeared to me, dropped her backpack on the ground, and incautiously dipped her face toward the stainless steel water font. I yelled, hoping to caution her before she jammed her teeth against the spigot, as I had yelled and successfully protected her on any number of occasions. I didn't exactly hear her front tooth break, but I felt her contact with the metal as a sympathetic shock through my body, and received a mental image of the chipped tooth as the shock traveled along my back.

She did not disappear. Sarah was still visible to me, chipped tooth, backpack at her feet. But she was immaterial. She vanished entirely only when I approached her.

| IX |

Ted woke me just after six-thirty. He'd made his way to our bed sometime after my return. Already he'd cajoled Paul and Patricia out of bed and gotten them started on breakfast. We held each other, contented ourselves with shared sadness and hope. Mute comfort was comfort nonetheless. Ted left me to shower, and as I allowed myself to retreat back toward sleep the doorbell sounded.

Clare, in jeans and a sweater, was accompanied by a tiny elderly nun in full religious regalia. Sister Urban's black veil fell to her waist, where a rosary-bead sash was looped around the layers of her black habit. Clare had assigned the ancient woman the task of answering our telephone for the day, a contingency I had not anticipated. Sister Urban excused herself from breakfast and seemed not at all interested in conversation. I watched her take up her post in the living room, seating herself on the sofa and making the sign of the cross in the air, as if to exorcise any lingering irreligious spirit that might interfere with her duty. Then, as reflexively as a sailor hoisting a mainsail, she swung the large crucifix into her palm, raised it to her lips, and launched into the first decade of the rosary. Her presence and her praying were like a salve. Not only could I see in her the icons of my youth, but I could relegate to her responsibility for keeping alive our request for providential intercession, a task I could not manage.

Clare headed for the refrigerator. "Sister Urban insisted on bringing her own lunch." Clare held up a venerable brown paper sack, which produced immediate laughter from my children. I smiled, embarrassed for the old nun and for myself. The bag seemed a completely ridiculous addition to the shelves of fresh and prepared food jammed into my refrigerator. Clare sat at the table. "Is there any coffee, Anne?"

"There will be in three minutes. Would Sister Urban drink tea? Patricia, go ask Sister Urban if she would like a cup of tea."

Patricia did not protest vocally, but her reticence was clear. I couldn't blame her. I was behaving as my own mother would in front of company, particularly church-related company. I was putting my daughter in her place—servant of her elders, obedient handmaiden of her mother. Why not Paul? More pertinently, why not me? Still, Patricia asked and Sister Urban declined.

This brief exchange brought to mind my own parents and the correct way of informing them of Sarah's disappearance. I knew before I seriously considered my options that I had tacitly opted for a policy of silence until at least the weekend was past. Despite the obvious ramifications of this choice, most of them based on my mother's sense of being wronged, I decided not to inform them. It was not a tormenting decision. As time and its promise narrowed, such practical considerations were increasingly easy to adjudicate. I was operating under unprecedented conditions, a military chief of staff issuing commands, dispensing with customary rules of polity and form. Anything, absolutely anything, could be justified.

| X |

Sister Clare's optimistic prediction of 150 volunteers proved to be only slightly inflated. By eight-thirty 137 adults and children were assembled in the St. Cecilia gymnasium, each wearing a photograph of Sarah as a badge. Two huge red plastic coffee urns framed a cafeteria table loaded with doughnuts. The general atmosphere was good-natured but subdued; not unlike the incoherent environment of a wake. Everyone observed some self-imposed limit on gaiety; conversations were conducted in exaggerated stage whispers. A metal chair tipped onto the floor had the effect of hushing the crowd. Many children and a number of parents paid a good deal of attention to Paul and Patricia. Ted and I were hardly fixtures in this milieu, and I experienced our near anonymity as I presume a pauper or an accident victim would experience philanthropic attention focused on him by the membership of the Rotary Club or the Junior League. I did not want to refuse the assistance, but I wanted to pass as one of the benefactors.

Celebrity status was soon thrust upon me. Standing on a chair, Sister Clare called the meeting to order and called me forward. Ted was meant to join me, but Officer Hall and two other policemen had just arrived and engaged him in a discussion. My confused attempts to think of something appropriate to say (I considered explaining my low profile in the school, even) were interrupted by the spontaneous applause from the crowd that accompanied my appearance next to Clare, who had descended from her perch and had her arm around my shoulder.

In the few seconds that followed, the applause continuing, I saw in the faces of parents and children the impossibility of translating my loss into anything meaningful. What I knew was only this: losing a child was nothing like what one imagines it to be. Even this did not seem to be pertinent information.

Oddly, as soon as the applause died down, I readied myself to speak. "Sister Clare has been more organized, efficient, and loving than any friend I could have hoped for. I applaud you, Clare." (Here, I turned to Clare.) "I expect to find my daughter Sarah. If not today, then tomorrow." (Had I just called for a second day of searching? Apparently I had. The attention of the police and my husband was now completely mine.) "The point is to look for anything meaningful—clothing, books— and to talk to everyone you encounter. Passing out copies of Sarah's picture will help if we don't find her today. If we attend to details, we can at least know where Sarah is not, has not been. This is essential." (Movement among the policemen here.) "But I am sure that Officer Tim Hall will be able to instruct us all. Please give him your complete attention. And I will say now that there is no way to repay your generosity in coming here today. Along with the Sisters who have been working since yesterday, you are all my hope. Officer Hall?"

No applause greeted the arrival of the police: business had begun. Ted joined me and did not say a word. He seemed to know that it was not the Anne he knew who had just rallied round the cause.

The only detail of Tim Hall's speech that interested me was the mention of my being partnered with him for the day. The crowd was instructed to follow orders from the two other policemen, Ted, and Clare. Grabbing a stack of photocopies as he left center stage, Tim Hall led me to his cruiser. I was still wondering if this was a concession (Ted having been selected yesterday) or if I was actually to perform a particular service.

As it turned out, I was occupied with filling out official reports and court-related forms and meeting with a series of remarkably disinterested town and county employees for the better part of the morning. The afternoon was spent in the custody of various advocates, private and public, who specialize in missing children. Over and over, the warning was repeated about the urge to despair sometime during the first week. Impressive statistics about the number of family members reunited after literally years of separation were repeated with various degrees of earnestness. Three of the people I met referred to a case in Alabama of a young boy abducted by an elderly couple and found after three years of benign captivity. The woman who directed the Children's Hope program dubbed this boy Rip Van Winkle.

Of course, I had beaten the advocates to the punch. I'd given up hope, other than the artificial variety that fueled my participation in necessary public events (including this series of informational interviews), within a few hours after Sarah's disappearance.

What my day left me with was a nightmarish corona to surround my despair. The range of plausible explanations for Sarah's state was as impressive as it was gruesome—kidnapping (for ransom, for literal sale of a child, purely for sport); acquisition of a preadolescent sexual partner or a starlet for pornographic films; expedited adoption by an odd elderly couple or a barren and desperate young mother; recruitment for child prostitution; simple or complicated murder fantasies. This was but the light at the end of the proverbial tunnel I was to travel in the process of becoming enlightened.

I was learning about the world. It was a strange, truly unthinkable place.

Officer Hall, who raced in and out of offices, answering radio transmissions and meeting with a fellow officer about another ongoing investigation, drove me to St. Cecilia's at six o'clock. He tried to prepare me for the futility of the day's search by telling me of the paltry evidence of Sarah turned up by the expedition: a Brownie uniform cap was recovered two blocks from the school, on a fence post. Apparently, a passerby had seen it in the street and hung it up for retrieval by the owner. It was hardly certain that the cap belonged to Sarah. I doubted whether even I could make a convincing identification without Sarah perched beneath it.

I responded to his description of the hat as if he were an intimate. "I think the one hope I harbor, Tim, is that she is dead. I know that must sound crazy, or self-serving. It's not. To hope her alive means what? I hope she's being tortured? Abused? What drives people?" Seeing the library, I yelled, "Stop, please. Stop! I have to get out of the car. Just a minute. I have to get out!" Though he was pulling to the side of the road and slowing, I continued to beg him to let me out until I was outside, racing toward the water fountain. I screamed her name, not waiting for a response. I grabbed the neck of the bubbler, trying to shake it loose from its concrete mooring. I called her name once more before she appeared at the rear of the police cruiser. She was still in her Brownie uniform, cap and all. Her backpack was missing. She avoided the few passing cars and made her way toward me. I knelt and the very act of reaching out my hands to her was force enough to displace her. Sarah was gone.

THE
BLINDED
PUBLIC EYE

| I |

Before Officer Hall and I returned to St. Cecilia's, a radio transmission warned us that local television reporters had picked up on the story of the search party and were interviewing for live broadcast. The policeman who radioed the warning mentioned that he had heard that the newspapers had sent out reporters earlier and that police headquarters had fielded a number of questions during the day.

Tim Hall, in his greater wisdom, convinced me not to speak to reporters until Monday. "They have all the pertinent, helpful information. All you'll accomplish is that you'll stir up a lot of crazies who will call in with ransom demands and false sightings." He said so with such authority that I agreed to circle around in the cruiser for an additional fifteen minutes. I realized that Clare had likely made several reports to the press already; for no good reason I was willing to delegate authority to her on all matters of crisis management.

The school was nearly empty when we finally thought it safe to return. Clare and Ted and a few vaguely familiar nuns were in the gymnasium. Clare was holding a clipboard. Paul and

Patricia were watching television on the floor in the far corner of the vast room. As if on cue, Clare walked toward Officer Hall, smiling at me as I headed for Ted.

Ted filled me in that he had refused to speak to the reporters, or to allow the children to be interviewed. "Nearly everyone else had some urgent information for the television people. There were literally fights about who ought to be on the air. The only thing that happened as a result is that one of the cops got on the air to say that there would be no public search party operating tomorrow. His reasons were—I don't know, Anne. He had some reasons. I think he realizes that if we turned up nothing whatsoever today, there is no reason to rely on anything but the information and the systems the police typically follow."

Less physically spent than was Ted, I mustered my indignation. "But the cap. That must constitute a lead. Someone found that cap. Who knows what they might have passed by without noticing?"

Ted looked at me as he might regard a noisy child at a concert. "Clare doesn't think it is Sarah's. It's too small. She also said that about seven of the caps are lost every week. Boys apparently like to use them as Frisbees."

"It was on a pole. Someone put it there. Some kid did not throw it there."

"The woman who put it on the pole found it on Friday evening. She says she finds all sorts of clothing and books on her lawn or nearby. Her fence is sort of famous as a lost and found for the grammar school. She never saw Sarah."

"I know you must be exhausted. But I want to question that woman, Ted. Don't you think?"

"Don't I think what? That you should? No. Two policemen and I spent half an hour with her. Anne, it was a cap like a million caps made last year. And nothing else all day. Not a hint of a possible sighting by anyone. Not even a false lead. It just seems inevitable to think she was taken by someone."

"Why is that inevitable? Is that what they said on television?"

"Who cares what anyone said on the television? It's a question of no one having seen or heard a thing. It's too clean. This town is too small for that sort of thing."

I was irate at the idea of Ted having arrived at a conclusion about Sarah's fate without having consulted me. Still, our capacity to respond to each other's questions—I mean, the completely banal capacity to speak coherently to one another—was compromised to the point of being nonexistent. We weren't talking to each other. We were standing next to each other. There was the appearance of give-and-take. But we had not managed to exchange a normal conversational piece of information. Apparently, nothing could be done to remedy this odd and new problem. We simply ceased to speak. Silence was less disconcerting.

| II |

At home we behaved like hostages: silent, cooperative in our newfound mute way, resigned, almost callous. This carried on for something more than an hour. I spent a good deal of that time reassembling our ransacked photo albums. Unwittingly, I had come very close to destroying the photographic evidence of Sarah beyond age five. Despite this, my attention was fixed on the health of my remaining children—and my apparent inability to provide them with a meaningful or even an alternative context for routine life. Every step taken in our home, every meal and every moment shared, occurred in the arena of darkness in which we were playing out the feeble game of hide-and-seek. We were the seekers.

As if it mattered, it seemed that we'd not only been cast into utter blackness at the outset of the game; we'd actually donned blindfolds—our familial sense of victimization. And like prisoners who'd been blinded so long that they no longer hoped to see again, the Fossickers let their heads hang, blind eyes to the floor, cast down in some sort of mourning. Or surrender?

Ted intervened. As if he'd been waiting for the moment we all assembled in the living room, he started to speak as Paul slunk in from the kitchen, a large glass of soda in his guilty grasp. "I was just thinking, about all the stories you hear. About the FBI giving people new identities? How hard it is, how scared the informant who's getting the new identity must be."

Silence, though interest had been stirred. I did not exactly stop shuffling photographs, but I knew that I would soon be drawn in. Paul, Patricia, and I were used to being drawn in by Ted. It was his single-mindedness that could not be resisted. He spoke his thoughts exactly as they occurred to him, without a storyteller's adornment or sense of structure. And he never felt compelled to highlight his story's point or even its point of origin. It forced one to attention, to participation.

Ted continued. "I was also thinking about all the kids who, well, who disappear. Runaways, kidnappings"—now I was caught—"just finding themselves plain old lost. And how not one of those things seems to apply to Sarah for me. I mean, I feel like I ought to be able to think something definite about her since I know all that. I can't make the connection."

Patricia spoke excitedly. "That's exactly, exactly what happened to me when Kerry and all the other girls were saying like, 'This happens all the time, you know,' or 'How 'bout Timmy Blandon who ran away and now he's in jail?' I couldn't care less, you know? I mean, I'm sorry for Mrs. Blandon, but like I feel like saying, like, What does that have to do with Sarah? They think it does, but I can't get them to understand that it doesn't. At all."

Paul, no slouch himself on school gossip, added, "Timmy Blandon is a drug addict, too. He sells to grammar school kids. He should be in jail."

Ted sat forward in his chair. "I wonder why it is that none of us can make those connections, like with the Blandons. If it wasn't Sarah, I mean, we would have said the same thing. I would, anyway."

Paul was on a roll. "Definitely I would. 'Cause you link up things together, like accidents or criminals. You think about it like it's all just news or something."

Patricia was crying, though without embarrassment, a feat she had not managed in more than four years. "It's just like nobody can think about how much you love someone who's your own sister. It's that Sarah wasn't just some kid who is, like, on a milk carton, you know: This Kid Is Missing." Now my daughter was sobbing, but still desperate to speak, to be heard. "I used to even ignore her. Now I wouldn't. I would play any stupid game with her. She has the greatest hair in the world, the greatest blonde hair. I want to brush her hair for her. Mom?"

I walked to Patricia and held her and, completely unprecedented as it was, Paul came to my side, tears literally streaming down his face.

I looked to Ted, thinking he might continue. But he was lost in a darker, ineffable sadness that he could not transgress. He nodded, shut his eyes.

I spoke, knowing that I was about to commit the first act of memory, though only dimly aware of the consequences. "You're right, Patricia. Sarah's hair is the perfect blonde. Yellow, really. But do you remember when I tried to make you teach her how to braid it? What you did to her?"

Patricia responded, quietly. "Paul helped."

Paul returned to his sweating glass of soda. "You showed me what to do. I thought that was how you braided it. How was I supposed to know? What? Do you see me going around having dreadlocks or something?"

I laughed at the image of Sarah the story restored to me. "It was braided all right. How many of those tiny braids had you made? Thirty?"

Patricia laughed. "No. Forty. Twenty on each side. Sarah kept saying it hurt, and it must have. I mean, like it wasn't supposed to hurt. But remember what she looked like after you made me undo them all?"

Paul yelled, enthusiastic now, mimicking me. " 'Not one hair off her head. You understand me? She loses one hair while you undo this mess and it's curtains.' "

Patricia pointed at Paul. "You were the clumsy oaf who kept pulling the braids instead of unwinding them. Mom, remember how she looked, though? How far her hair stuck out? It was like she was electrified."

I tried to keep at bay the urge to silence that made its way to the weakest border of any conversation. *Mom, remember how she looked.* I stood. "The truly horrifying part was that she liked it, of course. The sight of her with that hair. I will never forget it."

Never forget it. Silence seized on my mention of forgetting and asserted its right to rule over the gathering. Escape was my only reliable ally. A half-hearted offer by Ted to cook dinner served as my excuse. Milk and juice were needed. Supplies were needed. (I was relieved no one asked for specifics.) I promised to be back within the hour. Patricia and Paul retreated into magazines.

Just before I left, Ted caught me around the waist and held me to him. "Don't be gone too long. They need you around here. Thanks."

| III |

I resisted the urge to return to the library and actually drove the four miles to the huge supermarket that was one of my harbors in the world. I could think of nothing in the Fossicker larder that needed restocking other than milk and juice, but any small task promised relief from Sarah's absence. And I was out of the house. (I think this state of affairs was so preferable, in part, because it gave me the pretense of being on the lookout for my daughter. Perhaps, more to the point, though, was that both apparitions of Sarah had taken place outside.)

The oddity of a less than half-full parking lot and the gassy fluorescence of the store itself I noted with displeasure. Why was I shopping for food on a Saturday evening? How little did I want to encounter bands of giggling teenagers with armfuls of junk food? As I entered the supermarket I felt myself reduced by the circumstance. I felt like a lowlife. Alienated by the night-lit produce and the dim aisles dirty from a day's wear and tear, I appreciated for the first time my children's absolute repulsion at the idea of joining me on a foray into this very store. The whole setup—the repetitive goods, the overabundance of un-desirable cans of spaghetti and bread crumbs, the ridiculous carts that can never be easily navigated around midaisle displays of day-old, reduced-price goods—seemed designed to depress and humiliate the shopper.

Nevertheless, I had come for milk and juice. Though I know I am aware of this only in retrospect, I am sure that I mapped out the shortest route to the dairy cases in my mind, debated the tradeoff between low-fat and skim milks, whether to pay more for the product of a well-known dairy. These thoughts were probably layered between a few dozen other choices and strategies.

I know all this—I mean, I think about all this—because on this already overanalyzed Saturday night I had the odd privilege of confronting the mind of the American food shopper. My routine acquisition of groceries has never been the same.

Before I was within earshot of her, I knew that the woman in the flowered dress (it looked to be vintage 1940, a true housecoat) and baseball jacket (a hero jacket, royal blue trimmed with yellow leather) was a regular Saturday-night shopper. She had a cart in which were stacked a dozen or more boxes of instant rice and nearly four times as many boxes of Jell-O. When I closed in on her (she was directly in front of the skim milk) I saw that it was orange Jell-O, through and through. As I reached for skim milk, I heard her talking. I seemed to have entered her consciousness, though I was but a temporary aside. She was talking aloud, not exactly to herself, but in the hushed tones one reserves for that type of thing.

She said, "Skim milk always seems like a good idea till you drink it. Bad on cereal. Turns coffee sort of green. I hate all the sizes. Generic milk! Did you see that? Milk ought to be milk. Forget it, I can get milk at the corner. Really, that's too much, generic milk. I should've bought that veal. It was cheap. Does veal always turn gray?"

I was transfixed. I simply leaned on my cart and trailed her.

"Yoghurt is terrible. Why not sour cream? For the rice. How would I do that? I like gravy better than sour cream. Or butter? Yes, two pounds." (Here she retrieved her butter.) "I hate margarine. I really hate those plastic tubs. I always feel like I have to save them and I end up with moldy bits of things. Remember the soup that turned solid? I should've bought that veal. The next time I see it here it will cost twice as much and I'll be sorry. What about veal and rice? Frozen peas with that and gravy? Frozen peas are the greatest. Chicken and frozen peas and gravy."

Abruptly, she pulled a U-turn and headed for the frozen-foods section. As she passed me she said, "Veal is not always the greatest."

I was completely happy for the duration of my short stay. I felt I'd been exposed, another madwoman-shopper cataloguing my unsolicited opinions, my marginal preferences, summoning everything I knew about milk as it existed in its packaged form.

How did I ever learn to identify thoughts that merit speech? How did my children learn? Closeted with my own running commentary, which seemed oppressive after I was made aware of it, I made my way through the streamlined, fifties-style conveyor belts. When I felt the night air my mind reeled back to Sarah. Involuntarily (as far as I can tell) I prayed for her well-being, telepathically demanding the attention of the powers that be. Then, already frustrated by my oversensitivity to my silent discoursing, I yelled aloud, looking up past the streetlights, "Bring her back."

Clearly, this was the sort of thing that gained nothing in the speaking. Knowing this, and in honor of the woman in the baseball jacket, I yelled, "Fresh veal is pink veal." To call a close to the incident, I switched on the radio and joined the audience of silent thousands.

| IV |

Sunday elapsed like a hymn. The first verse was the familiar ritual of the Fossickers madly rushing to shower and don approved clothing for church, settling into their customary pew— three from the front, left of the aisle, Ted letting each member file in before him, pass by him at Communion, the Protestant benchmark in the Catholic arena. The refrain was sounded as we left church, politely limiting our conversations with parishioners and priests who'd heard about Sarah on the evening news; the refrain ended when each of us was handed a photocopy of Sarah by a young girl at the rear of the church, who repeated rather unspiritedly the phrase, "Have you seen this kid?" (Clare had written that refrain.)

Next verse, a sad breakfast of bacon and eggs, normally a happy ritual. Again, the refrain, as the four of us joined Clare at the minimall and leafleted the Sunday-morning newspaper-and-doughnut shoppers with photocopies of our disappeared fifth.

Verse three, late lunch at home with Clare, the sole believer among us. She ended the verse with a sort of Amen: "If you can make yourself believe that she is not coming back—I mean, that is hard to believe. Would you have believed it if I'd asked you a week ago? Well, if you can almost believe that, why not just believe what's easier to believe, that we will find her?"

The final intoning of the refrain was a long and drawn-out affair, involving intermittent stimulation of memories of Sarah by Ted or me (we'd tacitly agreed, I think, to make each other and Paul and Patricia talk about Sarah).

Finally, Ted surrendered to the children's desire to make a search of outlying areas by car. It was his idea of a compromise, I think, having declared that on no account would they be allowed to stay home from school on Monday. I did not join them. I knew my evening's plans. I had to inform my parents that unless they had kidnapped Sarah (a thought that was not entirely jocular as it presented itself to me), their total number of progeny had been inexplicably reduced by one.

| V |

One of the odd comforts that inevitably accrue in the midst of a tragedy or miracle is the proof one receives of the constancy of particular notions or facts. I imagine that in the wake of Galileo's reorganizing of the universe as sun-centered, scientists, theologians, and thinking people of all bents were tempted to scrutinize even the most unrelated physical phenomena, just to feel the salve of the known, the reliable.

My conversation with my mother provided a peculiar solace, albeit indirectly. Her questions (she has a knack for making even simple declarative sentiments into questions) as I recall them; then, as now, my responses are irrelevant:

When?

How long were you planning to wait until you told your father and me?

You are absolutely sure she didn't run away? You do know that children, even good children, run away, don't you?

Who is this Sister Clare? Why is she so concerned about Sarah? Is it possible she had something to do with this?

Do you honestly believe that children disappear?

What are the police doing for you?

Are Paul and Patricia with you now?

What does Ted propose to do about all this?

Have you told your sisters already? Did I tell you already that your brother, Richard, is living with a divorcée? And I mean, living with her, and that he lost his job?

Carol didn't tell you about Richard? You're not in touch with Theresa at all? Ever?

When this all blows over, do you think you could talk to Carol about maybe pulling herself together a little? Did I tell you she chopped off all her hair?

Your father is fine, why?

I'm sure there is nothing we can do, is there?

Why didn't you call me right away?

How much do you think the police care about one little girl with all they have to worry about?

Do you know how to go about getting her picture on the milk cartons?

Will you call me again or should I call you? Are you keeping that little job of yours?

You don't mind if I just tell Theresa about all this, do you?

| VI |

By midnight I was the only Fossicker awake. I sat by the telephone, which Ted had outfitted with a recording machine to take messages so that I wouldn't be tethered to the house. We'd agreed that he would return to work and I would not. For a time. His schedule was flexible enough to allow for shortened days at the office and time off as required. My conscience was inflexible enough to maintain the implicit link between Sarah's disappearance and my employment.

I reviewed the catalogue of atrocities documented by the various advocates of America's missing children. In several abusive or dangerous scenarios I managed to place Sarah, gauging her reactions, her instincts, overestimating her capacity to survive. I denounced my earlier wish for certainty: I argued now that she could survive trauma and live to return to me. Still, I balked. I simply could not resolve to have her live through torment. I could not cling to such a hope.

Unmindful of the fact that my decision was of no practical value to Sarah, I opted for the nonexistent middle ground. *Sarah is alive and unhurt.* If wishing and hoping were my only resources, I would make the most of them.

| VII |

Monday morning never quite materialized. From the moment I opened my eyes until well after my two remaining children and Ted had left me alone in the house, storm clouds chugged into town in ever nearer and nearer reaches of the sky. Like some sad Victorian heroine in a Hollywood romance, I presumed to understand the significance of a dawn that brings on a gradual darkening.

Patricia and Paul joined me in the kitchen, silently ate from bowls of cold cereal. We were all waiting for Ted to join us, each of us hoping he might have something to say.

Exasperated by his father's tardiness, Paul finally said, "I guess it might rain today."

Patricia said, "What a genius."

I smiled, as if I knew what was being said.

| VIII |

Just after seven-thirty, Paul said, "We've missed the bus."

"Tell me something I don't know," Patricia countered.

It was obvious that both children understood they were not to leave home before their father appeared. This was by no means a tradition. On those rare occasions when Ted drove them to school, the children were alerted well in advance. It was not at all uncommon for one or both of the children to leave for school without seeing Ted. And Ted often left for some far-off site at such an early hour as to elude even my gaze.

For a few minutes more we all listened as the water from Ted's shower drained through the pipes that descend through a kitchen wall. I entertained the notion of Ted having committed suicide above us all, veering off immediately into a consideration of whether I would sell the house he'd built. I decided I would sell the house, probably move to Maine. If Paul and Patricia did not want to be moved from their friends and familiar environs, I would simply make them obey. Having lost a child and a husband, I would prove a formidable opponent. I could make them do anything.

The water stopped running. Ted yelled, "If the kids are still here, Anne, tell them to stick around for a minute. I want to see them."

In a tone of voice that had something to do with love and

something to do with my dependence on Ted, I said, "Isn't he great?"

The disproportion embarrassed my children. Mocking me, Paul said, "Isn't he late?"

Patricia brought her bowl to the sink, hoisted herself up on to the counter, and sat there. Paul retied each of his sneakers. It was as if they'd caught me necking with Ted.

| IX |

Ted in white chinos, a light blue shirt, a plaid madras tie, penny loafers; a tall, strong man; stiff short blond hair, still slightly damp at the crown of his head, arranged in a decidedly barber-shop style; his eyes gray, nearly transparent in harsh natural light—say, on a beach in Maine. When this Ted walked into the kitchen Monday morning, I took note of him as I would size up a stranger. He might have been an insurance assessor, a bachelor assessor, come to provide an estimate of the damage sustained by the Fossicker family. I wondered if he ever thought of himself in this way; I do not believe he would have had cause, ever, to figure me for a competent, appealing stranger in this setting.

Patricia and Paul looked to Ted. I was so happy to see Ted looking so alive that I almost exhorted our two children to acknowledge the remarkable fortune that was theirs to have such a man for a father.

If we'd all remained encased in that initial silence just a moment longer, I might have asked Ted to pull Sarah out of his pocket, willing to rely on magic in the absence of a miracle. I wanted to believe he could do anything.

| X |

Ted asked Patricia to join us at the table. Once she was seated, he took Paul's hand in his own; then we were all holding hands, linked up in this way as the rain began to fall in wavelike rushes, one layer of clouds after another giving way. After a loud clap of thunder, Ted said, "Finally. That's better. Because I remember that it stormed hard the day after my parents were killed. It had been so long since the last rain that the dust rose up, bounced up, and from eye level it was raining mud. I'd never seen that before. I remember thinking that I had never seen such a thing before as mud falling like rain. And I thought that was just fine. That the world was changed. That my parents died all at once and then it was raining mud the very next day and I was all of a sudden living in some different world. It took me years to figure out it was the same world I'd always lived in. It took me years to figure that out. The rules didn't suddenly change. The world hadn't chnged. It's just that such things happen in this very world. And I woke up this morning and had a shower and I hate to admit this, but it is a world where Sarah gets separated from all of us. I won't say I know what that means or how you have to act now, as a result of that. But there you have it. Right now, if I were God? I would wrap you in my arms. That is what I would do as God. I would want to be your God that way. I would have Sarah in there too. She would belong with us. I would want to hold on to all of us. I would not let go. And I suppose that is just one of the reasons I am not God. What I do know about this world and being in this world, though, is that I am like God in how I love you and I love you, Sarah. Even if I were God that wouldn't have to change. It is already."

In blind, divine union we let the rain fall. Twenty minutes passed, maybe more. As the rain ebbed I stood, kissed my children's heads. They moved to collect their bags and coats. I walked to Ted's chair, held his head between my hands. He took my hands and said, "Please outlive me."

| XI |

My assignment for the morning was to contact one of the only agencies devoted strictly to finding missing children; that is, an organization without a particular categorical imperative about the condition under which the child was separated from the home. After a brief initial conversaton with one of the staff members, I agreed to a second telephone interview with a case worker who would be assigned to me before the end of the day. Involving volunteers located in an upstate New York town exposed the dimensions that my quest now encompassed. Peevishly, I conjured images of Sarah on a steamer crossing the Atlantic against her will or perhaps without her knowledge.

I hesitated before putting in a call to Officer Hall; wrote a note reminding myself to call Clare at lunch time. Then, with as much disdain as I could manage, I addressed the God who had failed to hold the Fossickers together in his embrace. After all, despite a lapse and a great many impertinent assaults on the tenets of churchgoing and obedience that my parents had passed on to me along with the customary threats and unmanageable promises about the quality of life after life, I had charged back into the relative bounds of the Church.

Admittedly, it was a technicality that allowed me to reassert my standing. The unbaptized state of our first child, Patricia, forced me to reconsider the sagacity of my secular state. I would look at her for hours at a time, reconsidering my right to withhold from her the rite of passage that I'd doubted but never denounced as it applied to me. This, and no small desire to wed myself to my family in the wake of my marriage, led to the uncovering of a pertinent detail by a young Catholic priest who asked Ted and me to call him Freddy. Unwittingly, Ted and I had been married by an ordained Lutheran minister. In the modern Church, our marriage was therefore licit but not sanctioned, or legal but not blessed—it was, in any case, a recognizable marriage in the eyes of the Church. Essentially, this meant that as a Catholic in this situation, should I divorce Ted, I could not remarry. The real coup, though, was that Ted's first marriage was not licit or legal—not even visible in the eyes of the Church. So, I'd not become a heathen or even suffered tacit exclusion from the fold by binding myself to him. Ted's marriage, as far as the Church was concerned, stood outside of history.

With a brief, decidedly unceremonious blessing by Freddy in the presence of no one else, we became a married couple with full right of access to the baptismal font. With Patricia soon cleansed, we took up the practice of church attendance. Ted never thought of converting; he considered Catholicism a personality trait, symptomatic of his understanding of his parents' missionary zeal. Harboring no end of doubts and discomforts and a shameful degree of disbelief, I carried, and occasionally attempted to shape, a personal faith. I believed that I could achieve a rejuvenation of, or an intimacy with, my spirit, my soul. I did not lay claim to this; like money in a retirement account, rebirth on this scale was held in private reserve.

As naive or ridiculous as it may seem, I was dismayed when I began to confront religion and Catholic ethics in my children. Choosing parochial schooling had been an issue of educational quality. Church had been an opportunity and a social context. So I lazily thought. My tolerance for dogma was limited, not to say nonexistent.

What had I expected? Para-Catholics? Or, as Ted would say, What are you going to do now?

It was not whimsy, though, this drive to be saved but not bound. I did not bray at Jesus and the failures I ascribed to him in jest. I believed entirely in the separateness of my soul—a separate, complete Anne. I believed in another world, perhaps a coexistent world. I believed that occasionally the spheres of soul and body overlapped and something wonderful or even miraculous happened.

Principally, I lacked a tether that would bind soul to body, belief to living. Thus, like my parents before me, and my sisters and brother alongside me, I shuttled between the world and the Church, between life and death, willing to believe in another world and entirely committed to my existence in this one.

Typically, it was in Sarah that I saw the distortions I had wrought. Sarah, lover of regimentation and rite, who could forget to put on shoes before leaving the house but who had memorized all necessary prayers within weeks of her first exposure to organized religion. Sarah whose First Communion, still a year off, had been in the planning stages for more than two years. Sarah who liked to bless herself with the sign of the cross, a habit that gave me hope during the days after she'd disappeared. Sarah who was a soul as clearly as she was my daughter.

Gnarled and irresolute, the unmanageable idea of Sarah not here, Sarah gone, implanted itself in me as a new icon of my faith. Is that it? I only knew that I was alive in a terribly miraculous world. A mountain had moved.

| XII |

The rain lasted for three days, enough to dismiss my romantic notion that heavy rain and the subsequent clearing would renew my hope. When it stopped, sometime midmorning on Thursday, the abatement seemed only inevitable—heavy rain cannot fall forever. Children disappear forever. No correlation. No hope there.

In the meantime, Paul and Patricia had gotten themselves immersed in a great buzz of activity generated by Clare. There were small-scale searches, leaflets to be made and distributed, assemblies addressed by local law enforcers, Child Awareness Day to be planned, interschool networks to be forged. Paul and Patricia were now celebrities. Annoying as this was to me, I could hardly convince them otherwise. It was a desirable end; in fact, they had been catapulted out of social obscurity by means of their sister's disappearance. This did not mitigate the simple joy of attention in the form of telephone calls, name recognition, authorized excuses for missing classes, prominence on various committees.

The tragedy had lost its familial focus. With Paul and Patricia away at school and Ted at work, I was forced to welcome the personal pain of longing for Sarah, regretting her brief unhappy moments, punishing myself with all manner of psychological abuse if I discovered myself in a lapse—perhaps eating lunch and not devising a plan of action for the next half hour. Disbanded, the family ceased to exist, really. Each of us was alone with whatever sense of Sarah we'd accumulated before she left.

And time passing—I was alone with that. Thursday I woke with a fresh panic, aware that she was unseen for nearly a week. Already, our helplessness and despair were ritualized, various tasks acted out for the benefit of the actors with no practical regard for Sarah or her return. If someone had asked me what I was doing with my days (the sort of impersonal, standardized taunt that Ted did not bring to our marriage), I would have said, "I am trying to locate my youngest daughter, whom I will never find."

| XIII |

The volume and variety of mail addressed to the Fossickers increased so dramatically that I installed a small file stand near the front door, into which I would drop the many sympathy cards, letters expressing support, requests for interviews, and copies of lists on which Sarah's name and description had been entered. Transcripts of the three-day investigation into Sarah's disappearance conducted by the local television station arrived on Thursday with a note from the series producer. I filed that alongside the clippings from the local newspapers and radio-bulletin transcripts. In an adjacent folder I filed several fliers I'd received that detailed the histories of children "presumed missing" throughout Fairfield County and as far away as Indiana. We had already become a new hot spot, a color-coded pin on some national map of disasters involving children. These initial efforts to forge a national consciousness were uncoordinated— various personal crusades whose tactics and proponents became increasingly alarmist in response to the paucity of public concern and the minimal government funding and manpower available. Already a new vocabulary was being coined: Missing Children, distinguished from Runaways and Parental Abductions, to elicit the sympathy that was deemed a prerequisite to a generalized public reaction. A Missing Child could happen to anyone.

The categorical Missing Children seemed to me the juvenile counterpart of the Missing in Action. America had learned to live comfortably with the idea that some young men are just lost in a war. Oddly, sadly, the popularization of the phrase did not impel the citizenry to demand an explanation or to recover the missing soldiers. Missing in Action became a reality, a fact. America believed in Missing Men, relegated them to the ever-lasting limbo that houses missing limbs, missed trains, and missed opportunities. *Missing:* a circumstance that can be mourned, decried, forgotten; a circumstance that has a life eternal.

A second source of my despair I located in the ineptitude of the media coverage. As I had become an unwitting archivist of available literature on the topic, I saw that every broadcast and print report relied on the small body of available literature for its presumed facts. Sarah's case, even her personal history, was cut and pasted to resemble the stories of other Missing Children. The media's assessment of her plight, the reported likelihood of her recovery—what passed for an analysis was simply a generalization from the few and randomly assembled precedents. In this way, the media simply propagated inadequate methods of searching for, protecting, and thinking about children. By making personal tragedies into something for broad and even national consumption, the media inevitably became a conduit for pooling our despair, sharing our ignorance.

Of course, I had already identified a sufficiently painful and irrational explanation for Sarah's disappearance—my determination to be a Working Mother. I knew it was unlikely that any media report would identify this as the root cause of a national epidemic. But I was certain that I could not go un-punished for Sarah's fate. No matter how completely assimilated the notion of the Missing Child in the culture of the 1980s, I knew it to be an unnatural state of affairs.

How I had longed to call myself a Working Mother. And

within a week of Sarah's disappearance it was obvious to me that a Working Mother is the unglamorous equivalent of the celebrity who retains the services of a ghostwriter to produce an alleged autobiography.

We are not mothers biologically. It requires an act of the will or, at least, an act of surrender. If you choose not to accept the responsibilities of the biological reality you have acceded to, you must secure the services of a nanny or a nurse. Even the stupidest woman does not expect her young to raise themselves. All the elitist and libertarian notions we have invoked will not compensate for the simple and sad fact that Working Mothers essentially give up their children for adoption. What more pertinent hallmark of a faithless world can one imagine than this: that a mother sees in the child she has chosen no satisfacory guarantee of the better future. Really, it amazed me when I considered the option of public day care, or defended other women's choices based on the availability of state-run centers. The state that failed to accord women voting rights until it was to its own advantage? The state that shipped off a generation of young men to Vietnam and pretended not to notice that thousands of its erstwhile representatives were missing?

The very least we could do is to raise up a professional surrogate-mother class. Or a volunteer corps.

I had so long accused society of cultural amnesia, failure to learn the salient lessons from its tragic history, that I determined not to ignore whatever could be culled from my own tragedy. I resolved to be willing to offend my sensibilities, to denigrate whatever principles I held as sacred. None of them had saved Sarah. They were not sufficient.

On this Thursday morning I resolved to begin again. I decided to think beyond myself, to act and speak in spite of myself. I did not doubt my capacity to complete this heroic transformation. I was girded for the battle. Along with the mail that I filed after only a cursory examination, I had received a small box wrapped in brown paper. It was addressed to "MRS. FOSSICKER, MOTHER OF SARAH FOSSICKER."

Inside the box was the Monday edition of a local newspaper with a picture of the search party organized by Clare. Within the large group, it was easy to make out both Paul and Patricia. The sender had drawn around their likenesses a large noose, in red ink. Beneath this rudimentary message was some tissue paper. Inside the tissue paper, also red, was Sarah's Brownie cap, cut into thirty-one pieces.

| XIV |

In my innocence I had cajoled myself until I believed in a random universe. In that fool's paradise a child could just disappear. A mother could lose a child and dedicate herself only to various attempts to comprehend her loss. In my confusion I'd consigned myself to a permanent state of benign sadness. It would be my lot to acquire the virtues of tolerance and humility.

As if wishing and hoping and praying might make it so.

Then, like a fragment of a dead star fallen from its orbit, the noosed image of Paul and Patricia and Sarah's shredded cap fell into my life. Like a fallen star? No. Something more akin to a cross burned on my lawn, blood smeared on my door. It was not mine to ponder some intergalactic mystery. I had been issued a warning. I was living in harm's way.

| XV |

I had spoken to Clare and told her to bring Paul and Patricia home to me before Officer Tim Hall returned my call. After a prolonged debate on the topic, Tim Hall challenged one last time my intention to warn my children about the threat that had been issued. "Tell me once more, Anne, why you are certain that the threat is imminent and that by frightening them you can protect your children. Explain that to me once again. I still do not understand that part. Explain it to me once more, for my sake, before you tell them."

To a woman in my state, people don't make simple statements.

People do not feel free to say, "For God's sake, don't tell them." This was a new twist for me. I had to translate expressions of doting, relentless concern and exaggerated confusion into warnings and advice. People had taken to addressing me as a woman in a certain condition, speaking to my circumstance. It had yet to occur to me that I was so visibly reduced; I convinced myself that I was surrounded by cowards.

Ted's secretary telephoned to tell me that my husband was on his way home. She asked me if I was all right and I pretended to be very busy, thanked her for her concern, hung up. I tried to concentrate on preparing some kind of lunch for the gathering, again was interrupted by the ringing telephone. I was sure it was Ted's secretary calling to apologize for having sounded condescending. Annoyed, I said "Hello" as if it was the last thing I had time for.

Sarah said, "Stop looking for me."

Immediately our connection was severed and the electronic hum signaled the telephone company's readiness to place my call. But I didn't know how to call Sarah. I didn't even remember how to hang up a telephone. I sat with the receiver in my lap, ignoring the computerized voices and buzzes exhorting me to hang up and try again. Sarah's voice had vibrated along wires and through transmitters. Recorded or live, Sarah's voice had warmed this machine pressed into my lap. Sarah's voice was here.

INVOCATIONS

| I |

PAUL AND Patricia sat motionless on the sofa. Clare stood beside the sofa, staring out through the large picture window. Tim Hall was seated, stirring sugar into his coffee. I moved back and forth between the kitchen and the living room, accomplishing nothing, waiting for Ted to arrive and intercede.

I was so afraid the telephone would ring.

Without warning, I retrieved the package from the shelf near the front door and displayed the picture with the noose and the pieces of Sarah's cap. "It's a threat, obviously. I think you all better know about it." I was carrying the package like a tray of food, offering it to my children, then Clare. "What it means, who it is from, that's all anybody's guess."

Clare was shocked. "Guess?"

I tried to hold to my thin line of reasonableness. "Before you came, Officer Hall inspected the package. No postmark. It was hand-delivered. He's going to talk to neighbors about anyone near the house. Who can see all the way up here? I think we have to rely on guesses, hunches. That's for now anyway." I had lost hold. My two children were retreating before me. They had seen too much. Parodies of polite young adults, they seemed to

80

want nothing more than to be overlooked. I had scared them into submission. *What are you going to do next?*

I gave the package to Tim Hall, hoping that I could coerce my audience into simple, calm planning. "We have to deal with this. Of course. We're going to need a plan."

I was not only unconvincing. I was a torment. I had dared Paul and Patricia to make sense of the incomprehensible and wagged a death threat before them as nonchalantly as I might display a dirty sock I'd found under a bureau or a cassette tape left out of its appropriate case. I had unthinkingly asked them to explain it to me.

Patricia shook her head, speaking rapidly. "I'll just kill myself. Why not? I guess so. Like maybe they'll have a trade and they'll give back Sarah alive. Now they're kidnappers? Then what do they want to kill me for? I'll just do it."

Patricia continued to shake and twitch. Paul was still, not even daring to look at his sister. In this unprecedented, perverted atmosphere I'd created, he felt like a coward for not matching his sister's offer.

I approached Patricia. "My God, that isn't the point."

She stood, estimable in her confusion and rage. "What is the point? What is the point? What is the point? The point? You mean it? Why? What did we do? What are we supposed to do now? Who are you kidding? We know the point. What? Like me and Paul are gonna hide? Where? Like we're just gonna— you don't even know who sent it. I don't believe this."

I yelled, to stop her. "Patricia, this won't help."

"What will? The police? Like they found Sarah, I suppose. They can't even find her and you think they're gonna help me and Paul. Who are you kidding?" She pointed at Tim Hall. "He gonna live here? Go to classes with me? Do you know how easy it is to kill somebody nowadays? How would you know?"

Timidly, Paul said, "May I be excused?"

Before I could answer, Patricia screamed, "Nowhere. Stay here now. Nowhere."

Paul obeyed her.

Clare had not moved. Only now did she engage my stare. She was smiling, condemning me. "Ted just pulled in."

| II |

Silence—a desperately hopeful silence—greeted Ted. Eventually I provided him with a summary of the events immediately preceding his arrival, purposefully avoiding Sarah's phone call, which I had yet to introduce as evidence. Of what? With occasional interruptions from Patricia and Tim Hall, the story filtered through to Ted who, all the while, stared at the noosed picture and the shredded cap as if they were artifacts of postmodern art.

He put them out of sight, on the table near the door, then assumed a central position and spoke softly, quickly. "It's too late to wonder about who should see this, of course. Everyone has. Seen it. Right? That's done. And unless Tim Hall knows something I don't, it seems perfectly obvious that, just to be on the safe side, Patricia and Paul are due for a short vacation. I really think this is a hoax or something. I think there must be a simpler explanation than that someone wants to do in the Fossicker family. As far as where they should go—"

I yelled. "Not now. Not here. I don't care if it is paranoid. Not in front of everyone."

Ted seemed to want to move toward me, but he only pivoted. "Everyone who? Officer Hall? Clare? Me?"

I did not want to have to speak my accusations. "It can wait, can't it?"

Clare sat next to Paul on the sofa. "Can it? Wait?"

I tried to ignore her, tried to dismiss the ominousness of her moving nearer my children. "There are other considerations. What does this mean for Sarah? Isn't that worth a few words? Or have we given her up for good?"

Ted turned to me, angry. "Stop it. Who are you helping? Is this a competition? Who cares more?"

"It's not a competition. But it is a contest." I had meant to sound conciliatory. I could see that I had failed. "Someone is competing with us for her. Someone wants something. The cap." This too was greeted with silence. "It doesn't mean . . . Someone is telling us something. Like they might harm her if we're not careful. Like we have to be more careful who we talk to about anything."

Tim Hall said, "The cap means something. I'm not sure I could agree that it means she's . . . It's not direct evidence that she is alive. I mean, whoever sent this cap may have her—but that's not clear at all."

I wanted Clare off the sofa, away from my children. I felt her presence now as a dare. "And you? Clare? Can you tell us what it means?"

"No." She smiled.

"Why not guess? You have a right to guess."

She smiled again. "I don't want to guess. Can't we try for fingerprints? Or is that silly? People are careful, people who send such things as . . ." She looked at Tim Hall, who dismissed the possibility of fingerprints. "Well, I still think the hand-writing, the cap. That is something, means something."

Tim Hall interrupted. "That will all be gone over, of course. I really doubt it's going to give us much—"

Ted chimed in. "People are so smart about fingerprints and evidence now, aren't they?"

"Cop shows." Tim Hall stood. "But we're more sophisticated about fibers and trace materials than ever. We can give it a thorough going over and see—"

"As to what it means about Sarah . . ." Clare was not prepared to speculate herself, but she wanted the issue aired.

"Does it mean something, Tim?" Ted actually sounded hope-ful.

I could not suppress my enthusiasm. I had thought I should wait until Clare left, but I could not. "Sarah is alive," I said nonchalantly. "I got a phone call. Right after your secretary called, in fact, Ted. I wanted to wait . . . I shouldn't have waited . . . I thought it would be better . . . She called. Sarah. Sarah called."

The moment of silence that followed my revelation gave me courage. "We didn't have a conversation. In her little voice, very seriously, she said, 'Stop looking for me.' Then someone cut the connection. But it was her. And she is alive. And this package, it has something to do with—someone trying to scare us? Punish us? I don't know why, but that hardly is as important as that it's happening and we still have time. Her voice was—it was her voice!"

Tim Hall said, "On the telephone in this house? She called you here?"

"Of course. It was here."

The calm silence in the room unsettled me. Finally Clare said, "When, Anne?"

"Not an hour ago. I was just getting something together for lunch, when I heard . . . What does all this matter? Her voice." My children would not look at me.

Ted said, "We certainly have a lot to figure out." He was staring at Tim Hall, staring him down, in fact.

"She's alive. My God. That counts."

Clare said, "Of course she's alive. I believe that."

But you don't believe what, Clare? I was waiting for someone to explain what had happened since I mentioned the phone call.

Tim Hall said, "It's the only thing to believe."

As opposed to believing she called?

"What? Do you think I made this up? The call?" I addressed Ted.

He said, "I believe, really believe, I mean, that you heard her voice."

But not that she called, really. I felt ridiculous, having to defend myself this way. Why doubt me on this? "I heard the phone ring. I said, 'Hello,' and Sarah said, 'Stop looking for me.' And then—nothing. What is there to doubt? It's not like when I've seen her."

With that *It's not like when I've seen her* I was undone. I saw shame and fear replace doubt on the faces half-turned to mine. Like wind, my words flew through the room—wild, bothersome, unaccountable. Tim Hall sat again, in deference to this display.

For the first time in my adult life I honestly believed that I had nothing to lose. (Only in retrospect do I know that such a stance is the stupidest sort of optimism.) I continued. "I don't think I see her in the flesh. I mean, I think she's there and I think that I see her for some reason. And not just, like, I want to see her. She wants to see me, too. Right? But the call, it was her—Sarah, the real Sarah. I should know the difference. She's my own daughter."

While the adults in the room searched their imaginations for an appropriate or even appeasing response, Paul spoke, driven to practical terms by my speech. "There is that police cassette machine. I mean, we have tape recordings of everything. Is she on that?"

I was overjoyed. "You're a genius, Paul. Get the machine— do you know how to replay it?"

Paul obliged, brought the machine to the living room, set it on the floor near the couch. He appeared to have been won over by my confidence, which stemmed my panic.

With my approval, he started the tape with the call from Ted's secretary, and I said, "I hate the way I sound. Do I sound like that to all you on the phone?" No one answered. I said, "It's the next call. Listen."

For almost a full minute we strained to hear the impurities of a blank cassette tape played at full volume. Twice Paul adjusted the machine, to provide for optimal monitoring of my conversation with Sarah. Soon he returned to his seat next to Patricia, the tape player spinning the blank cassette toward its conclusion.

You are unreliable as a witness, Anne. I wanted to say as much. I also intended to announce that I was aware that I was somehow reduced. Before I admitted to my own disintegration, I reeled back one more time, trying to establish the unreality of the phone ringing, Sarah's voice coming to me. I only managed to see Sarah on the front lawn, running toward the open door of a light brown sedan that had pulled to the curb. As she closed the car door I apparently fainted dead away.

| III |

"You fainted," Ted said gravely, as if I might need to be convinced of this fact.

Clare was standing by the couch and holding an open bottle of ammonia like a torch, which I vaguely remembered having been used to rouse me. Without my asking, Clare told me that the children had gone to their bedrooms, that Officer Hall had responded to a radio call and would be in touch later in the day.

I said, "I never faint."

Ted nodded. Clare nodded. It was just the sort of thing a woman in my position is expected to say.

Why say anything?

| IV |

By five o'clock Ted's patience had been defeated. By me. I had not spoken a word. Automatonlike, I had packed my suitcase on command—we were all going to Maine for the rest of the week, until the police could guarantee the safety of our remaining children. I had resisted the urge to explain to Ted my growing distrust of Clare, a distrust that infuriated Ted and with horrific implications that were not lost on Paul and Patricia: Who to trust?

The telephone rang several times and I refused to acknowledge it, much less answer it. I was sure it would be Sarah delivering some message for my ears only. I didn't want to start that up again.

I was preparing dinner while Paul and Patricia and Ted packed the car. Officer Hall had spoken to Ted and told him not to leave before he and Clare arrived with some information. I noted the arrival of the police cruiser with less than normal interest. In my state of noncommunicativeness I found a kind of hollow in which my imagination and my stronger emotions could be laid to rest.

Tim Hall's information came in the form of a truly funny-looking little girl. Though I had not intended to join the session, Ted came to the kitchen and said, "I don't care if you want to be a mute partner, you can not abandon me now. Stand next to me at least. Or is that too much to ask?"

Voicelessly I said, *I have made Ted cry*. Even this could not deliver me to the surface where I might speak. I did follow him into the living room.

Clare had again taken a seat on the sofa with the children. I looked the other way; I rued the fact that my hope of keeping our whereabouts from her had been foiled already.

Pointing to a very small, pale child, Tim Hall said, "Mr. and Mrs. Fossicker, Karen Flynn."

Ted said, "Hello, Karen. You are a very good person to come here to talk to us. Do you feel all right?"

Like a spasm, I got the idea that little Karen Flynn was being offered to me as a replacement for Sarah. To the horror of everyone gathered I seized this as my opportunity to utter a few words. I actually said, "I don't like the looks of this one. What about that hair?"

Karen Flynn burst into tears. Before any adult could move, I retreated into the silent kitchen, honestly uncertain as to whether I had spoken aloud.

It was lucky I had left, after all. I listened to Clare and Tim Hall coach the child to stop crying and deliver her testimony.

At last, Karen said, "I didn't tell 'cause I thought my own Mom and Daddy would say I'm bein' bad. That's why. Today I told 'cause I heard the principal callin' Paul out. I told that Sarah was really cryin' when I looked at her in the hallway. She was leavin' forever 'cause her own was bein' bad."

Clare asked, "Karen, Sarah's own what? You said Sarah told you her own mother was—"

The child spoke again, emphatic now. "Sarah said she was

leavin' school 'cause her own mother was bein' bad. She was cryin' when the lady told her that."

Nothing more could be coaxed out of the child witness. Sarah had told her nothing about who this lady was who'd told her about my badness. If this young child with the ridiculous mop of black hair was to be believed, Sarah was dragged away from home by some woman who rather effortlessly convinced my youngest daughter that I was bad.

Thank you, Karen. That will be all. There is certainly nothing else to say.

| V |

Not surprisingly, the dinner I presented to my family was virtually inedible. I offered no defense for the hashlike substance I earlier believed would be a sort of quick chicken gumbo. Relieved to see that their father had not ventured beyond his first taste, Paul and Patricia asked for permission to leave the table and finish packing. Ted said, "Remember, Patricia—Sister Clare will probably sleep in your room. Leave some space for her things, will you?"

Clare guarding the home front. I was nervously reviewing the range of personal information she could acquire during her stay when Ted suggested that I call my parents to let them know we would be away. He assured me that Clare would call neighbors and friends who might be alarmed by our absence. Another defeat.

After a few minutes Ted said, "I'll call your parents. I suppose you realize that will only make them worry more about . . . No, I don't know what you know. Or think. I don't know."

Ted went to the telephone and I retreated to our bedroom, planning to secret anything I suspected of having talismanic significance, anything Clare might be able to exploit. My charges against her were still unformed, but I was willing to rely on instinct.

Finding little of even potential harm, I sat on the bed and

quietly lifted the receiver from its cradle on the bureau. Is this why I had come?

I believe Ted heard my intrusion, but immediately thereafter my mother answered her telephone. I had won entry.

Ted was matter-of-fact. He recounted the contents of the package I'd received and relayed the various theories. To my way of thinking, he overemphasized the prankster theory; of all people, my mother need not be given an excuse to dismiss the seriousness of the proceedings. When Ted finished, having briefly detailed our plans to retreat to Maine, I heard my mother draw a deep breath, sharply, as if she had taken in the shock all at once. In truth, I was gratified.

After an uncomfortable, sad pause, she said, "Ted. This is impossible. Who would threaten the whole family? This is impossible."

Ever the model of simple sense, Ted replied, "It is impossible and it is a fact. You can imagine the effect it's having here, Eleanor."

My mother was stalled, somewhere between terror and indignation, occasionally lunging toward one extreme. Her voice was thin, piercing. "No, it is impossible. Good heavens. And how can you be sure it is little Sarah's cap? This is the second cap, right? Wouldn't Annie have sewn Sarah's name in the cap? Oh, no, this is not how these things go. How are you going to keep this from Paulie and Patricia?"

Ted was deft, though pointed. "Anne has dealt with that. I don't think I have anything else to tell you that will help. We're having a phone installed in Maine. We'll call soon. I just wanted to let you know, in case you tried to reach Anne."

"She doesn't seem to want to talk about this, though that's not exactly new. Ted, I had to drag it out of her. It isn't right. I am her mother, Ted, you know?"

Wearily he said, "I know." After another very odd silence (my mother is capable of imposing silences that convey the entire range of human emotion), Ted rather spiritedly said, "You know, Eleanor, I've half a mind to put the kids on a plane and hide them away with you in Arizona until this thing stops."

"What do you mean stops? The threats?"

"And Sarah."

Impatiently my mother asked, "You still think the two things are really related?" She seemed to feel she had already provided sufficient evidence to the contrary. "Anyway, you can't exactly run away from this thing, can you? Ted? It still just seems impossible."

"I know, Eleanor. Maybe it is . . ."

"What does that mean? Ted? Are you there?" My mother's voice asked pleading, stubborn questions. I hung up my extension and carried my suitcase downstairs. Clare was seated in my living room, her own knapsack at her feet. My replacement?

I took stock of her still-bandaged hand, the weakness that lack of sleep had painted on her face. Clare followed me to the car. She handed me an overstuffed manila envelope on which my name was written in cursive lettering that recalled grade-school writing tablets with exemplary samples provided by a middle-aged nun. "This is from Lilian—Sister Urban. She wanted you to have it, though I tried to tell her you'd rather get it from her directly. She was writing it when I got back to the convent. Don't be afraid of me, Anne. I'm trying to help."

It was not, to my way of thinking, the stuff of which reconciliations are made. I was tempted to laugh at her.

"I'll do whatever I can to convince you. You can rely on me. Anne, I really have to help somebody."

Unprepared for any show of weakness from my alleged nemesis and afraid that I might exercise my new talent for fainting, I begged her. "Please let her go without more . . . Whoever is doing this, can't you see you've won?"

| VI |

The car ride to Maine began with Patricia's accidental admission that she'd told her best friend, Sue Ameron, that she was being secreted away. When Ted calmly asked her if she had considered that the trip was not supposed to be a public event, she countered with the news that Paul had taken the opportunity to inform his best friend, Bobby Ameron, as well.

Dismissively Paul said, "Bobby promised to keep it a secret. He keeps secrets."

Patricia was as certain about Sue's trustworthiness. "Duh. I told Sue to keep it a secret, too. No kidding. You think I wouldn't do that?"

Paul went directly for the weak spot in his sister's defense. "You told Sue it was a secret? Come off it. That's like begging her to tell everybody. I bet half the freshmen know it before they even get to school. I can't believe you told her it was a secret. How dumb can you get."

Patricia was not disinclined toward a fight with her brother. "Not as dumb as Bobby Ameron, that's for very sure. Even Sue says he is the dumbest kid we ever met. Remember when the Amerons' curtains caught on fire when he put real candles in the windows? Last Christmas? That is dumb, Paul, and that is your friend, the dumbest of them all."

Paul hated these attacks on Bobby, who was perceptibly slower than average. It raised his ugliest temperament, a kind of surly, low-grade anger. This time he simply said, "Shut up about Bobby. And he is not dumb. Ask Mom."

Several times I had tried to calm Paul by distinguishing between intelligence as measured in school and intelligence as savvy—which is both common sense and that more elusive characteristic that I would dub street smarts if we'd lived in a city or town with even the slightest aura of tradition or specificity. As it was, Bobby Ameron had an urchinlike appeal. He was not hip to mall behavior and other suburban rites; he knew something about himself that most of his friends did not. He somehow caught on to the idea that the world was a hierarchy for good reason, and he made a perceptible effort to play to his level. When there was a fight or an accident or a rule broken and Bobby was implicated, he simply shrugged and crossed his arms over his chest, as if to say: Right you are, I was caught out. You're not surprised, are you?

Had I been capable of conversing, I would have said that Bobby Ameron possessed a kind of grace. I don't suppose that it would have vindicated either of my children's positions on the question.

After a long silence Ted said, "I'll have to let Officer Hall know that the Amerons know we're in Maine and let him handle it. Did you tell anyone else, Patricia?"

Of course, she was offended. "No. Not that it's anyone's business. Anyway, it's my life."

I was certain an argument had begun. I looked at my tired husband and tried to make him understand that I would support any tack he adopted. Apparently unaware of me, he said simply, "But, Patricia. Your life really is part of my life. Like Paul's is. That's not just something I say, you know. And Sarah and your mom. I know everything seems pretty rotten sometimes. I just want us to be safe is all. I'm not angry. I want to help us. Are you two still scared about being in the Maine house?"

This was evidence of a conversation I had missed.

Paul said, "We agreed not to tell the Amerons the name of the city in Maine. They only know it's on the ocean. Nobody ever remembers Boothbay. So we really didn't tell, Dad."

Patricia added, "I guess we are still sort of feeling, like, weirded out. Like, what next. But in Maine we're safe, I think. I think you were right, about no one being able to harass us and stuff. That might be all it is, the package. Right?"

Ted looked at me before responding. "I said it before and I'll say it again. I do think it's got the look of something a prankster would do. But trouble usually makes for more trouble. And I'm betting this is the sort of thing the police are used to dealing with. Remember how calm Tim Hall was during it all? He's got some ideas, I bet, and it's just gonna take a day or two for him to track them down. I get the sense that he is best at exactly this sort of investigation."

Paul was audibly relieved. "And don't forget how he said they can test for incredibly small hairs or pieces of cloth and stuff and trace it back. That's the part that will make it easier for him."

"You know what else, Dad?" Patricia was reclining in her seat. "When you asked us to make up our minds how we're thinking about Sarah from now on? I did. Like, not on purpose. Not like, okay, now I believe she is alive. It just came to me. I think of her being alive."

"I know she is," said Paul. "I mean, just how you know some things and you know you don't know about something else? Like that."

Ted only said, "It will help both of you to know what you think." He twisted the rearview mirror and saw that they were both nearly asleep. "It definitely helps me to know what you think. Good night, you two."

Almost simultaneously they said, "Good night, Dad. Good night, Mom."

Reflexively I answered, "Good night and God bless you both." I was surprised enough to feel that my children must have been startled as well. I could only manage to say, "I promise breakfast will be better than dinner."

Paul said, "Good."

As I had not done for years, I watched my two elder children fall to sleep. *Sweet dreams, Sarah. Mom loves you.* And with that I knew the dam would be broken, that in time I would have at my disposal a strength to match in magnitude my sorrow. I did not know how it would be manifest, or even if I could control it. It was enough to have been made aware of its lurking presence, to understand that I was not spent.

| VII |

We rode in silence for more than half an hour. It was Paul's hollering that interrupted us.

In response to some dreamed accusation, he yelled, "She is not. She's good. She's good." With nothing more than a few somber, incoherent mumbles he subsided.

Amiably, Ted commented, "Well, you've got one staunch defender."

I had not understood that Paul was indeed denying the charge leveled by Karen Flynn. *Sarah was leaving school because her mother was being bad.* It was as if Paul had followed me across the boundary, into an alternate piece of time in which Sarah spoke, in which I had something to say. An immaterial world in which he could remain convinced of my goodness.

At once I believed it was urgent that I make something clear to Ted. It was not comfort or even protection I was after. I wanted him to know what he was dealing with, to understand the ostensible proportions of the illusions or delusions or unnatural wonders I'd exchanged for facts.

Of course, I couldn't bring myself to simply start. Embarrassed by my hours of stony silence, my infantile refusal to be engaged, I burdened myself with the responsibility of saying something that would serve as both apology and dismissal. I felt compelled to acknowledge the ridiculous reaction and I felt completely incapable of explaining it. Initially, I took my discomfort to be a good sign, a normal reaction. Understandable shame. *But she did speak to me.*

I guessed that women who hear voices and lay claim to apparitions are not protected by the rules of fair play. Still, I reasoned, even prophets and witches must have the occasional desultory conversation.

In a voice that only ever speaks to me, I said, *And you still haven't uttered a word. What's wrong with you?*

| VIII |

I failed to break through. I contented myself with noticing the freakishness of small towns lit by streetlamps, the perceptible changes in air temperature as we drove north.

When we were within twenty miles of the house, Ted made a pitch for unity and calm. "I am not exactly sure what you have in mind, with your suspicions of Clare. But I feel like it's up to me to ask. Or, I guess, to say that I think you've got it wrong. I've been trying to come up with an explanation. For why you want to suspect her—want to not in the conscious way, I mean. I didn't think of an answer. But it is clear to me, anyway, that she wants to help. I'd go so far as to say she has a need to help us out. That's a puzzle of its own, I guess. Why is it so important to her to be so kind? She has been more than good, Anne. You've said so yourself up to now. She wouldn't harm Sarah, as I see it, anyway. And she knows that being away from all of us is hurting Sarah. She can see that. She gets that. So that's the thing that is illogical about suspecting her." Ted paused and I suspected he believed I would respond. But he was not waiting for me anymore. "I can't keep it up without you talking to me, I can't talk about things. I feel completely stupid. See, right now? It's like talking to myself. Only out loud. I feel worse than stupid. I feel terrible. Maybe you have to. Not talk, I mean. But it's killing me, Anne. I hope you didn't know that already. I've been trying not to let it get to me. But, as you would say, it is a fact. A goddamned fact. And I need you. I get scared, too." Ted did not look at me. "Now you know. I had to tell you."

I moved toward Ted, still mute. I took his hand in mine. But I hadn't touched him. With my refusal to speak I had finally managed to sever my connection to Ted. The circuit that channeled Anne into Ted and Ted into Anne so unflaggingly as to make one's concerns and desires indistinct from the other's was broken. I could not get through to him. I feared that this was evidence that Ted was not getting through to me.

Again and again I told myself, *Ted's voice was here.* But you couldn't prove it by me.

| IX |

With a solemnity bordering on the absurd, we escorted our exhausted children into hastily made beds, prepared our own, ascertained that the telephone company had indeed revived our wires (we'd brought a telephone from home). This was accomplished in utter silence. Before he actually got into bed, Ted said, "I do love you, Anne."

"I love you, Ted." It was neither a fact nor a fiction. And it was certainly not speech of any meaningful kind. It was one more corner of a sheet tucked under the mattress, another step taken along the path of least resistance.

I saw no advantage to being in bed; Sarah was unlikely to feel free to put in an appearance in her parents' bedroom in the middle of the night. Instead, I settled onto my couch in the living room, considered and then decided against removing one of the boards from the plate-glass patio doors. I hoped the presence of her personal sofa might be enough to draw Sarah inside.

She didn't appear, at least not while I was awake. But in the hours before I fell asleep in the freezing room I did nothing but dream of her. I was stringing together images of her from various years just at the point of departure from this strange house, as if memory actually existed as a contiguous videotape that I could splice and edit and reassemble. This particular configuration had a nightmarish quality: Sarah aged, but her sadness and reluctance to leave adhered to each of her incarnations. Played again and again in my mind, the fixity of her emotions acquired a voice: *Why do you give me this and take it away? Can't you see I don't want to go? Why can't we live like this forever?* Year after year I cajoled, threatened, promised—I did everything in my power to convince her that hers was an inappropriate response, an impossible desire. I tricked and teased her away, the surest way to trick and tease the innocent Anne who could not accept or understand the need to abandon this very state of bliss.

Having reviewed this length of memory so often as to have it entered into me as a permanent highlight of my collection, I finally absorbed its meaning: I had prepared her to be an accomplice to her own abduction. Little Karen Flynn reported that Sarah had been crying, sad and no doubt frightened by the news that her mother was bad, that she would have to live without her mother and her family. *We can't live like this forever.* Sarah knew that. Sarah had learned that an emotional response, a private and even holy desire, was an untenable indicator of necessity or propriety. Sarah had learned to scold and cajole or otherwise circumvent her innocence.

That's a good girl.

| X |

I woke slowly, pleasurably warm. In fact, I felt so ridiculously good that I laughed aloud. This had the effect of more fully rousing me. Only then did I see that I was wrapped in a quilt and, more to the point, I was wrapped in Ted's embrace. Ted had a blue wool sweater pulled on over his bathrobe. He was just staring at me, taking me in, reabsorbing me. Then he arched his back and pressed his ribs against mine, as if he could relinquish his separate frame and let himself run into me. He didn't speak and I heard everything he had to tell me. He took in what I could not say. And at a depth below my life with Ted, at so far a remove as to seem ancient, I recognized the dam that had yet to give way, the pressure on it gaining though the source remained unknown. *There is more to come.*

But then and there, I had all I could do, all I could comprehend, to attend to my unearned awakening.

| XI |

My first attempt at conversation began about an hour later, in bed with Ted. We'd observed a moment of silence to determine whether we'd woken the children and decided we had not. "Ted, I've seen her. More than once. And I spoke to her on the telephone. And I've got to tell you that I really don't believe I'm nuts. Despite everything." It was, admittedly, a weak opening.

"I'll tell you, Anne, I believe you. But exactly what I mean by that? I don't know. I accept what you're telling me. But I have to say it's not like I think you're a seer or something. I mean, I believe these visions of Sarah, and her calling. They're real for you. No, more than that. I believe they are part of reality for you. Of your reality."

I wanted more, of course. "What about your speech the other day? About your parents dying. That there is only one world. One reality."

Ted seemed to really think about this. It was a familiar sight, Ted actually rethinking a position because of an apparent inconsistency I'd pointed out. Whether he intended it to be or not, this habit was vaguely unsettling. It had the effect of making me doubt myself. Often enough, I had to literally repress the urge to say, "I made it up. Forget it."

Finally Ted said, "There *is* only one world. That still seems true enough. I mean, of course. And not just in the dumbest way. In the sense that there is only this world ever. Ever."

The "ever" was a twist. "I don't know if I get that, but the point is, Ted, either I am nuts or I am seeing Sarah, who in this world's terms is not here. She may be dead—"

Ted would not let me go on. "She is alive. I know that."

This sparked my anger. "You know that, Paul and Patricia know that, even Clare knows that. But she visits me. She calls me. And I'm not convinced she's not . . . I could lie. I could pretend that I was convinced. When I see her I sure as hell know it is her and that she is alive. But then what? She's not here. She's not on the goddamn tape player. And so what? She's contacting me? Her spirit is calling back to earth? Tell me. Why me?"

"Her spirit is her. That's what I mean." Ted said this as if he understood it for the first time. "I know that is so, Anne. It's not like her spirit is separate from her. That is why I believe you see her and hear her. I don't know how to make this plain, but I do believe it. I think we expect to understand things but we don't act like it's the way the world is. If you know, really know, that you aren't inventing Sarah, and that she really is where you can talk to her, make a move. If that's what you believe, why can't you make yourself act on it?"

"Suddenly I feel like Mr. Put Your Hand Right Here in This

Gash in My Side. The doubting Thomas. I get to see Sarah because I don't believe she is really alive?"

Ted was unwilling to take it this far. "I don't see that, particularly."

Silence descended, an unhappy reminder of the relative novelty of conversation. We seemed to both sense that like patients temporarily laid up, we'd be better off not stretching this exercise to any extremes.

Rome wasn't built in a day. I figured Ted knew as much.

| XII |

Friday morning began again with Paul and Patricia refusing to leave their respective beds; they both felt sick. Of course, the house was underequipped, to say the least. The few aspirins I'd packed seemed inadequate to cover the possibilities. Neither Ted nor I had given any consideration to logistics, and the need for a thermometer, medicines, and other supplies raised the question of our visibility. Were we meant to be hiding in Maine or had we come simply to achieve a diversionary distance?

Ted said, "I don't suppose we have to make it a conspiracy. I mean, it's not as if the CIA is on our trail. No one told us to keep a low profile."

As I listened, I managed to assemble an impressive list of various kinds of organizations—particularly cults—that might undertake kidnappings, harassment, even direct confrontation and violence.

"Our choices are not great here, Anne. We don't have anything but some beans." Ted was not willing to adopt the cult theory I'd temporarily adopted.

"We have artichokes, too. And a corn muffin mix. Food! No wonder they're sick. Food, Ted." I'd gotten excited mid-sentence.

"What about food?" Ted was starting a list for the trip to town he was determined to make. "You want me to buy something in particular?"

"They came home from school yesterday before lunch—a meal I did nothing about. And none of you ate dinner."

Ted took a defensive posture. "You didn't eat a bit of it. How can you blame them? Or me?"

"No. The point is that's why they feel sick. I bet. No food. They haven't eaten enough for mice in the last twenty-four hours. And I'm sure their metabolisms are running at full throttle with the . . . with it all."

"You want to make a list? We can give them something for breakfast. A treat. A proper breakfast."

I started on a list after pouring hot water into two mugs for instant coffee. I sat by Ted, sipped from my mug. "It's terrible and I don't even have any of that powdered milk to color it. Please buy real coffee. Never mind, I'll write it down with the rest of this. Do you think they'll have a melon? Or any fruit? Well, check." Ted was not writing or responding to me. "I'll shut up now and just write."

"I want to know how you arrived at the decision to show the cap and the picture to Patricia and Paul. I was trying to think of the best way to ask you. But that's what I've been thinking about. Did you ask me something I missed?"

"Do you think they'll have any melons?"

"I can look."

I had every intention of avoiding a discussion of my motives. "I think fresh fruit would be the best way to start, on empty stomachs, I mean. Maybe apple instead of orange juice. Cider may be ready up here. That would be a real treat, especially for Paul. Get a lot if they have any." Aware of the flagrancy of my tactic, I put the list aside. "It was my instinct to show it to them. Despite Tim Hall. I think it was the right thing to do. I do, Ted. That is a fact."

Almost piously, Ted replied, "You mean, you'd do it again? If you had it to do over?"

"Spare me, Ted." I walked to the boarded-up patio doors. "I won't have it to do over. Can't you see that this is the point? Would I go to work full-time knowing some dope of an old lady would steal her away from us? No, Ted. I would not. Would I put her in day care so that when I think about her I think as much about the hours we didn't spend together? No, darling, I would not. Would I have had her at all had I known she would be stolen and maybe beat up or raped at the age of six? I don't think so. No, I doubt it, Ted. Look at me, Ted, and ask me another hypothetical question. I told them because they have a right to know. More than that. I told them both about drugs years ago. Everyone knew I told them that. You knew I told them about sex and birth control and not getting diseases and that didn't seem to be a problem. This is part of the world, your old one-world theory again. This is the way it is. I was going to lie to them, maybe? I should have kept it a secret?" I could not easily move into the anger that I sensed just beyond my present state. Nor could I generate a single tear. "This is the seventh day Sarah has been missing. And the fact is, that is the best explanation for everything just now—bad dinners, hours without talking, no milk for freeze-dried coffee. It's all the same to me. I'm winging it here, Ted. Aren't you?"

"Winging it?" He was smiling.

"Go ahead. Make fun of me. What the hell, I'm—"

"No, Anne. It's the milk for the coffee part. It's just like you." He was having trouble speaking at all he was laughing so hard. "It's perfect."

I felt both vindicated and slightly ridiculous. "I don't know why instant coffee is such a hoot."

Of course, this only sent Ted into worse spasms.

Finally he won me over. The sight of him laughing undid me. I sat by him and we laughed. And it didn't give way to tears. We'd remembered how to laugh. If fumblingly, we were coming back to life. We didn't consider what that might entail.

| XIII |

"One other question before I go." Ted was standing near the front door, shopping list in hand.

"If they don't have any melon at all? Get some canned pears." I was really concentrating on the boarded window, wondering if it wouldn't be worthwhile to remove at least a portion of the weatherproofing for the weekend.

"No, Anne. Not a food question." Ted sat next to me. "A Clare question. I guess. That's my question. Were you just having a sort of nervous reaction yesterday? Or do you really think she has some motive that she isn't making clear?"

"You want an answer before you go get food?" I hoped to emphasize the impracticality of that.

"You mean now? Yes. That's why I asked you now." Ted glanced meaningfully at the still-closed doors to Paul and Patricia's bedrooms. "At least a start on an answer. I mean, you sound as if you still suspect something about Clare. What?"

I tried to come across as uncharacteristically meditative, serious. "I think about Clare putting her fist through the window—an overreaction, to say the very, very least, Ted. It is not a normal thing to do. I put that next to the organized search—that was her idea, not mine. And the Child Awareness Day and the dozen or so other events she's organized in about a week's time. A week—it's as if she had time before Sarah disappeared to lay these plans. Anyway, I put those next to each other in one frame. And her staying at the house while we're here. All this—and this is just for starters—I put those things together. And I ask myself, What's wrong with this picture? This is a woman—"

"A nun." Ted wanted to make this clear.

"This woman taught Sarah in kindergarten along with twenty-five other kids. She doesn't teach Sarah now. She never taught Paul or Patricia. And suddenly she is dedicating ninety percent of her waking time to finding this one child? And she's smashing plate-glass windows?"

"Once, Anne. Which I thought she explained to you."

"It's not the one thing, it's the lineup. My God, Ted. She said I shouldn't be afraid of her. Why should she say something like that to me, of all people? What am I supposed to think?"

"You do understand, don't you, that you aren't making the slightest bit of sense in terms of why you suspect her—in terms of her motive."

"I'm not trying to make a case about her motives. I'm telling you where my suspicion started, what gives me the sense that . . ." I was yelling. I did not want to yell, to be cast back into the realm of the irrational, the unreliable. "None of this strikes you as strange? Worth a second thought? The hand through the window, four or five phone calls a day to remind me of a meeting I have with a social worker, to inform me of the existence of yet another regional or national hotline for Missing Children?"

"She's obviously a person who needs to be involved. And, I might add, a person who is good at getting things organized and off the ground. Sure she bugs you with all her scheduling and planning, Anne, but let's remember this is all a service to us. Remember, she's a nun."

I lost it again, of course. "Ted, you keep telling me that. It's like reminding me that Sammy Davis, Jr., is black while I explain how I can't stand to watch him sing. What? Do you think I have trouble retaining facts? I know she's a nun. I also know that it's making me crazy that she seems to have more of a stake in my finding Sarah than even I do. There's no room for what I feel about Sarah, what I need to do. I can't have twenty minutes of feeling lost without a pick-me-up from Clare. Well, I need to despair. I need to just sit around and curse people and the world and the fucking police department. Because she is gone. I don't need Clare telling me we'll find her. I don't need Clare's stupid reminders that we haven't exhausted all our resources. I need to let part of it out without a happy face staring at me. Doesn't she ever just feel terrible and lonely and sad? Why can't you hear this?"

"Hear it? Who can't hear you? You're practically hollering, Anne. I'm sorry." Ted was sitting really still, like a visitor at the bed of a laid-out psychotic.

"I know. I've gone overboard. I can't make the simple frustrations stay simple. They get built up with everything else.

Clare is not the point. But she is a part of the point." *Say something that makes sense.* I could see that it had gotten beyond me. I could not reel in the facts I'd strung out with the fears and sadness and the simple confusion.

"Maybe she only wants to be your friend, Anne, is all I'm saying. Maybe that's what she means."

"Maybe so." I had gone beyond the point of conciliation.

"What I guess I want to say is I don't believe Clare would hurt Sarah. I don't think she's responsible."

"Enough, Ted. Fine. I can't imagine why I said anything in the first place. She's a nun, after all." In fact, I had no idea what I really feared in Clare, what disturbed me, or why my slight discomfort with her style had recently taken on an aspect of suspicion. I wanted to explain to Ted what it was like when she told me not to be afraid, told me to rely on her.

Maybe you're just hard to get close to, Anne; you certainly shut me out yesterday. That's what I heard Ted saying. That is what I knew Ted had a right to say.

Before the silence became a circumstance, Ted pleasantly rushed off to the store, promising to cook breakfast when he returned.

Cursing the proficient cleaners, who had removed every old magazine and newspaper from the living room, I cast about the empty bedrooms for something to read. In Sarah's bedroom I waited for a few minutes, finally gave in and whispered, "Sarah? Come here for a minute, please. Mom wants to talk to you."

Nothing. She hadn't heard me.

Paul and Patricia were still asleep. I declared this a positive sign, after much consideration.

In my suitcase, which I'd not unpacked, I found nothing in the way of a reasonably warm outfit for the day. I extracted a wrinkled dress and tried to remember what had possessed me to pack that. Beneath the dress was a manila envelope, which I figured must belong to Ted. I turned it over and read my name in the large script. This pleased me enormously. I stuffed the dress back into the bag and carried the letter from Sister

Urban to my sofa. I could pass the time until breakfast without
further retreat into self-examination.

| XIV |

Inside the manila envelope were two white legal-size envelopes,
both chock full. I was amazed and tantalized by the labeling of
the envelopes as a series (parts I and II) and by the note on Part
I, which warned, "It is important that you read this before
opening the accompanying envelope."

Don't put beans in your ears. Eat anything but the apple. Sister
Urban's instructions had the quality of both a warning and a
challenge.

I luxuriated in the choice. I put the envelopes on the couch
and tried to guess the nature of the contents, particularly interested in Part II and why it required a preface. Then, showing
herself in possession of an impeccable sense of timing, Sarah
appeared on her sofa. Her presence did not startle me; I'd been
expecting her since we got to Maine. She sat with her legs tucked
under her.

Without greeting her or even acknowledging her arrival, I
said, "Who gave you those overalls, Sarah? They're very pretty."
She was wearing pink corduroy overalls and a white turtleneck.

Sarah didn't exactly answer me, though she was paying attention. Then, as if I was seeing her for the first time, I realized
her hair had been cut right to the top of her ears. Before I could
ask who'd done that to her, she said, "What's in the envelopes,
Mom?"

I picked up the envelope containing Part II, anxious to keep
her with me. "We'll open the wrong part first. Let's see." I tore
at the seam and withdrew what felt like a lump of tissue paper.
Piece after piece fell to the floor as I peeled furiously. The final
thin sheet was girded with Scotch tape. Trying to undo the
wrapping I said, "It feels like a bookmark, or maybe a scapular."
Still fumbling with the band of tape, I looked up. Sarah was
standing by the door, holding her tiny hands in front of herself.

She was sobbing, and when I stood she screamed, "Don't look at me, Mom. Stop looking at me!"

Panicking, I held the half-unwrapped gift in my palm toward her, but she was gone before I could speak. Defeated, I looked at what I had unwrapped: three more shreds of brown felt sliced from a Brownie cap. Spontaneously I conjured an image of Sarah seated in a wooden chair, weeping, as scissors sliced through her cap and her hair incautiously. I could only see a bit of the veined forearm and the tensed hand that furiously drove the blades. Unable to expand the frame to reveal the face of Sarah's tormentor I just screamed her name, time and again, to dispel the ceaseless squealing of the scissors' blades.

| XV |

Here, another narrowed stretch of time for me to wonder at. It is obvious that I passed through the space of several minutes—so obvious as to be a fact. But the breadth of the passage is impossibly small. I cannot even thread my hand into the space now, let alone reconstruct how I slipped through.

I know that Patricia told Ted that I woke her with my screaming; that she ran to me, fully expecting to find Sarah with me. Before I stopped, Paul had joined us; following his sister's lead he shook my arm to make me stop my frightening chant. As Patricia tells it to Ted (she has never acknowledged the incident to me), she spotted the bits of Sarah's cap I'd let fall to the floor and with those she was able to shut me up. She asked me over and over, "Where did you get them? Where did they come from?" When I finally answered I only said, "Wait for Ted." Apparently, I held their hands and sat with my children next to me on Sarah's sofa. No one spoke until I said, "Sarah's been here and gone again."

Thrust into an untenable position of responsibility, Patricia quietly said to Paul, "Don't worry. I think she's just having her period. Sometimes this happens to women and it does not mean they're crazy or anything." (When Ted told me this part, he looked expectant, as if I would recall that Patricia made such a comment about me. I did not, and I could see that this made Ted sadder than ever.)

I remember Ted arriving with two bags of groceries and Patricia and Paul immediately running to their respective rooms, slamming the doors. Ted put the groceries on the floor. Feeling the need to ward off questions I stated simply, "Don't ask me."

Ted went to Patricia's room. A moment later they walked together into Paul's room. I put away the groceries, anxious to know what verdict the family tribunal had reached, wishing I could at least be informed of the nature of my crime.

| XVI |

Ted came to me in the kitchen. "It's all right. I just want to talk to you. Okay? Come on." He might have been speaking to a frightened cat. His voice was like a whimper, which in no way conformed to his physical presence. His movement toward me and then away toward the living room (drawing me with him from the kitchen) was a wave. I had no notion to resist. We were seated on my couch. "You saw Sarah again."

"In pink overalls. And with a haircut. I know it's harder to believe when I give you this kind of description, this level of detail. But those are the facts."

"What happened then?"

I realized that my calm in recalling the visit with Sarah was disconcerting to Ted, but I could not imagine a more appropriate demeanor. "She got herself over by the door—I didn't see her walk there exactly. She just got herself over there. Then she wagged her hands at me and told me to stop looking at her."

"At her or for her?" Ted seemed confused.

"At her." I could see Ted was finding it difficult to supply leading questions. "I tried to show her the pieces of the cap but she was gone." Ted said nothing. "I don't think she saw them." After a slight pause I added, "I said that without thinking, Ted. That she didn't see the hat pieces. I don't know what I mean."

Calmly Ted stood and walked around the room. "You look better now. When I came in you didn't look . . . here."

"I don't know what went on."

"I think you better know." With that, Ted delivered Patricia's account of my screaming and the moments up to his return.

Hearing my actions recounted by a third party was of no practical use to me. Ted might just as well have been reporting to me about Patricia's ability to fly or Paul speaking in tongues. I did not doubt the veracity of the report, it simply meant absolutely nothing.

After a long silence, during which Ted actually removed one of the boards from the patio door, I stood up, resolving to adopt a confessional tone. "I suppose something is wrong with me. Stress, you think? I don't know why not. Who am I to doubt it? There is such a thing as temporary amnesia. Right?"

Ted was staring out through the hole he'd made. "You think it's that?"

I felt his serenity as a kind of mocking. "No. I actually believe I am a goddamned schizophrenic. I think my good self is telling the bad self that the bad self hid Sarah. In an abandoned factory. You think that's it?"

Ted didn't turn to me. "Are you going to keep trying to make me angry? I just want to know, Anne. I ask because I'm so confused right now, I want you to know how easy it would be to just get angry." He waited, then turned to face me. "You have two children in this house who are scared out of their minds." With no buildup, he was yelling, "Where did you get those pieces of the cap? Where did they come from? Why did you bring them up here? What is it? Why, Anne?"

This is an accusation. Is that really you there, Ted? Talking to me? I turned to the sofa, then to the sofa Sarah had chosen. "There was a letter with the pieces, Ted. Part One. I was supposed to read it first but I didn't. Didn't you see a letter? Part One?"

"I have the pieces of the cap, Anne. There was no letter with them." Ted said so as if this fact was incontrovertible. I could see that I had exhausted his capacity for trust. Any argument from me on the point of the letter would have simply forced him to deal with me as a maniac. He said, "I don't know what 'Part One' even means. Who would? Can't you understand that? What do you mean by Part One?"

He means "Part I" is some other crazy thing you've said. Like the pink overalls. Cowed by my inability to even re-create the outline of events involving the letter and the wrapped cap shreds, I said nothing.

"I'm going to make some breakfast. If you want to rest for a while I could bring you something in the bedroom. It might be nice." Ted was talking to that cat again.

I went to my room. Not only could I summon no self-defense, but I actually sensed the comfort of a descent into craziness. I could pack, walk into town, and get onto a bus heading toward Arizona. I could shave my head and be admitted to a hospital. Anything would be possible once I was down deep enough.

I saw the door to Paul's room open, as if he were sneaking a look at me or trying to figure out if the coast was clear. *He's hungry.*

Paul did not come out of his room for breakfast before I secreted myself in my room. Still, he had caught me out. I was his mother. I knew as much. Visions and all, I was not lost. This knowledge came to me slowly, ruefully. For more than half an hour I sat on a cold bed in Maine trying to convince myself that there had been no Part I, whatever it was. Insisting on its existence when it was nowhere to be found could hardly improve my lot or ease Ted's mind. Still, I believed in Part I. I was willing to believe the letter had disappeared. I wouldn't have been averse to believing that Sarah had scooped it up on her way out. I was willing to believe the most implausible account of its fate, but I could not shake my faith in its existence.

I put on slacks and a sweat shirt, hoping that it would be evident that I had chosen sensible clothes. I brushed my hair which, even after much struggling, did not look particularly sensible. Still, I was satisfied enough with my reflected image to launch into several practice explanations in front of the mirror. Aloud, I said, "Despite what has gone on this morning, there is a Part One." Dissatisfied, I sat on a chair and continued. "There is no reason any of you should want to listen to me but I have to find the other part of the package from Sister Urban." This fell short, too. I began again, in new spirit. "First off, I am sorry. I know you cannot understand me right now—"

"Can I come in, Mom?" Patricia did not let on that she had overheard me talking to myself.

I backed away from her, certain I would not be able to speak to her.

Seeing my retreat, she shook her head back and forth, then held out Part I. "How did you know about this? What does this mean?" She began to shake, literally trembling as she held the letter toward me. "I took it when I heard Dad's car. I just took it all so he wouldn't see what you'd done. I mean I thought you did do it—the cap. Here, hurry, Mom. Read it. Are you mad? I didn't want him to know if you were—read it!" She ran up against me and could not stop trembling. "Hurry up and read it. Should I get Dad? I know I wasn't supposed to read it first, but I was still thinking you did it. I didn't tell him yet. We have to leave, don't we? Now?"

I was already concentrating on the first of four longhand pages from Sister Urban. I made my way to the bed as I read.

Patricia said, "I'll get Dad."

Ted arrived as I neared the end of the first page. He said my name three times.

"But there's no time, Ted. Sit with me. Please, just read."

As I passed the first page to Ted, he turned my shoulders toward him. "Part One?"

"Believe it or not." I could have just stared at Ted forever.

"I'm sorry and I love you and you know that and, I know, just read."

"I love you and you know that and I can't make heads or tails of this so far. Naturally."

| XVII |

Dear Mrs. Fossicker,

You will forgive me for my caution about the enclosures and the order in which I think they are best confronted. Perhaps it is only the residue of too many years in the classroom. Despite what you may later think or believe I am impelled to write more out of my sense of sympathy than my sense of urgency.

I hope you can find some comfort in knowing that I have had you and your lovely family in my daily prayers since I learned of the tragedy that has befallen you. At the risk of seeming silly, I must tell you that I do firmly believe that Jesus has heard our prayers.

Your two elder children have been the source of much pride for all of us associated with Saint Cecilia's. Every day they are seen to be making something positive and loving of the terrible sadness they carry. I have been around children too long not to know that this is a reflection of the home. You and your husband have raised a lovely family. The one day I spent in your home left me with a sense of the sharing and joy that are the hallmarks of love.

Despite what may now seem to be the case

such simple and essential joys do endure. I know I sound like a Holy Roller, but I believe She is alive. You will be reunited. I believe this is so.

Please believe.

Pardon me for my long-windedness. I realize every second now is precious. I have a story that you must know. Please bear with me. It is important.

My given name is Lilian Nissen. Until I entered the

novitiate I lived in a small town, Dalton, in western Massachusetts (it is where Crane stationery is made).

Many years after I'd left, my niece was involved in a sad and confusing liaison with a laborer at one of the Crane paper mills. What followed was a child born out of wedlock and a failed attempt by my niece to at least secure the poor child's financial future by filing a lawsuit.

I expect it is unnecessary to go into the regrettable outcome, particularly as it manifested itself on the young child's life in the small town of Dalton. Although we all believed at the time that my niece had struggled on rather bravely under the circumstances, it later was made known to me that, in point of fact, the child had carried not only her public burden but the anger and distress of her mother.

page 3

Sister Clare is my grandniece, the child of whom I have been writing. Difficult as it may be to believe, she comes to us with this as her personal cross. We all know how uncomplainingly she carries that cross. This has been true of Clare since she came to our novitiate and dedicated herself to service for Jesus Christ.

I am a firm believer in the power of prayer and Clare's life has proved to me that Our Lord can overcome the highest odds. In all honesty, she has found her faith tested. She has sought the counsel of others and their prayers.

Still, Clare's life is not free of trials today. For reasons I do not understand, the disappearance of your youngest daughter has deeply affected Clare. I do not refer only to her emotional and spiritual energies, which she has delivered entirely to the cause of all children in trouble, including your beautiful little girl. I refer also, in confidence with which I believe you can be trusted, to Clare's torment. She is beset by the fate of your daughter. Night after night she worries over the efficacy of her prayers, the correctness of her efforts. She pushes herself, vowing that more can be done, that better prayers can be uttered on the behalf of the missing child.

page 4

Of late, this has led Clare to convince herself that there is something terribly wrong with her, with her faith as well. It is her present contention that she must seek the help of a doctor or even a hospital or even other means to deal with such critical questions.

All of this will be dealt with only with Clare's good in heart, God willing. Clare has never been prone to even the most petty violence. I know she would in no way harm a child or do anything to frighten or upset a child. I know this is true.

Mrs. Fossicker, what is contained in the accompanying envelope I found in Clare's bedroom. I do not know why, but she had cut several little caps into tiny pieces. Next to the pile of felt scraps was a paper bag, torn apart as one does to make a wrapping. On it was your name and address.

These are terrible facts and I must sound cold, repeating them so simply. But I do not believe adornment is called for here.

Briefly, I beg you to confront Clare. Please, go to no one else first. Give Clare a chance to make clear her intentions. Ask Clare herself. I believe in the hand of God working in all our lives and pray that your actions are guided thereby. You and your family remain ever in my prayers.

Sister Urban, O.C.

| XVIII |

When I finished reading I handed the final page to Ted. My reaction to the letter was displaced entirely from its potential meaning. I was so surprised to read confirmation of my suspicions of Clare that I could only wonder if I had not in some way provoked her retribution. The idea of actually being in possession of an instinctual sense that was capable of puncturing the surface of reality did not please me or give me courage. It frightened me. I felt that I was harboring something preternatural, or that something unnatural had taken hold of me. *Why am I granted visions of Sarah? What makes me see her?*

Ted was determined to stick to the human territory. He carefully folded the pages and returned them to the envelope. "You were right. You were right. I don't know how to apologize for doubting you when you knew it was—"

"Don't start." I walked toward the small window and leaned on the locked shutter. I did not want to begin to ransack the store of events that had accumulated. *Too much has happened.* I tried to explain this to Ted. "It's crazy but there isn't time to understand now. I have visions, I have instincts—maternal instincts? I don't know. I have completely senseless self-pity that I turn into punishment of you and the kids. I forget terrible screaming fits. I faint. I can say I'm sorry until I turn blue in the face, Ted. Will that keep the visions away? See? I don't even know what to do about the letter. It only makes me hate the way I've treated Clare, the way I've made fun of her and resented her organizing everything."

"We have to do something. I think we have to call Tim, Tim Hall."

I was so confused that I believed it would be best to do nothing at all, to simply let ourselves be delivered to our fates. "What are you going to say? Ask him to arrest Clare for having a bad time growing up? He's just going to think I got to you with my suspicions. Stick around, Ted, and maybe we'll both see Sarah."

My worst always called forth the very best of Ted. This is not as neatly complementary as it may seem. It allowed me to quickly retreat to my weakest, least-responsible posture. Not that I actively solicited Ted's strength by allowing myself to weaken. It's that I had so often seen him rise above me and swoop down to pick me up on his flight to higher ground that this turn of events seemed a natural pattern. It allowed me to look back on my incompetence and failure and see them as benign twists of fate, as being necessary—along with Ted's heroics—to the generally pleasing outcomes we achieved.

On this occasion Ted simply announced that he was going to call Tim Hall, explain the contents of the letter from Sister Urban, and ask Officer Hall to stay with Clare at the house until we got home. "Pack, Anne. Okay? Tell the kids to pack, too. We can talk in the car. We will all talk. I mean, Patricia read the letter already."

I was packing as he spoke. "She told me. I'm sure she's told Paul. I would if I was her. Ted? I'm right to think it's impossible that Clare has her, right? That's not what this means, right?"

"Everything is possible. That's our problem." He left to call Tim Hall.

WHOSE CHILD IS THIS?

| I |

WHILE WE waited for Officer Hall to telephone with instructions, we each efficiently completed tasks assigned to us by Ted. I cleaned out the refrigerator, packing whatever food could be salvaged. Paul and Patricia stripped linen and collected the few bits of laundry we'd dirtied. Ted replaced the one board he'd removed from the patio doors. These things done, we waited together in the living room, the car packed for another journey less than twenty-four hours after our last departure. Though well fed and rested, we were exhausted—individually and as a group. What remained of the family had achieved emotional exhaustion. Uncomplainingly the children acquiesced to commands and the possibility of being shuttled around without forewarning. Our casual conversations were brief and lifeless: "Did you pack my book?" "I think it's in Paul's gym bag." "In the car?" "Do you want it?" "No. Just wondered."

The new and still-encoded information provided in Sister Urban's letter was not received as an insight or a caution. None of us seemed willing or even inclined to speculate on its meaning. Too much had happened. We became a reactive unit, satisfied by our ability to manage internal affairs in such a way as to minimize the likelihood of sustaining additional damage.

To no one in particular, Paul said, "It's good that Sister Clare is the one who did the noose picture. I kinda doubt she'd kill us." He was watching his father arrange the contents of his briefcase. "It's sorta weird to think about a nun's bedroom. Maybe it's just that I never thought of it before."

The telephone ringing had the odd effect of paralyzing us all. It was clear that no one was anxious to know anything more than was absolutely necessary. I shook my head to signal to Ted that I had no intention of flirting with another fiasco on the telephone. *Let Sarah talk to someone else for a change.* Ted handed his briefcase to Paul and after his initial "Hello?" he said absolutely nothing until "Thanks, Tim. We should be there by seven-thirty or eight. We'll call you—no, that's fine. Right." Ted didn't even bother to hang up. He just disconnected the cord from the wall.

"Don't bring that telephone back if that's what you're doing, Ted." I was delivering this as an urgent message. "I only mean we don't need it at home. Every time I subscribe to a magazine I get another telephone in the mail. Whatever happened to transistor radios?"

Ted reconnected the cord and only then turned to me. "Clare isn't at the house. And she isn't at the convent. Tim Hall is having a man stationed in the house. He's going to try to track down Clare. Of course, she may have only gone out for some food."

Patricia was quick to react to the idea that had certainly occurred to all of us. "All of a sudden, no one can find her?"

It was tantalizing to think that Clare had Sarah. It gave Sarah a place. It gave us all another path to her. But this also required us to cast Clare as the sender of the picture and the cap, a woman who could inflict punishment. To no effect I said, "I hope she doesn't have her."

"She couldn't. I mean logistically. We've been with her. Or she's been with a class." It was clear that Ted had at least considered the possibility.

"I know we have to get going, Ted, but did Officer Hall get in touch with Sister Urban?"

Ted collected his briefcase and led us out of the house as he spoke. "He tried to get Clare at the convent, but he doesn't want to question anybody until he sees the letter, until he can show someone the letter. I mean, he doesn't want to be in a position to make a lot of accusations without some evidence. He's doing what he can." We took our seats in the car and left the house in Maine without even so much as a glance back. As we approached the entrance ramp for the highway, Ted said, "He is going to detain her if she returns to the house." It was almost too hard for Ted to say this. "That's why the cop is at home. I just hate the idea of her being treated like that, no matter what."

Annoyed, Patricia said, "Well, I don't."

Paul said, "Me neither."

Buoyed by her brother, Patricia continued. "She drew that thing on our picture. What? It's okay for her to do that to me? Forget it. Anyone else would get killed if they did it. Like say it was a boy in my class or some kid that hates Paul who did it. It's completely against the law, you know."

I did not understand exactly what was preying on Ted, but I could see that he was consumed by his effort to withhold his anger at Patricia's speech. I turned to her and with nothing more than a slight smile, I tried to tell her that I understood what she meant and that her father could not be expected to discuss it at the moment.

She called my bluff. It was a new stance for her. No longer was it enough, this all-knowing silence I offered. She would not release me from her gaze. She had something to say and she was daring me to try to stop her. Her mouth was slightly open. Her body was completely still. I could see her anger at her father's apparent lack of loyalty. I could literally feel her fear as a pressure holding me in place. There was a strange and distracting hint of a smile on her lips, as if she might laugh at me. And I know I didn't see the half of it. I was suddenly aware that this was Patricia, who had chosen to explain my screaming to her brother; Patricia, who had hidden and (even more amazing) restored to me the letter that might have been misunderstood by her father.

Paul turned away, unnerved by what he could not see. I knew I was watching a child give birth to a woman. *It will be years of labor.*

Patricia received this and stored it in her heart. Then a smile, not mocking, but pure. *We are the same but we are not one.* The daughter knew that she had to make this known to the mother. Casually, diffidently, she stated: "I just hope for everybody's sake Sister Clare didn't do it."

| II |

Within an hour both Paul and Patricia were asleep. Ted had not spoken since his abortive interchange with Patricia. My confused attempts to make something hopeful of Clare's life history and its intersection with mine produced nothing so enduring as a ridiculous picture of Clare in handcuffs seated next to a fat policeman on my living-room sofa.

Quietly, Ted said, "Sarah really loved Clare."

Of course, my impulse was to adopt Patricia's line of reasoning. *The woman is a maniac.* But I could see that Ted was not so much conversing as he was working his way toward solid ground. I trusted his sense of direction in these matters. I tried to follow.

Ted continued. "I doubt all kids go for Clare so much. She's sort of overpowering, I imagine. Always in motion. I wouldn't think most kids go for that in grown-ups. I mean, I think I see why Sarah would. You know. How she'd get you to write down her chores in order on Saturday mornings?"

I was drawn in. "The best ever was her complete insistence that I tell her which piece of clothing to pick up first. No kidding, she wanted the socks in some sort of numerical order. It's true that I can imagine Clare having complete patience with that

sort of thing." I couldn't carry on with homey depictions of
Clare. This was asking too much.

Ted seemed to sense my tenderness and moved with more
direction toward the territory he'd staked out for himself. "I've
been trying to think of all that from Clare's angle. How Sarah
surprised her. I mean, Sarah playing into her strong suit. I mean,
the Brownies. The more I think of Clare and that way she has
of making herself seem sort of out of place and indispensable.
You have to use your imagination and think how Sarah would
never make her feel out of place. That somehow makes sense
of the package. In some small way."

"I don't know what to think of it."

"Anne? I'm sure Clare doesn't know where Sarah is."

"Damned if she does and damned if she doesn't."

Ted reached his hand over and laid his palm against my
forehead, a gesture I'd never seen him perform. "Not that this
exactly follows. Last night, when I fell asleep and didn't even
know you were planning to sleep on the couch? I had a dream.
It was why I woke up and realized you weren't with me. Otherwise I probably wouldn't have found you until morning. Anyway, it wasn't a real dream. In the sense that it wasn't a story
dream. It was just that I was still a kid, about thirteen? And
my parents were still alive. And that kid—me, as a kid, I
mean—I dreamed about you. Just like you are now. And I
knew that my parents were going to die and about Sarah. How
you know things in dreams. And I—the kid in the dream—I
knew it would be all right."

| III |

Only seconds after moving across the Massachusetts state line
Ted had to bring the car to a complete stop. After a brief
standstill we made our slow way behind a van to the top of a
slight incline. At the top we could see that traffic was backed
up for at least a mile.

Paul was awake. "What's going on? Why'd you stop?"

Ted said, "Looks like an accident."

I saw no evidence to confirm this. "It could just be commuters. There's a lot of new high-tech on the North Shore. I bet it's just that." I liked to think that I had a special understanding of Massachusetts, having been born only minutes away from the state capital.

"It doesn't look like commuters." Ted seemed annoyed. "They look like travelers."

"The van? So what?" I was trying to see as many other cars as possible before I continued. "I don't see another van. Most of them are small cars. Commuters."

"Anne, it's late for a big commuter rush." Ted *was* annoyed.

"Listen, at Aerohead everyone is on flextime. You can't tell anymore by the time of day what is what." Even I hadn't found that persuasive. "Anyway, we'll find out soon enough."

Rather sullenly Ted said, "I bet it's an accident."

He reminded me of Paul, taking the last word like that. "Are we taking bets here? Or can you see something from your side that I can't?"

"How did you know?" Ted smiled. "There's a moving van or some kind of truck right across the road. I can see it from this side. It must not be too bad, though. I don't see any ambulance lights."

Just as Ted finished speaking, the van in front of us lunged forward. We were moving at almost full speed, heading for the scene of the mishap. As we neared it, traffic slowed again as drivers satisfied their curiosity.

"Oh my God, Anne." Ted whispered this. We were passing a line of four cars. Each had obviously been towed into the breakdown lane. They were so collapsed as to be comical, like props in a movie chase that ends with the villains' cars being crushed in a junkyard compactor. The truck had been moved enough to clear a single lane for passing cars. Just beyond the line of cars the breakdown lane was literally paved with glass, a few suitcases worth of clothing, and two desks, virtually intact.

"It must have happened hours ago," said Ted.

Excited, Paul began a litany of questions. "What happened, though? You think they died? All of them? They just gonna leave that truck there all night? Look. They must have been in it too."

Paul pointed at two young girls, not older than fifteen, who were leaning against the guardrail behind a row of flares. One had her arm over the other's shoulders. They were both smoking cigarettes, their faces turned away from a man in a business suit a few feet away. His left arm wrapped in a makeshift sling, he was staring directly at each car that passed. I was sure he was responsible for the accident. He seemed to be daring someone to stop and ask what had gone on.

"Somebody must've died." Paul was buckling his seatbelt as he spoke. "It's pretty easy to die in a car. They should do something about that."

"Four cars. There could've been ten, twelve people killed." I could not shake the image of that man's face, the girls who wouldn't look at him.

Ted was trying to find a local news report on the radio. "That's only what they couldn't tow away. There was enough glass there for ten cars. It's sobering."

Eventually we heard a traffic report that sketched the details of the accident whose aftermath had slowed our progress. As far as anyone knew, the desks had dropped off a station wagon in front of the trailer truck; the driver of the truck tried to avoid them (they'd eventually bounced safely toward the side of the road) and had ended up sweeping seven cars off the highway. A total of thirteen cars were reportedly damaged, and eleven people were treated for injuries. Three people died, including a three-month-old infant girl. The mother of the baby and the driver of the truck were both hospitalized.

After the report, Ted asked Paul to make sure Patricia was wearing a seatbelt.

"I always do, Dad. It's Paul who says they're stupid."

Paul protested. "I do so usually try to put them on. I mean, unless it's like we're going to church or if I have something on like my uniform."

Patricia said, "That will help a lot if a car hits you. Good thinking, Paul. Your basketball shorts instead of a seatbelt."

Impatiently, and nervously, Ted insisted, "Keep them on. From now on, always. No matter what."

Patricia had slept through the excitement. "Okay, Dad. We got them on. What's the rush all of a sudden?"

Paul seized this as a chance to establish his version of the accident, an account he would give to friends, teachers, and to anyone with whom he traveled in a car for at least a month. I listened to his thrilling, tantalizingly slow chronicle, which involved as many facts from the radio bulletin as it did from his own observations.

Accidents will happen.

Of course, I could only measure the fate of the survivors against the fate of the Fossickers in the wake of Sarah's disappearance. Which was worse? Which would I choose? Another session of *Truth or Consequences;* you're always a loser when you don't know the truth and you can't predict the consequences.

Paul was unrelenting in his details. He had begun to describe the two teenage girls as "real sleazebags." I turned on him, but neither he nor Patricia took note. He had already moved on to the mysterious man in the blue suit.

Are you going to tell him that girls in leotard-tight jeans and cheap camisoles aren't necessarily cheap? That out-of-date shag haircuts and white high-heel shoes are indicators of nothing? And when he introduces you to a variation of this type will you congratulate him for overlooking the cheap cover and getting right to the contents of the book?

I didn't speak. I abandoned the children's gruesome detailing and Ted's apparent upset at the sight of the wreckage for a simpler question. *Why have cars at all?*

Childlike, I raised the question without a nod to history, technology, society, or commerce. I would not agree to the necessity or benefit of a form of transportation that could not be developed without the regular sacrifice of mothers, fathers, and children. I thought of all the billions of dollars committed to medical programs, industrial safety, strategic defense—all under the rubric, "If this saves one life it will be worthwhile."

For God's sake, what about cars?

I wanted to voice some of this, but I could not imagine that anyone would be particularly interested. Such an impractical and hopeless diatribe would only have given Ted and the children something else to worry about. I'd provided them with enough.

But what about cars? Really.

| IV |

It was ten o'clock when we pulled into the driveway. Ted parked next to a police cruiser. *Welcome home.*

Officer Tim Hall met us at the door and before we were inside began his announcement. "No sign of Sister Clare. She hasn't been here since this morning at least. She may not have been here last night. Officer Paul Corelli was here all day. Except for a few phone calls, there was no activity. Oh, a neighbor did bring some food by. It's in the kitchen, Mrs. Fossicker."

Too tired to even signal my appreciation to Tim Hall, I went directly to the kitchen to identify our benefactor. On the table were two bottles of wine with a note that read, KEEP THE FAITH, JANET AMERON. She was not exactly a neighbor, but she was the one woman with whom I had cultivated an ongoing relationship throughout my years in Connecticut. The Amerons had been in town nearly as long as we had, and unlike most of the transient junior executives' wives, Janet had designs on a life in the simple, personal terms that made sense to me. *Call Janet.* I hoped the gift would force me to call her; it was no doubt why she'd delivered it. She wouldn't call me until I was ready to talk. *God bless Janet and all the Amerons.* It seemed worth a try.

Inside the refrigerator was a box full of delicacies—every item purchased at a small fancy Italian-import market. I was relieved and comforted to see that Janet had the good sense not to send over a cake. On top of a slab of smoked fish was an index card with a second note. "It's a terrible time and nothing helps. I know all that, Anne. Just eat something delicious and keep the faith. I'm here, as you know. J." Another prayer of supplication from me: *Don't let anything happen to her kids.*

Ted called me to the living room. Officer Hall was the only one standing. He obviously had something to say.

I sat on the sofa next to Patricia. "I'm sorry. Thanks for being here, Tim."

Tim Hall seemed genuinely embarrassed by my small thanks. "I wish I had good news. Or even news. Listen, before I forget. All of you should know that your phone is being answered by a special operator. She'll screen all the calls. Whatever may or may not be the case, it's just a guarantee that you won't get crank calls. It will ring through here after she's checked the name and number, and you'll have to tell her to get off the line when you start talking. It may sound like a hassle, but I think it's a good idea. The answering machine will still work. She told me this evening that your mother called, Mrs. Fossicker. And I think there's one other message on the machine. I think it's a business call, Ted."

Patricia, alert to the possibility of eavesdropping, turned to me. "You mean I can't call somebody without somebody listening in?"

Tim Hall laughed. *Why don't you ask him if he has children of his own; he must.* He said, "Only incoming calls are screened and only before they connect with you. Any secrets are safe."

Patricia blushed her acknowledgment.

Tim Hall continued. "I tried to reach Clare at the convent and the sister I spoke to understood that Clare was staying here. Clare didn't teach today, though she'd told the principal in advance that would be the case."

Ted stood. "Did you speak with the other nun? The one who sent the letter?"

I said, "Sister Urban. The elderly nun who—"

"The letter." Tim Hall was suddenly very nervous. "I thought it would help if I . . . I wanted to have a look at it first. Mrs. Fossicker, would you mind if I looked at the letter?"

Did the letter disappear by chance, Mrs. Fossicker?

I tried to avoid being defensive. "It's in Paul's gym bag, with my book."

"I'll get it." Paul went to secure the evidence.

"I think it's too late to speak with her tonight. In fact, I think it's too late to do anything but get ready for tomorrow." Tim Hall seemed to be hoping for confirmation from us.

"You must be exhausted." I was determined to get him to trust me again.

Ted sat down. "Nothing at all on Sarah? Nothing new?"

The very mention of her name had the effect of dispelling what minimal comfort there was in sitting in a warm, familiar room with no apparent threat of imminent danger. The lights seemed to get brighter. All of us shifted in our seats, anxious, afraid.

Tim Hall retrieved a notepad from the file near the front door. "There are some more requests for her picture from various organizations. They came in the mail. And here's what was reported to us. Two elderly women in Hartford called. Each of them reported seeing Sarah. I checked out the reports, of course." He paused but would not look at me or Ted. "They make three or four reports a day to stations all over Connecticut. They live together in a nursing facility. They've been reprimanded—I even begged—but every time they see a television report they call up, give their names and address, assert they've seen the missing child. I'm sorry to have to tell it this way, but this is one of a lot of these kinds of calls that search parties and newspaper reports stir up. It was only that they were in Hartford that made me . . . Anyway. We also had a call from a woman who lives in Richdale—"

I yelled. "That's only five miles from here. That Richdale?"

Tim Hall did not look at me. "I'm sorry, really. None of this is going to be helpful. She was confused about the timing. She saw Sarah weeks ago. In a restaurant? I think she said the Old Gray Manse?"

"Moose. The Old Gray Moose. That was almost two months ago." Ted stood and moved toward the stairs. He yelled up to Paul, then came back. "It was when I got back from traveling. Just before we went on vacation. Remember, Anne? The Saturday night we all went to Greg's Pond after?"

I was lost. I could not raise my head even to look to Ted for comfort.

Tim Hall said, "The woman said she remembered Sarah because she was so lovely. It *was* a Saturday night, Ted. She was confused about the time."

Paul arrived with the letter. No one offered him an explanation for the pall that had descended in his absence. *Because she was so lovely.*

Patricia said, "Sit here, Paul." He must have been wondering if he'd done something wrong.

I couldn't recover even as Tim Hall began his reading of the letter. He asked Ted a few questions. Paul and Patricia asked to be excused. Before they left, Tim Hall announced that there would be two policemen outside the house for the night.

Paul could not let this go unexplored. "To catch Sister Clare, you mean?"

Nimbly, Tim Hall laughed off this possibility. "No. It's really just to discourage any pranksters, Paul. There's no call for you and your sister to worry that way."

After they'd made their way upstairs, plans were laid for Saturday morning. This included a visit with Sister Urban. Tim Hall asked me if it would be all right if he brought her to the house, as he didn't want to have the entire convent involved in the questioning. I could tell he still believed in Clare's innocence. I felt they had made themselves allies during the last week; uneasy as their alliance was, it still held sway.

I drew direct attention when I stood. As casually as possible, I said, "I could get some food or coffee together, I think. Otherwise, I have to be alone for a bit. I wish I could be strong for you, Ted." With that I began to cry, letting sadness move me as it would. Ted held me lightly and let me go almost at once.

I think Tim Hall wanted to reassure me; I think he thought part of my collapse might have been owing to fear. He said, "I did check the house myself, Anne. Everywhere. Clare is not in the house. I am sure of that."

There are no such things as ghosts.

| V |

I sat at my bedroom window for nearly an hour, comforted by the buzz of voices below me, convincing myself that Clare had vanished to join Sarah in some hideout where they would never be found. In the wreck of a house that I imagined somewhere in the Berkshires, I saw Sarah happily coloring at a large kitchen table, Clare presenting her with a bowl of soup. I tried but failed to imagine how Clare would support the two of them. Relatives? I could imagine Sarah being happy, if confused, adjusting to whatever rationale Clare had devised for their new life. *I have to go to work because my work at home doesn't keep me busy anymore. Dad's workers need him for one month so he can be with us most of the rest of the time. Nobody at the Girls' Club is going to be mean to you.*

Finding herself in a ramshackle cabin in the Berkshires with the always attentive and industrious Clare would not be the worst thing that ever happened to Sarah.

After Tim Hall drove away, I waited for Ted to appear in the bedroom. Waiting made me anxious. But I knew he would need his own time alone with whatever vestige of Sarah he harbored. I walked to Sarah's bedroom.

It was not exactly apparent in the light cast by the child-size desk lamp *what* had changed about the room. It was not as I'd left it. I turned on the glaring overhead and then the closet light.

The room had been cleaned—meticulously, painstakingly. Immediately I summoned the full force of my self-doubt. I would need to have solid proof before I reported my findings. This proved to be ridiculously easy to assemble. The linen had been cleaned and pressed. The mirror and both windows had been washed; they literally shone from the overhead light. I opened Sarah's bureau drawers and saw that her clothing had been rearranged; the layered stacks made it easy to see exactly what was in each drawer. The clothes in the closet had been arranged according to what appeared to be a color scheme. Every pair of shoes had been assembled into an impractical straight line against the back wall of the closet, heels to the wall. In each shoe was a folded sock. For no particular reason this was the detail that affected me most. On the floor, kneeling in the closet, I could see that the pairs of shoes were actually identified by similar socks. Otherwise, I guessed, it would have been impossible to distinguish pairs, since the arrangement included several identical shoes varying only slightly in size.

Clare was here. Even as I told myself this, I could not help but wonder why she'd spent her time to achieve these peculiar results. To shame me? To unsettle me?

I rummaged through the closet, then went back to the chest of drawers, expecting that I would note several missing items. If anything, the collection had increased, with the addition of jackets brought up from the downstairs closet and at least two pair of shoes I thought I'd given away.

The sight of those shoes with the little socks arranged to puff out of the top was truly confounding. In combination with the exacting arrangement of folded clothing in the bureau, it seemed a kind of violation. *These are a child's things. This is a child's room.* The idea of Clare so carefully and thoroughly tampering with her clothes—it made me believe Clare was capable of, or susceptible to, the demented passions I'd heard described in the last week.

Don't tell Ted. It was an instinct. I didn't think it was a sure bet, my word against Clare.

| VI |

I fell asleep in Sarah's room and did not wake until after eight o'clock Saturday morning. Ted and the children had only made their way to the kitchen minutes before me. My rumpled clothes and impressively messy hair brought smiles to their faces. The scene reminded me of a Fossicker family.

Ted was vague in his recounting of the conversation with Tim Hall. Apparently they'd talked mostly about Tim and his two children. Tim's wife had left him and the children more than four years ago, offering as explanation that she had realized rather tardily that she shouldn't have married so young—she'd been pregnant by Tim before her nineteenth birthday. Neither Paul nor Patricia seemed to receive any part of this story as noteworthy, which fact did strike *me* as being interesting. Other details of Tim Hall's life that Ted passed on: Tim lived with his children and his father in a house with a big yard; Tim's ex-wife lived in New Haven and visited often; Tim worried that the divorce would prove to be the most significant memory for the two kids he was raising.

How did you feel when your sister disappeared? They needed to be asked, I knew.

In the middle of our haphazardly assembled breakfast, a woman called to inform us that Office Hall would be at our home within the half hour. He was bringing a nun, not Sister Clare.

Amid the rush to ready ourselves I held to my memory of Sister Urban as she'd looked with her rosary on our living-room sofa, keeping vigil during the day of the city-wide search. The letter and this almost holy image gave me hope, real hope that one knows not as anticipation but as the calm that powers simple action. I believed she might manage not only to solve Clare's problems but also somehow to improve Sarah's lot.

After unnecessarily polite and solemn greetings, Tim Hall said, "I left the letter here. Sister Urban would like to see it."

Sister Urban was seated in a chair that was twice her size. Her demeanor was so off-putting as to make her seem mean. She stared straight ahead, as if she'd been falsely accused of a terrible sin. She grabbed the letter from my hand as if it had been written a decade earlier and was being dredged up to sully her reputation. As she had rebuffed my earlier attempt to thank her for writing it, she did not acknowledge my delivery. She read it over in silence.

For five minutes she held us in utter suspense. I half expected her to walk over and rap me on the hand when she finished. Ted looked equally confused. Paul and Patricia were literally huddled on the couch, on the verge of bursting into fits of nervous laughter.

When she spoke, it was without emotion. Her voice had a gravelly edge, making it difficult to assess her mood. "I would ask that the children not be here while we discuss this. You can tell them whatever pleases you, Mrs. Fossicker. I would prefer to speak with them out of the room."

Paul and Patricia were relieved when I glanced at them. They headed for the stairs. On her way by the elderly nun Patricia said, "Excuse me," then bolted after her brother.

Sister Urban continued to speak without really addressing any one of us. "As I told Officer Hall here, I did not write this letter."

I looked at Ted and Tim Hall. Both of them had adopted a no-interruptions policy. I was willing to follow their lead. Presently, I was just happy to see that they were indeed in the room. Already I knew I did not want to bear sole responsibility for witnessing this event.

"I also made it clear that I do not intend to divulge what I do or do not know about Clare to you people . . . who may be acquaintances of Clare's but are perfect strangers to me. I have not been able to make sense of why you have seen fit to draw her into this situation so, considering her . . . Though I am not here to judge. I understand this is an extraordinarily trying time for you, Mrs. Fossicker. But I would not have revealed Clare to anyone under any circumstances. Rest assured I have no need to do this," she waved the letter, "least of all to perfect strangers." She looked at me, as if she pitied me. "I cannot explain this. Perhaps you have some ideas of your own why she would do any of this, why she should feel this is necessary."

It took me several seconds to realize that she was asking me to venture an opinion. "I don't know. Do what? Who?"

She was carrying on as if this were the most predictable of outcomes, the natural course of events to date. "Surely . . . Sister Clare did teach your child for a full year. Surely, Mrs. Fossicker, Clare wrote this letter. I am asking you why." Her volume increased on the last sentence. It was a demand.

True to recent form, I yelled. "Where is she then? Why don't you know?"

Sister Urban shook her head and refused to answer me. She looked absolutely horrified. I am willing to believe that six or seven decades had passed since someone yelled at her. She had no response.

Tim Hall was lost in a private thought. Ted said, "What do we do now?"

With no explanation Tim Hall stood, literally pulled the letter from Sister Urban's grasp. "I'd like to take you back to the convent now. I'll have to speak to some of the other sisters. We'd better not spend any more time here. Sister Urban?"

It was clear that Sister Urban had descended into a kind of reverie. She'd heard nothing Tim Hall had said and looked at her hand as if she didn't remember what had become of the letter. She tilted her head and said, "I told the young policeman here that she was at the convent yesterday. After school. Clare. She said she was going to try to find her."

"Sarah?" Ted moved toward the nun.

"Is that her name? Poor dear." Sister Urban's eyes were closed. She stood. "Where are we going now, young man?"

"Home." Tim Hall led her to the door. He grabbed Ted's arm and said, "Stay put. All of you."

| VII |

For several minutes it seemed to me that the most important decision I had to make was whether to tell Paul and Patricia what Ted and I knew. It occurred to me that the absurdity of the events of the last week must have been magnified from their perspective. Moment by moment they were dragged into close range of trauma and despair whose timbre they could only marvel at, only to be drawn back to the remove of childhood, at which distance they received information and emotion as muted reverberations from a sphere that enveloped theirs but did not involve them. Before asking Ted his opinion, I wanted to know my mind. I left Ted in the living room. He was staring out at the two policemen who were leaning on a cruiser in our driveway. He didn't look at me, but I knew he was smiling when he said, "It must be a great time to be one of our neighbors."

I passed the stairs and momentarily failed to register the significance of seeing Paul and Patricia perched on a single stair.

Paul actually sounded hopeful, as if I might have something to say, when he asked, "What does this mean? We were wondering if this means Sister Clare did something like, I don't know, say, took Sarah, maybe?"

"Your Dad and I don't know anything more than you know." *Why have parents at all, then?* "You want to come into the living room and wait with us?"

They followed me, ran to their father, who hugged them both.

Ted said, "I'm just praying. For all of us."

For nearly half an hour we waited in silence. I believe some of us prayed. Others affected as prayerful a posture as could be sustained. Finally, Paul asked if he could go outside and talk to the policemen. When he left, Patricia went to her bedroom. I saw the mailman coming, watched Paul intercept him. Paul delivered the day's mail along with what had accumulated on the table near the front door.

A total of seven requests for pictures and biographical information arrived from individuals and organizations willing to add Sarah to their dockets of hopeless cases. These I filed, wondering if I had any reproducible pictures left. Other than these requests there was a letter from my brother and what looked to be an invitation from a woman who lived at the end of our street.

Richard's note was simple.

Annie,

Carol told me. I am so sorry. If you need the kind of help I can do, let me know. Maybe even just getting the picture around. It is so hard to believe this is happening to you. You read about it but it seems so real now. I am so sorry, Annie. I have an apartment in Roslindale now. My address is on the envelope. I'll have a phone soon. Maybe I'll call you if that would help. Give my love to Paul and Patricia and a pat on the back to Ted. I hope she comes home really soon, Annie.

Your only brother who loves you,

Richard

I read it over and over. I'd felt for so long that all my relations with my family had to be generated and sustained by force of will that the simplicity of his note was an antidote to pain. I was not entirely disconnected. There was a woman here and she'd once been Annie, Richard's sister.

Please do call me up, Richard. That would be just fine. It would help. I did not file Richard's letter. I kept it with me.

The invitation was from Sylvia Castine (a woman with whom I'd exchanged little more than a casual greeting maybe seven times—each time at the block party that was her annual good-neighbor event) and had been issued on behalf of "the friends and neighbors of the Fossickers." From what little information the invitation carried, I guessed that a potluck dinner was being held at the Castines' home at which the Fossickers would be exhorted to keep their sunny sides up. Even the most gregarious and recently arrived neighbors must have dreaded this event, scheduled for the following Friday night. I wondered if Ted would consent to simply refusing the invitation. I filed it for later in the day.

Paul came in and asked what Mrs. Castine had sent me. For no reason other than avoiding his question, I asked him to go and tell Patricia to come downstairs.

Ted looked up as I entered the living room. "It's been more

than an hour and a half." With that the telephone rang. He'd only said, "Hello, yes. All right," before lapsing into silence. I felt like I had to concentrate on every slight movement of his head and eyes and mouth, that in this way I was literally passing the time that would otherwise not elapse. "When, Tim? How long ago?" During this second pause Ted stared at his family on the couch. "I am going to, just so you know. All of them. Wait—please, if you can, come by. When you can. It might help for us to hear . . . Thanks. Are you all right? You're sure? Of course."

Only after he hung up the telephone did he see in us all the fear of not knowing. Correctly he guessed that we'd each conjured up a nightmare involving Sarah. "Not Sarah. Nothing about Sarah. Nothing new about Sarah." Again, his hands wiping his face, this time removing disbelief. He looked painfully sober. "Tim said he realized it or at least guessed it as soon as Sister Urban said the handwriting was Clare's. It all fell into place for him. That's why he wanted to get back to the convent so fast. Why he rushed. He knew then. Sister Clare is . . . the fact is, she is dead. Apparently she killed herself. Sometime last night. Sister Clare." Ted said her name as if we might not remember her. "I guess I don't know anything more than that . . . I mean, I don't know how yet. God knows I don't know why people do this . . . she must have been very sad." Ted paused, vainly hoping someone might offer him comfort or at least a chance to withdraw from the center of attention.

Why say anything?

Defying silence, Ted said, "Sarah really loved her. Sister Clare knew that."

| VIII |

I could not sustain any curiosity about the details of Clare's fate. But it did occur to me that the horrors attending the Fossicker family had become so plentiful as to be statistically significant in relation to the county or state totals.

Two lives lost. Sadness and fear would leak out of Clare's small bedroom in the St. Cecilia convent and flow into the hearts of fellow sisters, schoolchildren, and relatives living unaware of Clare at a two-hundred-mile remove. Blood flows out and away from the victim.

I certainly didn't know what we were waiting for, but we all sat in the living room, anticipating. I don't think there was one among us who was fool enough to hope for anything. We knew something unprecedented would happen. Chaos was proving itself to be inscrutable—abundant energy whirring in our midst without regard for matter.

Clare dead: At least I knew that order would not be born of this chaos. Another tenet of life that would not pass unscathed into my children's minds. Look for the phoenix? Birds are not born of ash. Maybe once some young winged thing got itself buried in the wreckage of a home or church and later was seen to fly away to freedom. You can make a symbol and story of that bird, but you can't make a bird out of shrapnel or the cinders of a child's nightdress.

Clare was dead. I knew Sarah would not be born again of Clare's blood.

| IX |

Each according to his need. One by one the four not-displaced Fossickers took their turns at making a general, aspiringly philosophical statement. Ted began, and the order followed by descending ages. If I ever really heard what the others said, I don't recall any of the phrases or even words chosen for this odd occasion. I certainly have no idea what I might have said. At the time it seemed so serious and necessary as to be ceremonial. In fact, I believe that it was nothing more or less than a chance for each of us to say aloud, "I won't do that. I promise." I do remember that some time after her brother had said his piece, Patricia said, "I have to go to my room and think or something. Is that all right? I'll leave the door open."

She's afraid she will want to kill herself, given the chance. I knew as much because I knew that same fear. I could actually imagine not being able to muster any resistance to such an impulse.

Paul finally broke down and asked the question, "I know you don't know exactly how or anything, Dad. But do you think you know how she did it? Probably?"

"Anything I told you would be a guess, Paul."

Undeterred, he continued. "That's okay. I know you don't really know. You can guess."

Ted was smiling: He too could see that there was something comical about Paul's artless teetering between innocent curiosity and morbid fascination. "I know I can guess if I want to, Paul. I wasn't asking for your permission. What I mean is I don't see the point of guessing. It makes it seem that what we should concentrate on is the how-she-did-it part, instead of thinking about Clare and how many people are going to miss her. How she can't be here when Sarah has come back."

Paul was trying to edge into Clare's story still. "There's no way she could have—I don't know. Had Sarah wherever she was when she did it? I mean, Sister Clare?"

"She was at home, at the convent. I'm sure she never knew where Sarah was."

Finally, Paul seemed to register his father's reticence. He turned on me. "Mom? What about the thing—the package? Does this mean she didn't do that, too? I mean, do we know why she sent it now? She did it, right?"

Ted looked at me as if he had no theory of his own. I tried to convey the idea that everything I said was unreliable. I shrugged, I tilted my head—adopted all manner of gestures to make it clear that I was not at all interested in becoming the spokesperson for Clare. I felt she had dared to speak the ineffable—that's how I thought about her suicide. I did not want to get myself into a position where I might be willing to emulate her efforts. "Well, Paul, first off—we will never know for sure, even if she left a note or talked to Sister Urban or someone else. We'll never know in a way we can trust to be true. I think that takes seeing a person talking to you, telling you. You know? Anyway, what do I think?" Silence was a way of saying *Yes, that was the question.* "What do I think." I was stalling, amazed and a little put off by my impulse to tell my son exactly what I was thinking. Oddly enough, I did just that. "I think Clare thought I was the wrong person to be Sarah's mother in the first place and that she thought I had botched things really bad since Sarah disappeared and she finally got so sick of having to cajole me and remind me and organize things that she thought if she scared all hell out of me it'd help. And as to why she went and—"

"That's a little harsh, maybe, Anne." Ted had cut me off decisively. His tone belied his utter disapproval for my exuberant response to Paul's question. "It certainly is hard for any of us to know exactly what she thought she might accomplish. It was a kind of warning. That seems right. Do you have any ideas about it, Paul?" Ted locked on to Paul's gaze as if to protect him from further interchange with me.

Grateful, and frustrated, I let Paul speak to his father. Of course, Paul did have a theory or two of his own. He needed to have his say. *But why not air the facts? The woman they found dead in her convent room thought I was a bust as a mother.* My frustration seemed to fade, but I knew it would not evaporate or disappear. It descended, gravitating toward the mass that swelled behind the wall that still stood within me. Veined with stress fractures, and perceptibly swayed by the pressure it withstood, that familiar damlike thing was bound to give way. Would it only be the anger and frustration and resentment that would flood me when the pressure overcame the dam? I didn't think so. *Something lovely is the most of what's behind there.* This, and this alone, was what I knew of faith.

| X |

Answering the telephone in our house was no longer a mindless activity. I wouldn't do it, which registered with my children and husband as a reminder of my impaired mental health, I'm sure. Whoever picked up the receiver had to deal with the police-appointed intermediary, whose responsibility was to record the Fossickers' stated willingness to receive the prescreened caller.

By the time Ted handed me the receiver and made his way back to Paul in the living room, my mother's tolerance had been superseded.

She was speaking as I said, "Hello?"

"Who is it now? I am the woman's mother."

"It's Anne, Mom. I'm here now." I tried to make it clear that I was sorry about the annoyance.

"It would be easier to just disconnect your phone, Anne, don't you think? Anyone can understand a busy signal. This makes it a chore to call you, darling, I must say. Is Ted still on the line?" My mother paused only for a breath: she'd obviously lost all hope of engaging in normal conversation. "I can just as easily ask you. I don't mean to—the point I am trying to make is that Ted said he felt like he might send Patricia and Paul to stay out here with your father and me. I hope he hasn't done anything like that already, has he? You know I would be thrilled, darling. But I would need some warning. You just can't ship kids out here without telling me."

A long pause tipped me off to the fact that my mother expected a response. I felt like I'd been listening to the radio. I had no idea what she wanted me to say. After dismissing a few possible responses, I said, "Oh. The children are here, Mom. We're all back from Maine."

"I called you at home, Anne. I know you're all back. Are you all right? I was asking about what Ted said, on Thursday. About sending the kids out here?"

"Oh, no." I tried to sound cheerful, thinking a show of emotional strength might clear things up. "The package was a hoax of some kind, Mom. A prank? That's why we came back. The kids are fine here. Back on the track."

"Did the police catch the person?" My mother was coming to life. I felt inadequately prepared for a discussion. "Anne? Did they tell you who sent it? And why?"

"Oh, the package? They say it's a juvenile. No names on juveniles. They're protected." *How does one make up lies so easily?*

"Ridiculous. If they're old enough to threaten a life they ought to be treated like adults. But I suppose at least you feel better now that the police know?"

A lie is often a drawn-out affair. "Immeasurably. It's a real relief." *Why are you lying to your mother?* "I got a note from Richard."

This drew real surprise. "Why is he writing to you? I've never known him to be much of a letter writer. Where did he say he's living?"

"Roslindale, I think. He has no phone yet." I thought this sounded like a lie contrived to keep Richard out of my mother's reach. "I'll be sure to tell you if he gives the number to me. It was a sweet note."

"Well, be that as it may, I don't expect you'll get many more from him. Do you?"

I could not penetrate the sense of the question, though I had the idea that I was meant to reassure my mother that I did not expect to hear from Richard again. "No, I doubt I will. He just wanted to say he was sorry. About Sarah." Saying her name was costly. I wanted to be done with this conversation.

Tenderly, my mother said, "I hope you don't worry too much about her. She'll pull through."

What about me? Say something to me. "I don't know what to hope for." Finding it easy to move from sadness to anger, I yelled. "I can't believe you'd even think about telling me not to worry. Really. What do you think I'm supposed to do with my time? Celebrate?"

My mother would not retreat. "I didn't tell you not to. I said I hope. What is so awful about that? What is wrong with you that you can't have a conversation with me about this? What is it that you won't tell me? Why are you acting like I'm a total stranger?"

I could not establish who was overreacting, who was fueling

what fire. *She knows you lied about the package.* "I'm sorry. It's almost impossible for me to have a conversation with anyone. It doesn't mean anything."

She pressed on. Why? "I wish I could rely on you to be— at least to tell me. What you think, I mean. Or how you feel. I don't want to make you . . . I just get the sense that there is something you're not telling me. Anne?" Again, a long pause, a demand for a response. I could not even invent a lie. "Anne? I don't mean to act so much like your mother. I'm only trying to keep up with what is happening."

Irrationally, I felt I was being set up to look bad. I could see my mother gaining the high ground and from there taunting me with her good intentions. It was this jumble of resentment that prompted me to lie when she cheerfully asked to "at least speak with my grandchildren." I told her they were out. More yet: "They've gone out. With Clare."

Why should God answer the prayers of a liar?

My mother said I was in her prayers and promised to call in a few days. I tried to imagine what it might be like if I never spoke to her again.

| XI |

Ted was smiling that sad smile of his. I realized that he'd watched me during my conversation with my mother. I could hear him: *What are you going to do now?*

He spoke after I sat down, having failed to address his un-voiced question. "I asked Paul to check on Patricia. He said maybe they'd play cards. It's bad enough I was eavesdropping. I didn't think you needed a big audience. I'm sorry, but anyway, I heard you. Why, Anne? It will only make it harder to tell her anything. You can't keep it up, the part—"

"I know Clare is dead. Is that your point? I'm clear on that. It was a lie, not a vision or anything." I could not find a tone that was not angry.

Ted was not put off. "I didn't think you were believing what you said. It's just more complicated when you lie to her. It's like with the job, you know?"

I'd lied to her for months about my part-time work at *Aerohead,* not wanting to hear another version of my mother's thinly masked disdain for Working Mothers. "Of course it's like the job. It's exactly the same. That's the point. I don't want to discuss it with her."

"You can't just say that?" Ted appeared to be honestly confused.

"You need more proof that I can't? No, Ted. I can't." I paused, hoping I might think of some task that would leverage me out of the discussion. I failed. "Of course, it's because half the shit is half true, or seems to me half true. Maybe I was nuts trying to work. She's a pro on the weak spot anyway. 'Why don't the grandchildren know each other?' 'What's so wrong with Theresa?' She dares me to reveal secrets. She'd only use the news about Clare to tell me how she could have told me this would happen. She knew there was something wrong with Connecticut— 'How can you just pack up and leave Boston and everyone you know?' You've heard her. God knows. I'd expect sympathy on this issue, frankly. 'You girls never seemed to need Brownies, you had girlfriends. And neighbors who didn't move every other month.' Why give her the opening?"

Ted pressed on, still looking confused. "And half of all that is true? Or some part of it all is true? Half of what she says—"

"Maybe a third. Some part of it."

Relentless Ted. "Is true? Is true in the way you feel what's right, what's needed, what's best? You feel like maybe the Brownies, or Patricia not wanting to be a cheerleader, or vacations in Maine instead of the hallowed Cape Cod—this all makes you a target for bad luck? For unhappiness? Half of that is what you feel is true?"

I yelled, an increasingly typical response. "Half of it is half of me. It's what I know. That half. I was happy on Cape Cod, and in Braintree. I know that. That half says maybe she's right. The other half is guessing, making it all up, thinking about options. But it doesn't erase the knowing. That's what is half right or half true. She did it. Here I am. That half makes it possible. I didn't run away. Carol didn't get kidnapped. These are the facts. Theresa, Richard. Mrs. Johnson pulled it off. No major mistakes."

I could see that I had moved him. In fact, it was as if he had literally been moved and settled into a new posture. I thought he was forcing himself to be silent as a way of acknowledging my anger, my frustration. But he was crying. *I have moved him to tears. Again.*

I felt myself withdrawing into narrower confines, beginning to descend into the tunnel that led away from Ted, away from the moment. But he would not let me go. He came toward me, grabbed my hands and lifted me, spreading my arms. *Like wings.*

Almost apologetically, he whispered, "Mrs. Johnson made a mistake. Everybody makes mistakes. Everybody. There's a difference, and it really matters, a difference between what you know and what somebody tells you. What you know—it's that you love Sarah. You know that. You know that. Please stop acting like you don't. No matter what somebody tells you or what you think they mean. You know that."

Opened up and moving back toward Ted I needed to know more, assure myself I would not retreat. "She's my mother, Ted." I looked for sympathy and instead saw something hard and sheer.

He raised his head above mine. "A lot of women are somebody's mother. Mothers, fathers—we're all just another herd of sons and daughters. We're not sacred institutions. I think parents are overrated." Ted moved away from me, sensing that I could stand on my own with falling away. "One faulty milk truck killed my mother and my father. I don't know why. Getting to be a father didn't make me understand that. I know what I always knew since that happened. I won't get to make Patricia or Paul or Sarah be something. If I lived forever I wouldn't be able to—and I won't live forever. They're not mine in that way. I know that. What matters about being a father are not the things that have to do with being a parent instead of just being a man. Anne, I can't look at anything in my life and say I know it's the best way, the only way, the final word. Except how you love me. Don't you know that's what I mean about feeling like maybe something your mother said is half right? I just want to love them—not change them; to make a difference, not to teach them. Just to take the lucky chance to love someone right from the start. So much of what my mother and father seemed to think about me was all tied up with how I acted, what would become of me. And they didn't get the chance to see it all turn out. No one ever gets that chance. So can that be the point of being in the world? Of bringing more people into the world? It can't, I know that. None of this is an explanation. None of it makes me understand why my mother and father got blown up. Why Sarah is not here. But these things aren't secrets. And there aren't formulas or good-luck vacation spots or sanctioned careers that make for happy-go-lucky living. You know all this, too. Act like you know it." Ted delivered this last bit as if it were a command. Then he laughed. "I made a speech, I guess. Not on purpose, really. Sarah's in the future for us now, Anne. I don't even exactly know what I mean by that. But it is the right thing for me to know that I miss the chance to watch her and to just like the way she does the simplest thing. The only thing I have going for me is that I know I love her. I don't think a half-truth is much next to that. In fact, it's nothing."

"In fact?"

Ted smiled, happy and embarrassed. "Just like you say. A fact."

If there is such a thing as immortality, I nominate Ted.

│ XII │

During his brief telephone conversation with Tim Hall, Ted forwarded an invitation to dinner. Tim Hall accepted. I was pleased, thinking Tim was not only the best-informed but the most insightful spokesperson for Clare. After a very brief and tentative discussion, Ted and I managed to make it clear to each other that we both felt it would be best if Paul and Patricia were not present—for their sakes and for the sake of Tim Hall. To facilitate this, I telephoned Janet Ameron.

"Janet? It's Anne and I've got one of those terrible favors I want you to do for me. Feed my kids dinner tonight. Keep them for a while?"

Janet, in perfect form, said, "Tell me what I need to know before they get here."

"Clare—Sister Clare?"

Janet spoke as if she was taking notes. "The kindergarten teacher up at school?"

"I'll tell you everything I know, if it makes it easier. The fact is, she sent the package—the one with the cut-up cap."

"You couldn't possibly have time to tell me why." Janet seemed to mean this.

"More to the point, she's killed herself. The police seem to think the two things are not related. I don't know what to think. Tim Hall, the cop? He's coming to dinner. Ted asked him and it's apparently going to be public, the fact that Clare is ... committed suicide. It's going to be a mess, isn't it?" The publicity that would follow on such an unlikely event had only just occurred to me. I realized that Paul and Patricia would likely be popular again, as sources of the details.

Bravely Janet said, "Sarah?"

"Nothing. Goddamn it." At least speaking to Janet I could muster some indignation.

"You call me when you can handle having the kids back. They could spend the night."

They could disappear. "I wish I felt up to it. I'm sure they'd prefer it. I don't think I could handle it, them not being here."

"I'd like to see you, do something. Jesus, Anne, I pray for you all. As if I knew how. Call me tomorrow. We could go for a drive? Anyway, you have to figure out some way to get me out of the potluck." Janet paused. "You're not seriously thinking about going? Ted too?"

"We could not go maybe?"

Janet laughed. I could just picture us driving nowhere together. "Listen, Anne. You hold all the cards. You need a refresher course. You don't watch out and when Sarah gets back there'll be an annual neighborhood dance in her honor, courtesy of Sylvia Castine and family."

When Sarah gets back. I couldn't talk.

Janet sensed what had happened, waited a few seconds. "She is coming back." Nothing from me. "Send the kids when you want. A warning: I am going to call you tomorrow and beg you to come for a ride with me." Still nothing. "You can always say no later." And still nothing from me. "Don't die inside there. Don't let that happen."

"I have to go. Thank you." I hung up before Janet finished speaking.

Any joy that made its way to me from outside the strict family boundaries registered as a betrayal of Sarah. The inversion of this wrongheaded reaction was a sort of compulsion to embrace Clare's suicide in its awful entirety.

Ted had already told the children of the evening's plans and without waiting for my confirmation of Janet's acceptance of the proposal, they raced to me, kissed me, left the house.

I said, "There you have it in the flesh. News travels fast."

Ted seemed positively thrilled by their animation and his pleasure was unqualified by the complications that fueled their enthusiasm. Finally he turned to me. "When are we going to eat? What time?"

"What food?" The notion that dinner had to be prepared had finally dawned on me.

"Do we have food?" Ted was reeling himself back into real time, Fossicker time.

"Janet sent over a basket of snacks—I mean, good things. Things we could eat as if I'd meant to make a sort of dinner out of them. Real food."

"They sound perfect."

I did not think Ted knew *how* good the food was. This seemed important, as if it might excuse my complete lack of forethought. "No, like a great pâté. Beautiful small breads. Some canned things I've never heard of."

"It sounds really great." Ted obviously was not interested in a predinner catalogue.

"Janet is good. She's something. I'm thinking about going to talk to her for a while tomorrow. I don't know, maybe not." I wanted Ted to tell me not to seek advice outside of the walls he'd built, to make a law that would solidify my fear of resuming daily life.

Ted? "She is great. I like that whole family. Even the kids. That is something. I hope you see her. I don't know. I think it helps. She may have nothing new to give you, to say, but it matters that it's coming from her. I've had people I hardly know call me at work, people who I think are there in the right way? It helps. It's good there are people who will blunder around trying to let you know they care. It's so tempting to think there's nothing to say."

I was not completely satisfied, to say the least. Hoping to sound ironic, I said, "The kids certainly couldn't wait to be released from dinner duty."

"Yeah." Ted was smiling again, as if he'd caught a glimmer of the trail they'd left. "I don't know what it means, really, but life goes on."

That's the problem. "Well, life calls for food. Let's not eat in the kitchen."

Before either of us moved we saw Tim Hall's car pull up next to ours in the driveway. Ted left me to greet him, I went into the kitchen, to make the best of dinner. *Sister Clare is dead, Sarah. I'm so sorry.*

| XIII |

Tim Hall was not wearing his uniform. He stood when I entered the room, looking less familiar in rather tight new jeans and a plaid sportshirt. *This is a sexy man.* Without his regulation blues and badges and buckles he might have been a young college professor or a lawyer. He'd tossed his suede baseball jacket on the carpet and shunned my offer to hang it up properly. *Who are you anyway?* He smiled, helped me carry trays, said next to nothing, and the whole while I felt like a flirt. When he sat on the sofa, next to Ted, I saw that the two could easily pass as brothers. Shorter and more ambitiously muscled, Tim Hall had the accessible, graceful sense of his own presence that was Ted's hallmark. It was such an oddity for me to be alone with two men that I began to feel self-conscious. I wanted to make some mention of their being men; to let them know that though I couldn't imagine it would make a difference of any kind, I knew that I was not a man. *They know that.*

Even when Tim Hall spoke I could not quite align the voice, the words, with a familiar source.

"It's nice of you both. To ask me over. You've had too much to handle without dinner guests." *What does he make of this food?* "My dad—you know I live with my dad? He has a poker game at the house every Saturday night. Gives me a chance to get out. He takes care of the kids."

Unsettled enough to ignore social graces, I said, "Where do you go?"

"Out. I date some. Date sounds funny to me. There are a couple of places—bars. I go there."

I felt like I was talking to a visitor from Italy or Australia. He lived in a different society. I wanted to know what it was like there, whom he met, what they did. I only said, "Not much of a dinner, I'm afraid."

Tim was making his way through the various bits with a sense of recognition that clearly left Ted and me in the dust. "It's great. Just the kind of meal I would have ordered—if you'd asked." He smiled and laughed. Ted laughed.

Ted knows what that means. I don't really know why, but I was nervous.

"How are Paul and Patricia doing?" Tim looked to Ted.

"They'll get by. It's pretty scary, I suppose." He looked at me, as if I might add to his assessment.

After a few silent seconds, Tim pushed a basket of bread and the pâté along the coffee table. "You really should have some. Even the bread is great."

What happened to Officer Hall? Who are you?

Ted seemed more than relaxed. He seemed happy. With the two men on the sofa separated from me by the low coffee table covered with a dozen little plates and bowls, I had the sense that I was secreted behind a two-way mirror and observing some kind of experiment.

Ted said, "How are you doing?"

"I'm going to see my ex-wife tomorrow. Ex-wife. It makes it sound so legal. Her name is Marilyn."

Of course.

"She sees the kids a lot, but we don't see each other so much anymore. It's harder when you don't hate them." Here he looked at me, the third wheel, the woman. "I think it would be easier if she'd gone off with someone. But she says she needs to live alone. I don't. I mean, I want to have a wife who I know is there for me." He laughed again. "I'd even give up my Saturday nights." *You wouldn't understand why that's funny, Mrs. Fossicker.* "The old problem, though. I love her. Marilyn. It makes you wonder."

Ted, now eagerly sampling the salads and bits of smoked things, said, "It's good the kids see her."

"It took me a while to admit that. I wanted to punish her. So I punished them, I guess. I don't have the answers." Again he looked at me, smiled. "I'm used to it all now, you know? I don't expect it'll happen, us being together again. It would be nice for me, but that's not what she wants. I mean, I'm not what she wants. Hardest thing I ever did was trying to explain all this to the kids. They hate it, I think. My dad's great, though."

Ted was enthralled. "Do they understand at all?"

Tim Hall actually blushed. " 'What must they think?' You know who said that to me? It was Sister Clare. She launched right into me, the day after the search. I got talking about something and told her about the divorce and she said, 'What must they think?' I never really thought about the kids having thoughts about it at all." He looked up at Ted. "Does that make me out to be really stupid? It just never occurred to me." Ted put his plate on the table, leaned back into the cushions. "Every time she saw me last week Clare would ask about the kids. Did I talk to them? Not like a nagging sort of thing. But like she couldn't wait for me to hear what they had to say." Here he stood. "Could I have something other than this wine to drink, Anne? A beer maybe?"

"Of course. Ted?"

"A beer would be nice. I'll get them."

I was already up. "I'll be right back."

Random thoughts carried me to the kitchen:

He slept with Clare. That's why.

He's irresistible.

He knows about Ted being divorced.

He can't believe Ted doesn't sleep around on Saturday nights.

Does he sleep with women at home?

Clare was in love with him and he di..'t even know it.

I found two beers and then leaned against the refrigerator. *Why are you afraid of him?*

Just the act of relaxing momentarily was enough to curtail my hysterical reactions. I listened to Tim and Ted without hearing what was said. *That's a man out there.* This did not register from his foreignness, but in the simplest sense. I was being made aware that my life, and the lives of all the Fossickers, were intersecting with other lives in a random but personal way. It had been easier to maintain my focus on Sarah, on my loss of Sarah, when it had been the policeman, the teacher, the lady at the center for Missing Children. But Clare's desperation and Tim Hall's unadorned presence—this was evidence of lives. My reluctance to acknowledge them had been a way of restricting the boundaries. In my narrow little world I could eventually make sense of Sarah's disappearance. At least that much seemed possible. But I could not make sense of a planet on which men like Tim Hall do not have happy home lives. A planet that cannot provide a woman like Clare with something other than the disrepair of her childhood to inform and move her.

Blame me. The choice is between feeling guilty and not knowing?
No contest. Blame me.

It was absolutely a reflex response to unanswerable questions.

"Why should Theresa have to be a widow?" (I went to sixteen moratoriums for peace during the Vietnam War; I weakened the spirit of soldiers who might have saved him.)

"Why doesn't Carol ever have a date?" (I don't get dates for my fat sister.)

"What ever happened to family weddings?" (I married a divorced man; no one would come, even if you were prepared to invite any of them.)

"Who would believe that after fighting tooth and nail to save our family home I would ever set foot in that hospital?" (Dad was out with the car. I made Theresa promise not to tell you I was vomiting. But when blood came up she ran for you and all I could think was how many times you told me that my crazy dieting would land me in a hospital.)

In recalling all of this I saw the oddity: I had never felt the martyr, never had a sense of having been assigned the blame, exactly. These questions were raised, cruel little riddles that commanded my attention. If any of my time was ever really spent in thought, it had been in this form: How can it possibly be that . . . It was always easy for me to see my part in whatever "impossible" had come to be. *I suppose you could blame me.*

"Are we out of beer?" Ted followed his voice to me.

"Found a couple." I followed him back to the living room.

"Sorry for the trouble." Tim took one of the beers. "Water would've been fine. I just can't drink wine if I want to stay awake." He rubbed his hands together. "This is the hard part, right? I told Ted already that one of the nurses recognized Clare right off. She's a mother of a kid at St. Cecilia. I don't think the sisters—well, of course, they're not going to announce that she killed herself. People *are* going to know. I say that just so you don't try to keep it a secret or . . . She slit her wrists. It's so rare that people who want to die actually manage it that way. It takes something unusual." He could not look at Ted or me. He was in front of Clare. "I can't tell you how physically difficult what she did is. She cut halfway up her arm, the long way. She would have died fast. I'm sorry." He looked at both of us. I think he was trying to get a fix on how much we could handle. We were like sphinxes. We could listen to anything. "The nurse—the one who recognized Clare—she kept saying it was so clean it was like a surgeon did it. You know she still had the bad hand from breaking the window. She just wanted to die. All out. I guess that makes me out to sound cold or something. But you knew that when you saw her. She wanted to be dead. It's hard to believe anyone ever does, really, but she did."

Ted smiled at Tim. "I feel like we should be saying something. Reacting. I can only tell you that we know how much Sarah loved Clare."

"I didn't see what I should've." *I confess.*

"I wanted to come here for two reasons tonight, Anne. One is just to be with the two of you. It means something to me, knowing the two of you. And I am not used to making promises, but we are going to find your daughter." He waited for me to look at him. "But I came here also because of what I saw today—and this is not the sort of thing that can be repeated. It's not like a secret, but ... The point is that Clare did what she did. Not because of you or Sarah or anything to do with you."

Reflexively I said, "That's nice of you. But it's a little difficult not to make the connection between—"

"I don't think you're qualified to make that connection. I'm sorry, Anne. What I mean is this. Clare loved Sarah. That was obvious. But she loved a lot of kids she taught. Especially the Brownies. Sarah's picture was one of sixteen Clare had framed and hung up on her bedroom wall, above her desk. All the sisters talked about her in terms of time with all those kids."

But Sarah is special. "The events involving Sarah were a little more dramatic than normal."

Tim Hall would not let me have even this much. "Friday morning Clare went to see a fourth-grader who's in the hospital for some kind of shoulder operation. She also left a note. To that Sister Urban." Here his voice broke. He shook his head, as if he could loose the hold of the pressing sadness. "It was an apology."

Tim would not submit to the sadness, but his efforts to resist paralyzed him.

Ted took over. "Clare's letter to you—the one we thought was from Urban—it was true as far as the details of her past. As far as Tim or anyone knows. Sister Urban won't go into any of it. The thing is, none of the other sisters knew the story as a whole. She'd made up a past when she went to live with Sister Urban. She said—in her note?—she was sorry for having exposed Sister Urban and her family. But she figured—"

Tim Hall broke back in. "She figured she shouldn't die without somebody knowing who she was. She said—and this is what I cannot understand about that old lady—she said she knew it hurt Sister Urban when she brought it up but that she had to say it all at least once." Tim Hall had struck an uneasy truce with his anger and sorrow. "That old lady won't budge. Even now. And as if it makes it all right she just won't stop saying how she's really not surprised, that Clare had never been able to turn her life over and start again. She won't fucking budge on that. I'm sorry." He grabbed his beer as if he intended to use it as a weapon.

Ted again carried on for him. "The other sisters are completely at a loss. As far as Tim can tell, Clare had this same effect on everyone. They all felt like they couldn't quite keep up with her or even exactly figure out why she did so much. In that way she had. But, well, you can imagine how impossible this seems."

Tim staggered back into the conversation. "They're great, those women. They're open to you. You feel it. Every one of them I talked to really racked herself, trying to get to some memory that might be a reason for what Clare did. But you see, none of them knew her and that kills them. Just the way they might start crying and keep right on talking, like you just can't stop crying but it won't control you. It's so hard to figure that Urban. Right in the middle of them all. And nothing. Just nothing."

Then why can I only feel sorry for that old lady? "Nothing about Sarah that is new? I have to ask."

Tim smiled. "My bet? Clare wasn't even thinking about Sarah when she offered to stay here while you were all in Maine. She was trying to get herself a cover story, so she could disappear and not be found for a while, until she had done what . . . She wanted to do this. Ted seems to have the best theory about the cap and the picture."

Ted was staring at Tim Hall. "Tim told me about the visit to the kid in the hospital. And Clare doing this thing about giving each of the Brownies a special merit badge at a sort of ceremony last Wednesday. Each kid got one for being kind or patient or something. I just said that I think she was trying to make sure . . ." Ted looked at me as if to say, I know this, then continued, "She was trying to leave everything—especially kids she loved—to leave them all as well off as she could. In her funny way, she was goading us all into finding Sarah." Then Ted shook his head, to escape. "As if we needed it. Anyway."

"She gave you the letter when you were leaving." Tim seemed to be thinking aloud. "The one she said was from Sister Urban. I don't know if she thought you'd read it and call here Thursday night, or what. As far as I can tell she wasn't at the convent Thursday night."

"She was here. I know that much. She cleaned a lot of things." I tried to smile as I said this. "She really cleaned Sarah's room. Really cleaned it." I couldn't see any reason now to take public exception to Clare's methods. She'd been aiming for some other order. "I didn't read it. Until Friday. I'd forgotten about it, the letter, till then."

"No. No. I mean it, Anne. It wouldn't have stopped her." Tim Hall displayed this knack for becoming strong in the presence of weakness; it was another link with Ted. "I don't think so. Remember the end of that letter? Her insisting that you talk to Clare before anyone else? Well, she was not answering the phone here at all. She was on a mission. I know this is hard, but it is right." He was looking at the ceiling, as if it were the sky. "She'd even got herself on to her bed. She was on her back, on top of an old sheet she'd put down. Her arms sort of spread out."

Like wings.

Ted said, "Coffee?"

Tim looked at his watch. "I think I'm going to leave. I'm meeting someone." He blushed again. "I don't mean to just dump all my problems on you."

I had conjured up a picture of Tim and his date in some terrible cocktail lounge, his awkward meeting the morning after with Marilyn. "I wish I could make it all go away."

Tim stood. He put his hands in his pockets. "I wish I could bring her back. Sarah."

And Clare. And Marilyn.

I was crying as much for Tim and Ted as for myself. "Oh, God, so do I, Tim."

Ted retrieved Tim's suede jacket from the floor, walked with him to the door. They shook hands tentatively, then draw each other into an embrace.

I would like to add Tim Hall's name to those nominated for immortality.

Tim yelled, "Good night. You'll see me bright and early Monday morning."

I joined Ted at the door. We watched Tim's car until its red lights were out of sight. Ted put his arms around me, held my back to him. Then he said, "Good night, Sarah."

Can you at least see her now, Clare? Does she look all right?

FEAR
OF
INNOCENCE

| I |

BEFORE CHURCH on Sunday morning, Ted mentioned to me that a house just outside of Greenwich that he'd long admired was on the market. I vaguely recalled the blocky post-war home that Ted had considered worth showing to the whole family three years earlier. "It's so much what it is." Ted said so several times as he circled the house set smack in the center of untended lawn only a few miles from Long Island Sound. It was obvious the kids did not share his enthusiasm for the "piece of American functionalism" that Ted vowed to buy should it become available. When Ted mentioned the house three years later, I recalled having fervently hoped that the owners of the dubious treasure might live forever—and stay put.

I hoped that Ted would overlook design integrity for the time being. "I can't imagine even considering making a move from this house until we . . . I can't even make conversation about the idea of leaving here now, Ted. It's not worth discussing."

"Not moving, Anne. Not now, anyway." Ted was sitting on the bed, a tie around his neck, no shirt on. "I want to go see it again. Just see it. It's not the kind of house the company could do well with. Obviously. Even as a shell it has nothing to do with this mock modernism," he said, pointing around the room, indicting the entire house. "This-shaped-room-flowing-into-shaped-room business. Anyway, I would not consider gutting that house. It's perfect in its way, Anne. Some kind of first. I mean it, it symbolizes what became of prosperity around here in New England. Sure, the typical house got smaller, didn't get the pillared-porch treatment. But there it is, announcing the new standard, a carved-out block of granite. Really, it looks like that. It was a promise at the end of the war, that people could expect—"

"Ted, I don't care if it was built by Harry Truman. I don't care if the asking price is fifteen cents and two war bonds. Can you hear me? I am not interested." *I will not be moved. I will not be moved.*

Calmly, dismissively, Ted said, "I'm gonna go down and see it today, just for my sake. I might see if Paul and Patricia want to come along for the ride. I'm not even going to ask anyone how much. Just a look. It matters to me. It's only a house I like, Anne."

"I think I'll pass." I couldn't look at him. "I'm sorry. Okay? Never mind 'okay.' I am sorry. I'm so frustrated I want to pick a fight with someone."

"Pick on someone your own size. Pick on Janet." Ted laughed. *I really think you ought to spend some time talking to Janet today, Anne.*

In lieu of the field trip to Greenwich, I called Janet and arranged to have her come to the house for lunch. Paul and Patricia were inordinately excited about the short trip. They even responded favorably to Ted's suggestion that they all stop at the Stamford Museum observatory on the way. I felt like I was the mean warden who'd obligingly agreed to a prisoner-release program. The children and Ted said goodbye soberly. Once outside, Patricia and Paul raced to claim the front seat.

Janet Ameron arrived almost as Ted and the kids left. *Be on my side. Stck up for me.* I wanted a little sympathy, even pity. It was not being left behind; after all, I had been invited. It wasn't even the prospect of beginning the second hopeless week; I wanted Janet to elevate the emotional pitch, to raise me from the ordinariness that threatened to displace the panic that kept Sarah alive, present.

Janet walked in, led me into the kitchen. It was evident that she'd already planned to put in as casual a performance as possible. "I'll make some coffee. If I were a better friend, I'd offer to clean the kitchen." She opened the refrigerator door; a plastic bottle of milk fell to the floor. Janet's espadrilles were soaked. "Anything else likely to happen when I try to find the coffee?" She closed the refrigerator, wet a towel at the sink, began to wipe up the spill. "Oh, no. Let me get it, Anne." Only then did she turn to me.

"I'm crying." As stupid as it must have sounded, it was true, except in the literal sense. I was not shedding tears. But the unmistakable feeling of warmth, the suspension of my sense of place and appearance, the draining of some private store of hopes and frustrations, the random conjuring up of images to feed the outward flow—I was crying all right. "I cry like this all the time now. Nonstop."

Janet came to me, hugged me. Only then, next to her, did I realize that her casual air had been a foil for her objective. She would listen to me, she would sympathize over coffee. But she had something to say.

Of course, I didn't want to hear it. I pushed away and finished cleaning up the spilled milk. That done, I started on the coffee.

Janet sat at the kitchen table. "I want to know what I can do for you, what you need to say. Anything. But I want to . . . first off . . . Anne, your kids are . . . Patricia and Paul, both of them, are worried. I mean, about you. I mean, how you're taking this."

Ever the polite hostess, I banged the stainless-steel coffee pot against the sink and dropped it into the basin. "Screw the kids, then. I don't want to take it at all."

After a long pause, during which I began again with the coffee, Janet lit a cigarette. "You certainly seem okay to me. I don't know what their problem is."

I remembered how to cry, all of a sudden. "Everything is turned around. I'm afraid to tell them anything. I could be wrong. I just know that I don't know. I don't know anything. And they probably told you about the phone call. From Sarah."

"And about seeing her. The three of us ended up spending almost an hour after dinner. My kids headed straight for the TV—cable movies without the censor." Janet came to the sink and doused her cigarette under the faucet. "That's not what worries them, I don't think. They have a feeling for what that is, I think. It's more about you, Anne. The yelling, they said. The scenes? I'm not saying stop it. I'm saying maybe you could tell them why."

"Do you hear yourself? Tell them why I'm crying so much lately? Why Mom doesn't want to hear about what the policeman told Paul about runaways? I don't know why, I don't know why, I don't know why." I plugged in the coffee pot, walked to the refrigerator, turned on Janet. Then I screamed. "Where is she? Where is she? That's why."

Janet retreated into a kind of therapeutic calm. "I think I understand that. What that is like. But take a look. You've got two other kids. And Sarah might not come back. You have to think about them, too. You owe it to them."

Might not come back. It was the only intolerable condition. "I don't owe. I don't owe. Do you hear me? I don't care. It scares me. It hurts. This is a fact. The way of the world. I can't make myself care enough about everything else. I know that. I can see what's happening. Don't play me for the fool." Talking did not dispel my rage, but it made it unnecessary to act angry. I could speak the truth. I knew that. Janet approached me, to comfort me. I waved her off. "You have to let me say it. Please, let me. Please. I don't care enough about Paul and Patricia. Or Ted even. With her gone. Can't? Won't? I just know I don't. Simple, the simplest things, they don't come natural to me. Dinner. Breakfast. I have to be reminded. Days of the week. I don't care enough to know. It is impossible, what happened here. It's impossible. Don't you see? I didn't do it. But everything sure as hell points to me, or to something I should have done, better do, didn't do. What is it, then? Fate? Luck? It's simple. If I didn't have a job I would never have gotten her that daily planner that Ted hated and which didn't help her with being afraid about day care at the Girls' Club. That's one thing. Or, I could have made a habit out of walking her or driving her to school. I would have loved to do that. I wouldn't have minded if I could've thought of that instead of thinking: Kids take the bus. That's another thing. There are a million. No, more. I could've done anything but what I did. So who cares? I did it wrong. Or it just went wrong." I looked at Janet. But I did not see Janet. I saw a superior being. A mother who had not let a child get away. A mother whose children could all be accounted for. "You don't understand. Why would you even want to try? I half believe it's trying to understand just this sort of thing that is the reason Sarah is gone. All my time, all my time almost, I spend it deciding, Is this okay for my kids? What does it mean that I want them to have friends? Is it bad to be a Brownie? Can I rely on my instincts? How do I know what an instinct is? Do people even have them? The list goes on. It's endless."

Then, as if I were some distraught lady in a soap opera and she my best friend and confidante, Janet shook her head and rather tentatively said, "Have you thought about talking to a shrink, Anne?"

The utter stupidity of her timing defused me. It was as if I had forced her to say something stupid, something people say to people instead of saying, I'm not interested in spending a lot of time having conversations like this.

Janet said, "Would it be easier to kick me if I stood by the sink?"

"I spent two years with that crazy, great therapist—you know? About marrying a non-Catholic? Or so I thought. Her name was Audrey, remember? Of course, having got back into the Church, that money could have been better spent on a pool, I guess. Anyway, I don't think a shrink is going to make me feel—"

"Stop. It was a remarkably dumb thing to say." Janet lit another cigarette.

"I wish I smoked. You look so happy when you light up."

Janet laughed. "If somebody opens a bottle of white wine at the same time, it's pretty much orgasm."

Let's have new lives, Janet, with no dependents.

"But, coffee will do," Janet poured two cups. "But I interrupted you."

"Thank God, I suppose." I sat at the table, opposite her.

"So talk. No more stupidity from me."

"Oh, that's what I wanted to tell you. I mean, what I was getting at, about not wanting to see a shrink."

Janet shrugged. "Anne, it was a stupid suggestion that I regret—"

"That's not it. The truth is, I talk to—just like I might talk to Ted, like I do talk to Ted, who always listens. I talk to Sarah that way." Janet was retreating. I wanted her to hear me. "I don't know how to make this seem—not strange—to you, Paul, and Patricia. Ted seems to . . . well, he's not so put off by it. That's all I can say for sure."

Don't tell me things I can't deal with, Anne. I'm not Ted.

I didn't. Janet heard me out and advised me on the familial issues. She posed solutions for Paul and Patricia's discomfort. She offered her services, services I knew I would utilize without the burden of repayment or even proper thanks. She left me with a promise to bring a halt to the planned potluck supper. What more could I ask?

I could've asked her to listen as a woman in the world tried to say words that might express what it was like to find herself beyond hope.

I don't hope for anything anymore, Janet. I don't know why, but being hopeless is what got me started with the talking to Sarah. I can see that much. But you know, it's obvious that while I'm doing that—also with Clare; I talk to Clare now, too—I am talking to myself. To someone who is me but not here. That's hard to make clear, in words. The reason I go on talking to Sarah and Clare is because I feel like the words get better when they get passed through Sarah or Clare. They are not just words then. And, that far away Anne might hear the better words. I had the impulse to say this to you, even before Ted, since you are a mother and somehow I thought that was part of why it was happening to me in this particular way. The facts are one thing, Janet. But the truth is I am afraid I'm looking for God. That's not what looking for Sarah is, but it is what it means. The thing is, the world seems the most unlikely place to find God. But where else would I look?

| II |

As it turned out, the Greenwich trip was something of a disappointment. The house Ted so admired had been abruptly pulled from the market. When I spiritedly asked to know the reason for the change of status, Ted said, "Estate had problems."

Ready and willing to discuss the house in its unavailable condition, I pressed on. "I think it might be going too far to call it an estate, Ted. Even if it is near Greenwich."

Ted, unimpressed by my late-hour interest, said, "You don't understand. 'Estate' as in family quarrels. I know the difference between a house and an estate, Anne." He shook his head. "I think I'm hungry. Maybe for a sandwich. The kids seemed to enjoy the museum." He left me alone in the living room.

Paul and Patricia came into the living room as he left. Hearing the rumblings in the kitchen, Patricia went to convince her father to feed her. Paul sat next to me on the sofa, an odd choice on his part.

"Did Dad tell you about the stars?" He was embarrassed.

"He barely told me about the house. Guess you guys didn't get to see it, really." I wanted to be clear on the fate of the house Ted loved.

"We saw it. Some lady, the daughter of the guy who died. I don't remember. We went to that museum with the room that is one of those things, though." Paul was tossing a pillow as he spoke, waiting for me to ask the right leading questions.

"What sort of room?"

"You know, Mom. The ones with the stars—like stars, I mean. You put your head back and they play some music like it's all outer space and dark except for the solar systems and some gases." The pillow was pressed between his knees.

I hoped I was following. "A planetarium?" *Why is he nervous talking to me?*

"Is that what you call it? With the stars, right?"

"Right."

"Anyway, I was the only one who could name any of the things—you know, like the dippers. There's the big one and the little one? I knew where they were. And I knew about the bear. And one other. I forget. Maybe it was a lady in a dress— an old-fashioned sort of dress?" Paul was bragging. It was lovely. "Dad kept saying this one thing was the North Star, and how you could tell everything from that." Paul giggled. "It was Venus. Some star." More giggling. "Patricia didn't even know there was a lot of galaxies. Later she said she knew, but she kept telling me I was a dope if I thought so." Paul looked at me. "You would've known more. If you came. I bet. You know that stuff."

He's not bragging; he's bolstering me up.

"Anyway, it's nice, this place. You should come if we go again." The pillow was now something to be hugged. "Even the house was good. Like Dad said. He was so mad it was . . . that you can't buy it, all of a sudden."

"I don't remember that house too well." I wanted to do right by Paul, though this seemed an elusive goal.

"I didn't either. The house is like that." The pillow was back between his knees. "Mom, I didn't mean to say nothing to Bobby Ameron's mother. I'm sorry." Paul started to cry. "I'm not scared like I told her. Really."

I just pulled him to me, wishing I could protect him, that I had protected him all along. "Sorry?" It was an unreal, brave tone I'd struck. "I was scared for a while. Sometimes I still am. Sorry for wondering? No, Paul." He was sobbing, guilt and fear and sheer humiliation pushing him toward me. "It's me, Paul. Remember me?" I held him momentarily at arm's length, then reeled him back to me. He was choking back tears, allowing some hint of manhood and what it might entail to dispel emotion.

"You sure it's okay?" He'd got himself turned sort of sideways on the sofa, face turned away from me. "You mad?"

I laughed—well, I managed to cough and smile, approximating laughter. "One last time. I'm Mom. I'm not mad. You want some dinner?"

Wiping his eyes with his forearms he said, "Do I have to have a sandwich?"

Be my mother, then. "You and I could eat something else. Say, pancakes?"

"With somethin' in them? Raisins?"

The child is there again. "Name it. How about apples?"

"Raisins, unless you want apples."

I want you not to know enough to ask me that. "Raisins are much better. Much better. Raisins."

"Can I go wash my face first?"

A real laugh from me, finally. "If you know one thing about me, Paul, you know I would never say 'No' to that question."

"That's true." He ran toward the stairs, up to the sports posters and pine cones and disorder that would be the child's last stronghold. And already the air in that room of his had been tainted; uncertainty and emotional demands had seeped in, like smoke, and driven the child into the years ahead, beyond the room. He would retreat, but he would not forget. He might never remember the name of that fourth constellation. But he will remember running from me to Janet to Ted and back to me. And I am afraid he will remember that when he finally ran back to his room the smoke had not cleared.

| III |

Ted was in bed, watching me. I was staring at my reflection in a round mirror above my bureau, trying to assess how I looked, checking the visible clues that Paul and Patricia and Ted might interpret.

Ted said, "See anything?"

"Nothing new. Isn't that odd?" I continued my investigation.
"What were you hoping to see?"

I thought about what Ted might mean, then said, "What's changed, about me."

"You want an opinion?"

I did not want to look at him. "All right, Ted. Tell me."

"Just a guess. You haven't changed. Yet. You know you ought to. It's time for some kind of change. I mean, isn't that what you're looking for? To make sure you didn't change without realizing it?"

I pulled at the corners of my eyes, erasing a year or two, nothing more. "Maybe that's it. Maybe it's only that I have to change."

Ted livened here. "Nobody ever has to change, in the real sense change."

I rubbed some cream into my cheeks and forehead. "What would you like to see when you look at me?" I didn't only turn toward Ted, I turned on him, daring him to answer.

"Oh, Annie. I'd like to see you smile is all." He was undaunted by my stare.

I returned to the mirror. "That would be nice for a change."
That is not what I am looking for.

| IV |

Monday morning's breakfast was short and somber. The children were contented to know that Ted and I both thought it would be best if they told the truth about Clare, if they were asked. It seemed unlikely that they would be let alone on the topic of the suicide. "No one knows why someone kills herself." This was the line Ted repeated several times. As to their absence from school on Thursday and Friday, and the inevitable questions they would face about the threatening package, we all thought the policy to adopt was one of defusing interest. It was all cleared up. Paul and Patricia rehearsed several versions of these phrases; they were obviously nervous.

Your sister is still missing. I withdrew from the kitchen as Ted and the kids made their final preparations, knowing that such a reminder would undo the frail calm we'd wrapped around the morning.

I heard Paul say, "We have to have some money, then," before the door closed; I'd not prepared lunches. In truth, I could not believe that I'd ever managed to negotiate my way through a rendition of the day's upcoming events while preparing breakfast and filling orders for sandwiches, fruit, and dessert. And impressive as this all seemed, I could not imagine why I had for so long forced my children to accept a lunch from home. Under the guise of cost savings I argued with them more than once a week. But as I thought of the fruit pies, the individual bags of flavored chips, the concession I'd made about bologna, I knew that it was not particularly cost concerns—and certainly not nutritional concerns—that impelled me. Honestly, I pity any woman who protests that she wants to be making sandwiches while the other human beings in the household enjoy a few minutes together before they scatter into the world.

The old-fashioned Working Mother. She doesn't leave the house except to shop, tend to household-related duties, and to make the occasional traumatic visit to the principal's office or the emergency room of the local hospital. And in so doing, serves whose interests? Was it that husbands actually wanted to have an adversarial relationship with their homebody wives? Did someone think it was a good idea to maroon mothers in quiet suburban neighborhoods so that their children could be amazed at their mothers' naiveté and dictatorial commitment to unreasonable standards of timeliness and order? Who was the beneficiary?

Was I a Mother?

Really, I was not. Or, I didn't think I wanted to be a Mother, anyway. As a woman, I knew just how Patricia felt when she asked me what to tell people about Clare and the package. But, the Mother I had learned to be forced her wise and wily way to the fore: Don't empathize, lead. Don't admit confusion, assert clarity. Don't talk to Patricia, advise your daughter.

I wanted to undo it all. I wanted to get in the car, go to Patricia and Paul, make them look at me, and say, "I am Anne. See? I am Anne who is your mother. But I can't go on being both Anne and your mother. I am going to be Anne from here on in. Do you think you can handle that? What I mean by this is . . ." But I didn't know what it meant, beyond feeling that I could no longer say that my love for Paul and Patricia had to be informed by a separate sense of what children need in the way of obedience training and discipline and order. My love for them was the same blank, interactive emotion as my love for Ted. It was not improved or ennobled by all the strictures and conditions that are inherent in the Mother's thoughtful, premeditated love.

So you mean we can stay out as late as we want, Mom?

Not exactly what I had in mind.

Instead of dashing off to St. Cecilia's, I dressed and returned to the kitchen to wash the breakfast dishes. *Someone has to do this:* the ancient bray of the laborer whose dignity has been traded for security or for peaceable relations—or just to avoid becoming someone rather than one who has to do such things.

I could just hear Ted. "What are you going to do now?"

After much consideration and, admittedly, after the dishes were done, I believed I knew what I would do. I would leave my family in capable hands and I would go looking for her. Someone had to do that, too.

| V |

Tim Hall said the magic words. He'd joined me in the kitchen after apologizing for arriving later than "bright and early," as promised. It was just ten o'clock. Staring into his cup of coffee, he said, "I am telling you again that the leads are only that. They might be complete dead ends. And we've had more than a couple dozen calls telling us how they saw Sarah walking a dog in Vermont, pedaling a three-wheeler in the parking lot of an abandoned shopping mall in Springfield, having breakfast in

the Friendly Ice Cream shop here in town. None of them follow
up. I mean, none of these reports can in any way be matched
with the facts. The dates are wrong. Or the little girl was Chinese.
Maybe she had—"

"I'll just have nightmares about where she isn't if you go on.
I've stopped with the . . . I think I'm as calm and hopeless as I'll
ever be, Tim. Who are these other women? They check out?"
I kept an image of my face before me, as in a mirror. *You look
rational. You look credible.*

"Preliminary checks are good. But you can see the problem
just from the fact that one of them is a Texas sighting and the
other is from Chicago. On the same day. The Texas woman is
in . . . I mean, she has Sarah placed in an airport. The Chicago
woman has her nowhere, but I spoke with *her.*" He stopped.

"What?" *You don't look so calm.*

"I feel like I still hate doing this to you, Anne. We're bound
to start getting reports from all over now. You can't—physically
can not—check them all out. I can't even screen them all. It's
that the dates and descriptions and just the sound of these women
are believable."

Looking desperate now would unsettle him. "I know. My hopes
are not up. I simply have to start looking for her. Physically. I
could always start roaming around town. I'd rather make a
more concerted effort. Yes?"

He handed me two photocopied pages. He stared at the doc-
uments. "The woman in Texas is older. Maybe sixties, is my
guess. Her name is Angela Sarcasi. She claims to have seen
Sarah seated between two women in the Dallas–Fort Worth
airport. On Friday. The day Sarah disappeared. That Friday."

I would not let my face speak.

"Sarcasi alleges that she noticed Sarah because of the Brownie
uniform she was wearing. That detail—and the date—she could
have gotten all of it from any of the mailers. There are people
who follow this stuff, Anne. Like recipe columns in a newspaper.
A hobby."

"You didn't speak with her?" *Good sober question.*

"I spoke with this one." He brought the second sheet from under Angela Sarcasi's report. "Emma Lafayette. She's a teacher. A professor at the University of Chicago. Teaches French, I think. This is the longer shot, and she is—well, enthusiastic? That type? Sounds young." He looked at me, Tim Hall, man. "I don't ask ages, of course. Anyway, she can't remember where it was she saw Sarah. She happened to see one of the fliers in Bradley Airport on Friday and it caught her eye. She'd come into Connecticut for a meeting at Yale. She saw the picture hanging in the airport and she called. She doesn't remember when she saw her even. She thinks it was that Friday. Not last Friday—"

"I know the Friday you mean."

"Anyway, you won't be able to reach her until this coming Thursday. She's gone to Boston. Then maybe somewhere else? The point is—"

"Thursday. Is that the point?" I was imagining myself on a cross-country trek.

"No, Anne." Tim handed me the two pages. "This Professor Lafayette—isn't that a funny name? The point, though, is it's the kind of surprised way she had with me. Like she was surprised that I thought she should remember when and where. She was obviously proud of herself for having put the face together with the girl she saw at all. And she is anxious to talk to you. But she did say she'd call if anything fell into place for her. And she hasn't called. Anyway, it's a start."

Start. Start. Someone has to do this. "The Texas woman? Sarcasi? I could call her today, even." I was holding the sheets casually, as I imagined they would be handled by a police investigator. "I could start there."

"This could turn into nothing." Tim Hall stood, walked toward the coffee pot with his empty cup. "The one thing to be sure of is not to tell them things. I know this is the hardest part. Listen, though. Feeding them clues or leading them on is only going to get you off on any number of wild goose chases. Both of them know you might call. That's been cleared." He left his empty cup by the pot, picked up his briefcase. "What you can hope to do is to jog a memory, maybe. Or, more often than not, you just end up knowing that it wasn't a lead after all. That's the thing you have to know. Right?"

Start. "I'll call you later."

"Marilyn never showed up yesterday. After all my blabbing to you and Ted. My ex-wife?" Tim seemed to regret he'd brought it up.

"Did she at least call you to let you know?" *Start.*

"Oh, yeah." He headed for the front door. "But that's not exactly the same thing, is it? As seeing her." He opened the door, turned. "I'll hear from you, then? And if you just want to think before you call any—"

"No turning back. I'll call."

I ran to the kitchen, separated the two pages, arranged them on the table, sat and stared at the two reports. I put a hand on each. *Mom is coming for you, Sarah.*

| VI |

"Mrs. Sarcasi? I'm sorry. My name is Anne Fossicker. Could I speak to Angela Sarcasi, please?" I had the telephone on the kitchen table. Angela Sarcasi's report was in front of me. I was holding a black pen just above a pad of yellow legal-size paper. I intended to take notes.

"Yes. I'm here."

"Oh. I'm Anne Fossicker. Sarah's mother." I steadied myself for her response, pen tip to pad.

"Oh? Do I know you? What do you want me for?" Angela's voice seemed to be coming from some other continent. And it sounded as if she were standing fifteen or twenty feet away from the receiver.

I was prepared for her confusion. "You reported a sighting of Sarah Fossicker to the police. She is a Missing Child. I am the child's mother. Anne."

"Oh. The little girl from Connecticut with all the nuns who

are out searching for her. Oh, my. And this is the child's mother? You found her, then?" Even this thrilling possibility failed to raise Angela's mind above the muddle.

"No. She is missing. It's that you saw her. In Texas." *Stop being stupid; listen to me.* "Angela?"

"Oh, my. Oh, and I thought you were about to tell me that you found her. You or one of those nuns. You see, we get the videotapes from local news stations that will cooperate with our bureau here. Oh, that's too bad." She intoned this last part as if she'd just thrown a gutter ball at the local bowling alley. "I hope you aren't letting yourself get too depressed now. I have forgotten your name. Mrs. . . . ?"

"Anne Fossicker." I immediately regretted the didactic tone. "Angela? I'm calling you to go over the facts of your sighting." Even to me this was beginning to sound like a conversation about UFOs. "You saw Sarah." *This can't qualify as a clue. It's a fact, not a hint.*

"You have some cause to believe she is in Texas, then? A lot of them come out here. Runaways. Especially in Dallas. Oh, and Houston. Though I've only heard about Houston. I'm from the East myself. Pennsylvania. I grew up in Bethlehem and lived there until my husband passed on. My sister lives here. I came here to be with her."

Would it help if I screamed yet? "I live in a small town in Connecticut, part of Fairfield County? That's where—"

"I don't know much about Connecticut. Hartford! Isn't that in Connecticut?"

Why is everyone you need to talk to insane or distracted? "Yes, Mrs. Sarcasi. It is. Not far from here."

"Yes. I miss the East. I love it here, of course. My husband sold cars in Bethlehem. Pontiacs. He had his own dealership, so I don't worry about money, God rest his soul. Albert never would have taken to the climate here. He was one of those men who like the cold. You know men."

She's nothing but another woman; ask her. "You didn't really see Sarah, did you? I mean, really see her there in Texas."

Silence. With one arm I would have embraced her; I would have at least threatened her with the other. "It's all right. I know."

"It's so hard to be sure. You know that, if you're a mother. You hope these runaways will stop treating their bodies like dirt and go home." Angela coughed several times. "There was a young couple living right next door to my home here. Their daughter ran away. To Hollywood, California. I didn't think they still went there. Starlets. And Cary Grant and all that. You'd think they'd be going somewhere else by now."

Sarah is another day away. I yelled, of course. "It is against every law in the book to make like you've seen a child. And she is not a runaway, Mrs. Sarcasi. Her name is Sarah. Does that sound like a runaway to you? Do you think a whole school of nuns would go on TV to search for a runaway tramp? Does that make any sense to you?"

"Perhaps it wasn't your child." She said so as if there was a lot to be considered. I was sure that Sarah was one of ten or twelve children she wished she'd spotted. "No. She's a young girl-child? No. I don't think so. I am sorry." And with that, Angela ended our conversation.

A young girl-child.

It was unthinkable that this is what had become of my resolve to go after her. *What are you going to tell Tim Hall? He'll stop feeding you names and numbers.*

I was certain of nothing more than the absolute necessity for action. I could not relinquish my role as investigator. One hundred telephone conversations with the likes of Angela Sarcasi might do me in, but I would not give up my right to this line of pursuit until I had some option other than standing at the entrance to the movie theater, the church, the doughnut shop, with a stack of fliers.

I dialed the police station and was connected to Tim Hall. I conjured up the reflection of my calm face. "Tim? Anne Fossicker. Would-be sleuth."

"You already started." He seemed to be impressed.

"One down. She's a very nice woman. But she never actually saw her. It came out after I got a good part of her life story." *Does this sound credible?*

"Are you all right?"

A normal woman would be disappointed. Act normal. "Of course. A little put off. I know you told me it would be like this. I'm keeping that in mind, to stay calm. It is better to know." I was convinced that if I closed my mouth this credible, reasonable Anne would go on speaking.

"I forgot to leave you reports, to fill out. Every call you make should be logged. For the file."

A file among many others in a drawer sandwiched between many others. "Should I come by and get some?"

"If you want. Or you can just type something up." Tim noted my anxiousness.

"It's that I'm going out soon." I was willing to say anything, do anything, to keep alive my chances for an active role. "I could just stop by, I mean."

"I'll leave some at the front desk. I won't be here. You wouldn't rather have me drop them off? Well, it's up to you—I forgot to tell you about the phone, too."

It's tapped now and my screaming at Angela was recorded.

"I'm forgetting a lot. The calls aren't being screened or intercepted here. Ted seemed to think it wasn't necessary. Anyway, as of today, you have just your tape recorder. Is that all right?"

"I prefer that." I didn't know exactly what that might mean, but it was meant to sound normal. It can be hard to approximate normalcy. I was just learning the ropes.

"Good."

So it did sound normal.

I realized that I would go to see Sister Urban. More leads. I would drive to the airport, maybe. Talk to some of the desk clerks, janitors. "I will come by for those reports. Will I hear from you again today?"

Tim Hall took this as a plea. "You are the first to hear when I know something, Anne."

Excluding your reasonable husband, who is less prone to the visionary side of things.

| VII |

Ted was not in his office when I called. I'd wanted to ask him why he hadn't mentioned the status of the telephone at home, since Tim Hall had discussed it with him. It was going to be a signal to him, a sort of warning. I wanted to be told from here on in. I would suppress any weakness, even deny any past lapses in sensibility, to be admitted to the world of action.

Propriety seemed an unnecessary impasse. I told his secretary to leave a message. "Just write these words: 'I appreciate being involved in the decision about the intercepting of calls into our home.' Sign it Anne."

The secretary said nothing, communicating her glee. The boss's wife was angry.

Having failed to imagine what I might say to Sister Urban, or even why I really wanted to see her, I finally decided to make my way to the police station and to her without further meditation. As I left, the telephone rang. *It's Ted.* I didn't answer. I did listen to the message as it was recorded, however. "It's Richard, Anne. I'm staying at Carol's—at home—while they exterminate at my new place. I'm working nights. But I'll be here, with Carol, till Wednesday. How do I sound on the machine? I'll call back."

Richard's finding himself a job almost convinced me to call him. It was a landmark of sorts. But Richard hadn't seen Sarah. He was outside the scope of my work. Someone else could call Richard.

After I collected the forms left for me by Tim Hall (I was encouraged to see that he'd left me at least thirty) I drove to the St. Cecilia convent. I went to the back door, feeling that much was my due, and to my surprise it was Sister Urban who opened the huge old oak door. She did not open the screen door that separated us.

"Sister Urban. I didn't expect you to be the one—"

She was unmoved. "Hello, Mrs. Fossicker. I answer the door when someone rings the bell. The others are teaching. It is a school day."

Unnecessary as it proved, I made a mental note that I could force my way to her, even if it meant pushing through the rusted screen. "I'd like to speak with you. For a minute. It's important." *What if she agrees?*

"Fine. Why don't you come in. Do you mind sitting in the kitchen? I have tea brewing. Perhaps you would like a cup." She led me to the cavernous yellow kitchen. Outsized appliances lined the walls. At the center of the room was a huge rectangular table with two dozen matching chairs. "The sisters eat in here." It was clear that she was used to introducing laypeople to the convent. "I could make you real tea or some of that herb tea the younger ones use."

Pick a chair, Anne. "Nothing, Sister."

She sat in what I guessed was an assigned spot. She deftly gestured to a chair not quite opposite her. I obeyed.

She toyed with her tea bag. "What is it you have to talk to me about? The police left only a few minutes ago. With an autopsy report, which they insisted I hear about. I thought I'd covered all the details with them."

"I'm so sorry."

"Yes, I suppose you are." She squeezed a lemon into her cup, returned the used fruit to the refrigerator, sat again. "It is a very sorry thing Clare did. She was a sorry child."

I was not thinking, just letting myself speak. "The letter she wrote to me, when she signed your name, I was hoping that—"

"The details of Clare's life are not going to illuminate her death, Mrs. Fossicker. I should tell you that whatever her early life might have been for her, one doesn't make a practice of justifying despair. No. I am not Clare's judge. But the act. All of us can judge the act."

Like wings. "It's just the suddenness—"

A real burst of emotion: Urban slammed her venerable hand

on the table. Like a judge. "Two nearly uninterrupted lines traced along the principal veins . . ." She closed her hands around the steaming mug. "Clearly this was a premeditated act. As to the details, I think I've had my fill of medical exactness."

"I feel that I didn't do what I might have. I didn't see this for what it was." *Blame me.*

"Are you accustomed to diagnosing despair of this severity, Mrs. Fossicker? I am not. I believe that one has to be realistic. Clare was punishing those of us who loved her." She eyed me, as if she'd unwittingly exposed a weakness. "Perhaps. No one could reasonably expect you, of all people, to have taken note of her needs. You hardly knew her."

Stay out of my way; this is my tragedy, Mrs. Fossicker.

"I am sorry all the children at the school have to be exposed." Again, she eyed me. This was an accusation. "Parents nowadays feel it is their bound duty to tell all to their first-graders. Oh, I know it is meant to be for their own good." She finally sipped from her mug. "I think one ought to take a good hard look at the evidence to see if all this so-called honesty is making children happy. They don't look very happy to me with their drugs and haircuts."

"I need to ask about Sarah. About whether Clare might have said something, left something?"

"She loved children. Your Sarah, too. It broke her heart to see that boy in the hospital—he's since been diagnosed as having cancer. Did you know?" Then she was telling me that I was one of the world's millions of distraught mothers. One of the millions. "It is tempting for each of us to think that ours was the straw that broke the camel's back, so to speak. In your case, Mrs. Fossicker, I should think you would know better."

"Why?" It was reflexive, but sounded no less ridiculous for that.

She was not interested in me anymore. Her patience had expired, as if it were operated by a spring and she'd forgotten to rewind it. She was beyond repair. "There will be a memorial Mass on Wednesday, for the school. Clare will be taken to the

Berkshires tomorrow morning. For a private burial. Is there
anything else?"

"I wish I could help you." *One of the millions.*

She didn't respond. She didn't move. I showed myself out.

Outside, near my car, I looked up to the second floor, trying
to figure which had been Clare's window. I chose one that was
blocked by a white shade. *What am I supposed to tell Sarah, Clare?*

| VIII |

Apparently, I actually believed I was on assignment. I drove
from the convent to the center of town, and having been given
perfunctory directions, I headed for Bradley Airport. Within
minutes of crossing the town line I saw the first of many signs
heralding Connecticut's international airport. The idea that my
alleged quest might take on international proportions did not,
for the moment, daunt me. *If that's what it takes.*

Smooth sailing it was not. After a few exit signs for travelers
to New York City, I started to get the idea that I had overshot
my goal. Instincts won out. I exited and re-entered the highway,
thinking to travel in the opposite direction. Nowhere was there
an airport sign. After forty-five minutes of dangerous driving—
slowing at each exit ramp and every sign, literally lifting myself
up in the seat to make out something that might indicate the
presence of jets or airstrips—I began to see frequent signs for
Boston and vicinity. It did not seem implausible that I would
drive myself some three hundred miles northeast of my intended
destination. *You lack the simplest skills.*

It took five or six gas station stops to convince me that I
would not have to call Ted. Young men in coveralls would draw
long breaths and begin to recite the familiar route to Bradley.
Each time, I would concentrate on remembering one leg of the
prescribed route, nodding my head as the miles beyond the third
or fourth turn remained in the vast American highway system
unknown to me, out of my reach. *She could be anywhere.* The
evidence was beginning to overwhelm me.

Once inside the main terminal (I was relieved to be in a little-league facility; LaGuardia or JFK would have defeated me), I simply strolled around. I told myself I was looking for signs that carried her picture. I saw none.

After I'd passed her station maybe four or five times, a young uniformed woman in a car rental booth said, "Are you looking for something?"

"Someone. She's lost. A girl. Her name is Sarah." Oddly, for a moment I was less interested in making her aware of Sarah than I was in this woman herself. She was lovely. Maybe twenty-five. One of those straightforward American women who turn their head slightly to the side to smile at you. But she was dressed up like a clown. She had a kind of red golf cap on top of her long dark hair. Her blouse was red with white pinstripes. Her jumper, which met her breasts like a bra, was blue, with a few white stars scattered about. And she was gate-locked inside her red, white, and blue booth with only a computer and a rack of keys to busy her. *This woman shows up in statistics as a Working Woman. Are they serious?*

"When did you see her last?" She turned her head and opened her eyes as wide as they would go.

"Weeks ago." I said so pleasantly. Even if she hadn't been trapped in her private carnival for hours she wouldn't have had an easy time with me.

"Oh. She's *really* lost."

"No. Not really." I walked away.

It was only the shard of the idea that I was doing something to find her that kept me at the airport for several hours. I ate lunch there. I asked janitors about the signs that used to hang in the terminal. I spoke to a security guard who told me I could get clearance to hang more. (I hadn't brought any, of course.)

One astute man I accosted (he was trying to empty all the ashtrays in the terminal before his supervisor came by for his predictable inspection) said, "I hear you asking a lot of questions, lady. But who says your kid was here? You gonna tell me you're sure it was this airport? Not some other airport? You gotta have some reason."

Hurt, I lied. "I have reason to believe she may be here. Or coming through here." When he did not respond, I thought I might force him to grant me the right to ask more questions. "I certainly have reason to believe she is somewhere."

He laughed and laughed, put a gloved hand on my arm. "Lady, you don't need a reason to believe that."

Still, I could not make myself leave the one evidently living being I'd encountered. "You like this job?"

He stood up tall, let the half-full plastic bag collapse beside him. "There's reasons, believe you me, there's reasons a man who's read books and made love ends up making himself do this work. You oughta know not to ask a stupid question round a man like that. Pretty, sad girl with a big house in Stamford or somewhere. A mean man would give you a scare, and then some. In my line of work, ma'am, you asked for it. Now, you take care." He picked up his bag and moved on.

It was mostly indignation he'd raised. Not in response to him. Indignation at the God who would not see fit to apportion tragedies with a little more in the way of fairness. *I could get killed. I could get myself hurt. And Sarah would still be lost.* It was ridiculous.

| IX |

I made it home just as dusk turned to dark—made it by way of several gas stations. Ted was already home, which surprised me, seeing as it had been his first full day at work in more than a week. He met me at the door. A single lamp was lit in the house.

"Are you all right?" He took my arm, led me into the living room. "It's after six."

I walked to the kitchen, turned on a light, and beginning to panic, walked back to Ted. *Paul and Patricia are gone.* "Tell me, Ted. What happened? What happened to them?"

Ted didn't say anything. He sat down.

I went to the bottom of the staircase. "Paul? Patricia? Paul?"

"The kids? Sorry. They went to the Amerons. Janet called and she ended up inviting them."

"Again?"

"You mind?" Ted was letting all conversation lead him. He was relaxed, as one is during an orchestral prelude. Theme after theme was implied and abandoned. *What is he waiting for?*

"I'm just surprised she wanted to. When did you get home?" I sat on the sofa, across from Ted.

"I called at three-thirty and you weren't here and I thought the kids might not want to be alone. I came home then. I figured with the Clare talk at school it might be a little bit much for them to come home and find nobody to talk to. It seemed that might help—me coming home." Ted was uncharacteristically verbose. "I talked to them for a while. It went all right."

"I'm glad."

"Well, anyway, it was all right. A little harder on Patricia, I think. She said a lot of her friends were acting like she had a disease. They were being really nice in that way people are when they want to keep their distance but not be cruel. We talked about that. How people think something like this is contagious. That's what she said it was like. She's angry about that." Ted looked at me. He was attempting to solicit something, but I could not see what it was he wanted. Finally, exasperation with my dullness set in. "Did it occur to you that you might leave a note?"

"Every time I leave the house? That's crazy, Ted. I'm usually the only person around when I get back." That actually seemed sensible to me.

"For the kids? That they might get to wondering where the hell their mother is—it didn't occur to you?—since their sister disappeared into thin air. Or calling me—asking me to come home to be with them?" Ted again took up his attempt to solicit something from me.

"Every day? Someone has to be here for Paul and Patricia? They're not that young. They certainly aren't used to having—"

"They certainly deserve it. In light of . . ." Again, the quest to get something out of me, to see something I was not bringing to the surface. "Well."

"I did a stupid thing. Today I went to Bradley Airport and searched for Sarah. That's why I was gone. I got completely lost. I spent hours getting there. It was a stupid thing in the first place." I wasn't remorseful. This was being delivered as an accounting. "This morning I spoke with a woman in Texas who thought she saw Sarah and didn't, as it turns out, and I had to do something. I talked to a janitor and a car-rental agent. But I can see that the whole idea—"

Ted hollered. "Yes. It was stupid. But that isn't enough." As always, the outburst had the effect of forcing Ted to relocate in the room; his pattern was to yell, to move, and then to look back at the spot from which he'd yelled—as if to dissociate himself from the anger. "It's one thing to act stupid, even to go on being stupid. Or confused or vague. But it's that you are choosing to be stupid instead of choosing to be with the two kids who need the hell out of you and me right now. Think about it. Suicide to them was like . . . I don't know, skydiving, or eating glass. It wasn't what people they know do. One thing after another like that for them. And now you are suddenly too distracted or stupid to take a drive with them or just be here for them? It's not good, Anne. It's not." Ted kept an eye on that spot he'd abandoned, to avoid it, I guess.

I was determined not to lose my right to search. This was the sole purpose I'd given myself since he'd yelled. "After I talked to this woman I went to see Urban—the nun—and I thought I would try anything as a start, to get myself going. I have to find her. It's almost two weeks. Someone has to start looking—really looking." I raised my hands, signifying surrender of something, though even I was not sure what it was I thought to give up. "I know everyone is going to pay some kind of a price. But I am going to call another woman in Chicago and I am going to go there if she thinks she really saw Sarah. That is a fact, Ted. I am just beginning and maybe this is just one more hopeless fool trying to do the impossible, but—"

"No, no, no. You don't have that choice. You don't get to be the fool who has the simple choice. You don't. You want to choose between Patricia and Sarah? Paul and Sarah? What does that mean? That Sarah is yours? You think you get to leave me hanging here while you try to find her? That's just the way it is? No. No. That's not it. I'll do it with you. Annie, anything. You can fly to India if that's what it takes. But not for you and Sarah. For me, too. And for two other kids who happen to be lost without their mother." He came toward me.

I coveted his strength and the presence of his strength. But I feared total surrender, even to Ted. *If you give up now she is lost forever.* I stood, holding my hands against his chest. "Please be the mother for now, Ted. Please make them okay. Don't say it's a choice. I can't choose. But I already chose. I have to find her. Somewhere." I couldn't think while I was still within his reach. He saw this and took his chair. "I can't do it all. It is that simple. I know it like I know you, Ted. I can't. And I have to do this thing. I can call people. I can talk to people. I can do that for her. Can't you do the other part for now? It's that when I try to go buy some dinner or take a drive I think I'm losing more time, wasting time. Tim Hall hasn't got all day for her. He can't. I can. Not to leave you and the kids. Knowing you're here. But not with me to help here. Not now."

Ted looked so sad. His voice came out as something strange and weak. "I can't always say it so you hear it, can I? And some things I haven't even made into words. You didn't make me have words for them before...I was so scared of having one kid and you knew it. Didn't you?" He bowed his head. "But you did it for me. You didn't make me talk and I was so afraid I would have to explain it and that you could easily out-argue me. You let me get it across to you and..." He looked at me as if he was straining to see across more than fifteen years. "You took all of that. What was scared and what wasn't so strong and what was better." Ted's hands were moving as if around an unfamiliar object. "Because you loved me, I guess, and that's what I was. That's what I had to offer. And then you brought things to me." He looked up at me, smiled. "A mixed bag, too..." I thought he was determined not to cry. But then he sat back, relaxed, and I saw that something that had been formed with his sadness was now simply overtaking it, growing beyond it. "I don't know. It's so great that's what the kids are from. That's where they began. We began there, too. I hope you get what I mean by this—you're not special because you love Sarah. Me and Paul and Patricia—we're the same, in that way at least. Just like you. It might be that it makes sense that you do the legwork. But we all want to. Those two kids would do anything to find her. They want to have more searches. They'd walk to Chicago if you said it would help. Now, I don't care about the mother stuff. My guess is that you do some things I don't do so well. Cooking comes to mind. But the point is me and the kids—we won't let you choose not to be around us. Maybe we could agree that you'll be our representative, you'll represent us. We're all dying to find her. You gotta know that."

I was numb and frightened by my inability to respond to the simpler message. I could sense the resistance to emotion I'd erected; I was still managing to stave off submission to the larger will of the family. "I know it was stupid to get started so unprepared today."

"It was a banner day for stupid decisions. All around. The phone was a stupid thing, not telling you. That was just forgetting. It's that thing of letting Tim discuss it with me and not making him wait for you or at least getting your opinion." Ted sat forward. "It made me feel special, stupidly. At the time, anyway. Now I just feel dumb. Which is not exactly the perfect solution, but it's making me practice what I preach—the kids got a sermon before. They had agreed not to go to school on Wednesday. There's a Mass for Clare. Why should they go? They said they felt like that because of the package she sent. Of course, it would make them feel better for a little while. It's that I thought maybe it was the stupid genes they had that would feel better. Not the other genes, the better ones. They said they'd think about it." He smiled.

"Stupid genes or no, Ted, they will go to that Mass for Clare. There isn't going to be a vote." I had raised my own indignation at their reticence by conjuring up the faces of Urban and Clare both.

"I think they'll come down on the right side. We'll all be there, Catholics and non."

Vintage Ted Fossicker: We'll all be there.

The very notion of being in a church crowded with strangers who knew the sad facts of my recent life, Clare's name and memory being invoked without reference to her fate or its complications, unanswered questions and unending sadness burning like so many votive candles—it unnerved me. *Anything but that, please.* The same woman who would make her children go— because she knew that in its simplest, oldest sense such an offering of hopelessness was holy and necessary—she would exempt herself without so much as a second thought.

Ted says things like "We'll all be there" not to call my bluff (though I expect this was not entirely lost on him). He says these things because he knows and loves the simpler, ancient—and maybe she is even holy—Anne, who can act without a word or thought. It's a girl-child, that Anne. She's used to overbearing strictures and protective leashes, but she still wanders beyond her confines and speaks to Ted. He catches sight of her and engages her. Though I've never gone so far as to acknowledge this, I'd known from their first encounter that she was safe with him, might even prosper in his presence.

"What time is this thing on Wednesday, Ted? I mean, I might have to be in Chicago."

He smiled, then turned to the ringing telephone and laughed. "What do you think about getting rid of the police operator who intercepts our calls?"

Showing off my newly won confidence I answered the telephone. It was Richard. "Wait a second, Richard." I yelled to Ted. "I won't be long, Ted. Is dinner ready?"

"I didn't know you'd put it in the oven. You want me to check?" Ted came toward me, grabbed me by the hips. "Your liberated significant other will go buy some dinner. Goodbye. Call Janet if you get the chance. She's probably convinced that we're either divorced or one of us is dead."

"Isn't it great that we don't want to get divorced? People have terrible lives together." I said so because it had never occurred to me that this was a remarkable feature of my marriage. I wanted to be with Ted forever. And I completely believed that he'd always felt the same way.

"It's a relief, all right. You'd be hell in divorce court."

Richard was yelling. "Hey, this is my nickel. Hey!"

"Sorry, Richard. You want me to call you back?"

"Actually, I am at Carol's." He was embarrassed.

"Oh, right. The bug men. Hey, you got a job?"

"At the Holly K. It's a new diner sort of place in Back Bay. I'm a bartender." He sounded so happy.

"So it's not a joint? Sorry, that sounds awful. The name made me think so, you know?"

"It's supposed to, Anne. I think, anyway. How are you? You get my letter?"

"It was nice—I mean I really liked getting it, Richard. Thank you."

Richard searched for things to tell me. He described his apartment, then he asked why I never called Carol. He didn't argue with my assessment of the two-decade decline in my relations with my sisters. Then he described the clientele he served, next mentioned that maybe my mother would appreciate knowing more about me, then related a few facts about Carol's redecoration of the house.

Richard wants to make it all right. It was the first time I'd seen clearly that I had abandoned the Johnsons without so much as the courtesy of informing them. I'd run away. The twist to the story was that I'd done everything in my power to obscure not only my trail but the very fact of my leaving. I was unassailable on this front. *Why?*

"Of course I don't mind if you tell Carol about the lady in Chicago—but remember to tell the Texas story, too. I mean, it's not exactly real progress, Richard."

But it wasn't that Carol wanted to know. Richard wanted to tell Carol that Anne wanted her to know: Richard wanted to reunite us all. Even as I commissioned him, I knew that it was a fool's quest, that at best I was granting him the privilege of carrying an envelope in which I would enclose no personal note to a woman who would take the envelope to her bedroom and make a secret shrine of its unbroken seal.

"Of course you'd be welcome here any time, Richard." Truth without meaning.

The conversation ended without resolves or promises. But I knew one thing more. People do run away. It happens. Whatever a strict accounting of the circumstances may show, it is never without cause—necessity, in fact—that a person runs away. It is only the tragic symptom that those left behind believe there to be no reason for leaving, let alone just cause.

Like a desperate child I'd run away with Ted; Ted, orphaned as a child and in marriage, and an emigrant on top of it all. *It's not impossible that we gave to Sarah—at her birth or by our failures—just cause to turn and run.*

I looked at the telephone, my old enemy, and replayed for myself Sarah's unrecorded plea: "Stop looking for me."

| X |

I did not leave the house Tuesday. I did not answer the telephone. Of several callers, only Sylvia Castine left a recorded message: "Looks like we're out of luck on the potluck, Anne. Scheduling problems. I'll be in touch. We're all pulling for you." *Thank you, Janet.*

I did dial Emma Lafayette's telephone number several times. I knew she would not be back in Chicago until Thursday, but her voice on her answering machine was curious enough to renew speculation about her reliability each time I listened to her recorded message: "Emma's machine. Speak to me after the beep." It was an unlikely tone and an even more unlikely message for a professor of French literature to adopt. *She's flighty and she won't even remember having called Tim Hall in the first place. She's smart and odd; exactly the sort of woman who takes note of a child's muted distress in a crowded airport.*

I didn't ever leave a message for Emma Lafayette. I was engaged in the activity of making my telephone call to her a three-day affair.

Tuesday night was somber. Paul was attempting to write an essay about the history of the automobile. After several apparently unhelpful responses from Ted and me, he stopped asking questions and turned to the dreaded encyclopedia. Patricia was studying for an algebra test. (As she explained it, "The teacher said it's just to figure out what we know. Like it's gonna count for your grade, though. So, if you flunk it, you'll be in a remedial group. With extra assignments. And, if you ace it, you get stuck in the advanced group and you really get extra assignments. So it's like you wish you'd get a *C* except that would be totally humiliating when you think about it. If you're not a jock and you get a *C* or something on the first test, you know? What does she expect?")

I felt incapable enough in the realm of algebra; the larger questions of expectations and achievement were completely beyond me. Lamely I said, "Do your best." Meanwhile, Ted had asked me to help him put together the final copy for a large-format promotional booklet that several advertising agencies had contributed to without much success. I knew it was a ruse, a way of distracting me and keeping me within reach of the kids. I was happy enough to make believe. I was still in the process of calling Emma Lafayette, of finding Sarah.

And the diligent Fossickers did take their shared sense of industry in the face of despair with them to church the following morning. We sat together behind the sea of uniformed students and unhabited nuns. Patricia and Paul said nothing about our accompaniment, but it was evident that their parents had managed the difficult feat of doing them a favor in public.

It was not my paranoia or a womanly concern that was lost on Paul and Ted; the Fossickers were somehow to blame for the tragic death of Sister Clare. At the very least, we were material witnesses. Heads turned. Whispers circulated. "Let us pray that little Sarah Fossicker is found, which was so important to Sister Clare." The tragedies had been publicly and ritually joined. We four were the survivors.

After the final blessing, Ted did not move. He let the entire school population file by us. Several teachers and a few brave children stopped and spoke to one or all of us. None of us responded in any meaningful way. You cannot engage stone. Like a life-size Station of the Cross, we accepted kindly visitors and curiosity seekers and hostile passersby as our lot. It happened; it did not affect what had already happened or what might happen in the future. The Fossickers were living history.

Before half the congregation had filed by I managed to invert the scene. Our bench as vehicle, we were being propelled past the stagnant line of children and the occasional adult. We were being hurtled forward at breakneck speed. Staring at the sanctuary as if we would soon be flying through it, I thought, *Stick out your arms, Jesus. Here we come.*

As I have known chases in dreams to end, the motion dissipated all at once. The church was empty. As clumsily as I might make my way out of bed, I attempted to stand and turn toward the aisle. Only then did I register the fact that Patricia was holding my hand, Paul was holding her hand, and Ted had his arm around Paul's shoulders. *Did you all see we were heading for a crash?*

I sat down. Ted turned to us, whispered, "If you'd all agree to drive to the office with me so I can deliver copy for that booklet, I'd easily be convinced that this is an Australian national holiday."

Assent was silently given to the proposal.

| XI |

From his office, Ted telephoned the school. Apparently the principal, Sister Martha, took it upon herself to advise Ted that she thought Paul and Patricia would be better off left to their own devices in school for the day. Ted told me later that he simply said, "I really appreciate your input, Sister." It was the sort of thing I wanted to know enough to say. *Who are you to*

tell me what to do? Were you there when Clare needed someone?
I could just hear myself.

Australian holidays were not unprecedented in the Fossicker
household and the only rules governing their observance were:
(1) all members of the family must be included in the activity
undertaken; and (2) a person over the age of twenty-one does
not have a vote in the decision-making process. *Who will vote
for Sarah?* Fortunately, consensus was reached too quickly to
allow for a formal count. (Frequently in the past we'd gone
through round after round of naysaying.)

"I have the perfect idea," Patricia said as soon as Ted returned
to us in the car.

"I'm sure to be against any perfect idea of yours." Paul folded
his arms, readying himself for a long process.

"Wait. Wait till you hear it." Patricia posed before she spoke,
to slow herself down, and to give us all the chance to savor the
idea. "We go to some place like a deli and buy sandwiches and
like salad or whatever we want for lunch. Then we get a newspaper—"

"Oh, this is really great, Patricia." Paul was establishing his
dissenting position.

"No, for the listings. Okay. We see what is the mall with the
best movies. And we pick two or even three and we just go to
the movies all day long. With our lunch. We go to them together
or else Paul can see some awful gory one and I can go with
Mom or whatever we want?"

Almost reverentially, Paul said, "It is perfect. It's exactly the
perfect thing. It's so perfect."

Though I initially doubted my tolerance for more than one
full movie, Ted was enchanted. And since the voting members
had so moved, we headed for a delicatessen that Ted frequented,
bought a paper, and within an hour were eating huge sandwiches
in an otherwise abandoned cinema. Since we could talk without
inviting the scorn of the serious viewer, we all took short trips
to buy a soda or a box of candy, knowing that none of the
essential plot details would escape us.

The barely adult manager was forced into duty behind the

candy counter and by the time that I, the fourth customer, asked for some popcorn, he sensed that something odd was unfolding.

"I'll make you a deal." He leaned on the case full of popcorn as if he'd often dealt with strange requests. "You finish this movie. Then you pay a group fee—say, twenty bucks? You can go to as many movies as you want until seven o'clock. You can go see ten minutes of this one, all of that one. I'll leave it up to you what the kids can see."

"No kidding?" I was undone. I couldn't wait to run down the aisle and announce our good luck.

"One other part to this bargain. I don't want to have to keep selling you candy every ten minutes. Could you buy a whole bunch at the end of this movie and then I could go read? I've got a lot to do. And watch the noise, just in case. Even out here we get some people who are dodging their boss or their girlfriend or who just come during the day 'cause they hate crowds. Agreed?"

I did something that had nothing to do with me and everything to do with the glee he'd incited. I kissed him. "You are a wonderful man. You really are." I ran back into the darkness and yelled, "We can stay for hours!"

| XII |

Overfed and overwhelmed, we rode home in near silence. Whatever had to be said about each of the three movies we'd sat through had been taken care of during what turned out to be three private screenings. Since we were all thinking along the same lines, Ted finally just said, "Sarah really would have loved that choice, Patricia. It's just the sort of thing she would think is perfect. We'll have to do it again. Don't forget that one." *Don't forget. Don't forget.*

The evening brought a return to the tasks of the previous night for the children. Patricia knew she could not escape the algebra test and Paul implicitly understood that any paper he'd written could suffer a rewriting, or at least a review to convince himself that he was "living up to his potential," a standard to which he'd grown accustomed. (During his first week in the second grade, he'd come to me for a definition of his potential. I did my best to accommodate the request. In a fit of misplaced rationality I'd apparently mentioned that living up to a potential takes time. It was this that he's relied on ever since, as a defense against any anxious teacher who exhorts him. "I mean it," he'd say. "When you think about how long I have to do it, I am living up to my potential. What? Does she think I'm gonna just do it all at once?")

Ted and I sat in the kitchen with various piles of bills and unread magazines. We hardly exchanged a word. It was not until the kids were in bed that he finally released the thought that had visibly held him throughout the evening.

"Sarah. It's not that I know this, quite. It's that, in church today? When they said the prayer that we'd find her? I thought about what's the point of asking for that. Like when we're all praying for the president to be peaceful or terrorists to be fair. I always think, Would I ask for a check in the mail? I mean, prayers like that bug me." He was speaking aloud, but not to me. A thought was taking shape. He was on the verge of knowing something new. "Who else would you ask? Right? I mean, the point of praying like that, why I think it should be reserved for certain things? I mean, it would make more sense to just ask for Clare back from the dead."

"I don't follow you, Ted. What is the point?" I was holding to the theory that finding a child, no matter what the odds, was a more likely proposition than resurrection.

"I think that I mean that what I don't like about religion— not Catholics, particularly, prayer, maybe?—is that all this asking for things is just all of us wanting to direct traffic. Why don't we just say, 'I think I better be God for a while.' What I mean about Clare is that most of us know it would be ridiculous to ask for Clare to come back from the dead, but it's just like that with other prayers. It ought to be enough to say there is a God. If there is a God. I mean, a *God*. Then everything is okay. We're all set. It's a matter of—"

"I don't think it's all right that she's gone. If that's what this is leading to. I cannot be bothered with all this passive acceptance, excuse-me-for-having-an-attachment-to-my-daughter stuff. That's crazy." I was not willing to consider a position that involved tolerance of Sarah's absence. Ever.

"This sounds like a kid, really. But if God didn't will it—and that much seems obvious—someone did. We have to think about that. You're right about looking for her. You don't let a child go in the world. I wouldn't think of not looking for you, Anne. But somehow with a kid, we let it go because it happens, because it's something we're getting used to." Ted laid his hands on top of mine. "It's not crazy to do what you want to do. We can't bring her back from . . . she may be dead and that is one thing. But a child is gone from here. This shouldn't happen. We don't need to go to God with this problem. He's not to blame." He laughed. "What's crazy is that you begin to think it is okay to say we need our jobs and to make up an algebra test and not let Sarah get in the way of that. We have to be sensible here, but part of being sensible is knocking ourselves out. For her."

I'm not all that reliable, Ted. Maybe I am a lunatic.

"When are you calling that woman in Chicago? Do you have other names from Tim?" He began to pace.

I was actually afraid that I'd finally worn down his sensible resistance. I could not imagine a future in which both of us were willing to upend domestic order to find her. "We need some kind of plan, though. We can't just up and start running. I mean, I've done that without much success. We can't start yanking the kids out of school to hunt around in bus stations." *Can we?*

"I really don't see why not. Anne, I mean this. What else are we going to do? It's Sarah." Ted was not alarmed when he said so. He was looking rather calm.

"I don't know what we should do, what makes sense." I was panicking. I had flash frames of the Fossicker four, two years later, applying for dishwashing jobs in a small, dusty town somewhere in Oklahoma. "I think I've been something of a fanatic on the issue."

"Well, what does it take to make me a fanatic? I mean, what am I waiting for?" Ted was still calm. I was only reassured to the extent that I judged these questions to be still unanswered.

"I don't think it helps to be a fanatic, Ted. Does it?"

He obviously wasn't sure. "You tell me."

"I think you are the one to say, Ted. You at least know that— even I know someone has to shop for groceries. My God, we have to eat." *How did I do this to him? How do I do it?*

"We have to think about this, maybe with Tim Hall here. Things have to change. You can't ask for people to come back from the dead, Anne. We have to remember that." Ted retreated into a consideration of what this all might mean.

If you were such a great God you'd get Clare back in operating form right now and save us all. What do you expect me to do now?

| XIII |

The morning departures were so calm and orderly as to be ridiculous. Ted was clearly preoccupied. Paul and Patricia were gathering their energies for yet another go at a return to normal life under intolerable conditions. I circumscribed all thought and the ascendant panic that was my response to Ted's preoccupation by forcing myself into a tedious and almost unresolvable silent debate about the very best way to deal with Emma Lafayette.

I allowed myself not to call Emma throughout the entire morning and even as several afternoon hours elapsed. I told myself Ted would call with a plan; Tim Hall would call with a legal ban on activity on the part of the Fossickers. But mostly I told myself that I would somehow succeed in ripping family life to shreds and not in the least advance Sarah's cause.

"Emma's machine. Speak to me after the beep."

She's not back in Chicago yet. She won't remember calling Tim Hall, never mind seeing Sarah. Which she didn't anyway.

"My name is Anne Fossicker. Sarah Fossicker is my child. You called the police here, an Officer Timothy Hall—"

"Mrs. Fossicker? This is Emma. Are you still there?"

When your worst, gloomiest predictions actually do produce the perfect result (as they are meant to; they're a way of fooling God into complying with our wishes), it is always unsettling. You feel both powerful and haunted. "This is Emma Lafayette?" Her voice was so adolescent that I actually doubted her.

"It's me, sister." She had been told about her voice by many callers.

"I'm Anne. It's about Sarah." And with that, I was weeping. *The last thing anyone wants to deal with on the phone.* "I'm sorry. I didn't expect you to be home."

What? Do you expect an apology? "I saw her, sister. I don't know if that only makes it worse. But I have one of those fliers right here in my apartment and I saw your little girl. I hope you're hearing me. No one wants to believe me. Everyone I tell says—I keep talking about it so I'll remember where. I haven't yet. But that only proves I'm stupider than a sow, not that I'm blind. Talk to me about her. Would that be okay? I'm sorry, honey. How are you? I'm just so mad at myself for not remembering."

This woman teaches at a university? This woman saw Sarah. Someone wants to help you. "We don't know anything more. I'm going crazy. You're so good to have called. You don't know how just that, hearing you say you know it was her. Jesus, do we miss her, you know?" Another wail. I didn't even bother to apologize. It was too much. *Someone saw her. As I see her.*

"She's lovely. She wasn't crying or anything strange. I don't think there was something like that that caught my attention. Praise be for that, huh? But there was something about her that—it was in the godforsaken airport. Oh, hot damn, sister. I just knew I wouldn't blank out totally on you. Do you hear me? O'Hare Airport. She was walking with a stewardess around the terminal I was leaving from. I know it now. What do we do now? Hey! Are you there?"

Sarah? Do you hear this? I am closer. Sarah?

"Oh, I hear you, sister. I hear you. Anne? You get a pen and start writing so you can tell the police and then you call me back. Maybe somebody should get to the airlines and find that stewardess? I'm sort of brainstorming here. But I'm on a roll now. I think we're going to find that child of yours. Don't you?"

I could not imagine what Emma thought of me. It took me something like three minutes to say, "Yes. Thank you." I sensed that I was coming apart, literally being severed. It seemed the worst moment for me to feel anything. It was incapacitating, but I could not suppress it. "Can I call you back? Later? Soon?"

"I'm here for the day and night. You are going to call me, though? Promise."

If I could talk I would just say I love you.

"Sarah. That's it. I can just see her, Anne. I can just see that face of hers taking you in. You'll see. All right now. Call me soon as you can."

"Soon as I can."

Soon as I can breathe. Soon as I can walk.

I tried several times to make myself dial the telephone to reach Ted, but I could not. I knew I would be unable to speak. *That face of hers taking you in.* As it was called for, I started to yell, not words, just grunts, or moans, as if the massiveness of whatever I was trying to release made it necessary to push and squeeze and jar my body into giving it up.

It is breaking. I must let it fall. Still groaning and crying and pacing, I saw the dam within me giving way. Stress fractures were opening into crevices, then ruts. And there, still trying to hold the dam in place, was Sarah? Her back was jammed against the distended barrier, her arms spread out behind her. As if she could stop it now. She ran away, and as if she *had* been positioned in such a way as to provide the final, pivotal support, the wall collapsed at once. I waited, frightened and enthralled, for the mass that lurked behind it to be unleashed, a tidal force that would sweep away the rubble and dust. But nothing followed on the thunderous fall but dust and echoes. Sarah was barely visible, her attention now turned to the still-invisible acreage behind the fallen dam. Impatient, she turned her head. She too had believed a sea of some sort had accumulated over the years.

Then she said, "What's all that?" She turned to me but I did not see her face. I'd turned to see what lived behind the dam: nothing. What I saw was a small patch of rocky soil and a surrounding plain of hardened dirt. Scattered on this landscape were a few familiar toys, small, dead, and stony stems that I seemed to know were things that I had put there long ago as seeds. I recognized the seeds as I might connect the young face of a childhood friend's uncle or mother to the almost shapeless, fallen features that it had become. As I saw more clearly, there were hundreds of these tiny abortive growths. I began to focus in on one, intending to catalogue each and every stump according to its origins. Then, in that not-quite-familiar voice by which I'd known her since she'd left me, I heard Sarah say, "I thought you said there was something terrible back there? That it would ruin everything." More bemused than anything, I turned to her, to try to explain. I watched her shake her little head, as if to reprimand me. Then she lifted her face. Not Sarah's face but mine. Not Sarah's voice but mine across the years. Sarah was not living deep within me. Beyond that wall, nothing lived. It was my petrified forest. A child's garden of earthly delights which were too frail to outlive the season of their planting. Embarrassed and frightened that someone might see what I'd believed could thrive, I'd walled them in and made the foolish child a perpetual guardian of the long-since dead dreams and secrets.

Let her go. Whoever has her. Let her go. Her name is Sarah. Don't dream on her. Her name is Sarah. Let her be.

| XIV |

I finally did call Ted. I had entered into an unappealing calm, as if I'd been under siege and was now living those awful moments of abandonment. My tormentors had been scared off but no rescuer was within sight. I could only huddle down, wrap myself in my own embrace, try to rein in my hopes and fears. Ted was not in his office and I could only manage to tell his secretary that he had to come home immediately, that there was an emergency of a not really bad kind. Completely unresponsive to my tone and unenlightened by the fact that this was not a characteristic exchange with me, she tried several times to elicit something more in the way of details. I hung up on her; I wasn't angry but I could not imagine what else I might say.

I also called Tim Hall, who promised to come immediately though I'd only said, "Something happened when I talked to that Emma in Chicago, Tim. Can you come over?"

Calm as could be, he asked me three times, "You aren't going anywhere right now, are you?"

I thought I might go shopping for a scarf. "Of course not."

Everything I tried to do was stymied by this unfocused apprehension. It was not that I expected Sarah to turn up, or even that Emma Lafayette would be a decisive witness. It was something more finite. As Ted had the night before, Emma, and even Tim Hall, had heard me for the first time. I had broken through my perception of the horror of Sarah gone and reached an open ground where those feelings that absolutely defied my ability to speak had voice, took shape. I had raised her up in some way. I had broken through to Sarah.

I heard a car park and assumed it was Tim. Instead, Ted literally ran to the front door, and finding it locked, began to shout my name.

"Yes. No, no." I meant to let him know that I was not under assault, that I was all right.

When he finally heard me unlocking the door he let out an audible sigh. "Thank God."

"Terrible message. But this woman, this Emma? Saw Sarah and now she remembers it was in the airport. In Chicago. She knows that for a fact. Knows it, Ted. And she gets that we can all work together. She said so. No clues from me. She just said so. She wants to help. If she can, I mean. But it's that seeing her part. Ted? Isn't this a start?"

"It's what we knew. She's out there." He stooped and picked up the pile of mail, carried it with him to the living room. "A letter from Carol, looks like. A lot of other things. From the national center, too." He gave me the mail, smiled. "Maybe we won't need to send out more fliers though. Right?"

"It's a start, right, Ted?" I opened the letter from Carol.

"Did you speak to Tim?"

"Yes. He's on his way. Sorry, I thought I would just quick look at what Carol has to offer."

Ted watched me as I read, as if anything that entered the house from now on would be treated as evidence, leads.

Dear Anne,

Have thought of writing and not done it only because I have been so busy with both the house (a lot of painting going on around here) and school and Richard's visit. He's here while his apartment is cleaned up. I suppose you know that.

I have Sarah's picture at school and a lot of the kids are putting it up around town. I hope every little bit helps. Can't possibly tell you how sorry I am. Words can't express . . .

I know how hard it must be to talk about it at all. If there is anything you think I could do I would do it if you asked. I know Theresa feels the same. Mom has kept us abreast of what details there are. She's really distraught for your sake. I know it isn't a help to hear that, but I mean only that she and I both feel like what you don't need is us bugging you by calling you; she really hopes you will let her know if she can do something. You know how she feels about her grandchildren. She was absolutely beside herself when she called me with the news that Friday that Sarah was taken from you. She actually thought about flying into Boston and getting a car and driving up to be with you. I said I thought she should wait and obviously she has, but she made her plans in case you needed her and I know if you need her she'd be with you all in a second. I know she's got everyone in Phoenix on your side, as is everyone here in Braintree who's heard about it.

Anyway, I am sure you are busy and I just wanted to pass on one address. My friend, Justine Arnold (I taught with her for many years—the one who drove the Corvette that Richard was so crazy about), lives in Chicago and Richard tells me you might need to go there, to talk to someone who reported seeing Sarah. If you do go, and you need a place, I am sure Justine would love to have you stay with her. She lives quite close to the airport at 2245 Camel Back Drive, in Skokie, Illinois. Do get in touch with her if you need a place.

I hope you and *all* the kids will come and visit really soon, Anne. You are always welcome.

My very best love to you,

Carol

Ted was still staring at me. "Anything new?"

"Sends her love. And a place for me to stay in Chicago—well, Skokie. A friend of hers."

"Nice of her. Isn't Skokie where they had those Nazi parades?" Ted didn't seem particularly interested in the Nazi population of suburban Chicago.

"Yeah. Sounds perfect. Anyway. Everybody sends their love. She said my mother's very upset about it all." *Less noteworthy even than the Nazis, I know, Ted. Tim Hall will be here soon.*

"You going to get in touch with her? Carol's friend?" *I am telling you I think you better go to Chicago.*

Neither of us could tolerate the idea of discussing these details. It seemed we were each trying to make the time pass more easily for the other until Tim arrived and set us in motion. I didn't even respond to Ted's question; we both sank back into solitude with our fragile desires.

Tim Hall, perhaps the most welcome visitor in the history of the Fossicker household, arrived within minutes. Ted and I greeted him with silence. We were just waiting for him to try to convince us that there was nothing for us to do. Tim only said, "You've got something real now. I spoke with her—Ms. Lafayette. I mean, Professor Lafayette. She's given the Chicago police a statement. The case can now be bumped up. To kidnapping. A lot more freedom with that. I know this might sound like a lot to ask, but I think it would be worth your while, one of you, going out there. You can deal through the local police there. I can set things up. It's a long way from being the end, but I honestly think it will help keep things rolling if someone is there who is connected to her. It can make a difference. I think you could start with the airlines. They'll be really cooperative. It's about the only kind of case they get good PR out of. That's a little harsh. Anyway. But maybe it's too much to ask right now?"

I felt like a contagion. Tim Hall's enthusiasm sobered me. *She was seen almost two weeks ago. In an airport. In transit.* "This is really a start, then? Right?"

Tim Hall put his hands on his head, as if he were containing something. "The thing that occurred to me on the way over here ... I mean, besides that she seems to be a really reliable witness. And none of this is a guarantee, you understand. But I can't go on denying what seems to be good luck. The thing that occurred to me, anyway, is that it would be very odd for someone to take her on a plane ride through Chicago if they weren't trying to hide her. I hope you don't mind this being raised, I mean it as a way to dismiss it. But if she was taken through an airport last Friday I don't think it was by someone who wanted to kill her. I'm sorry to even ... You know, though? And even more, it's—this is all premised on If This Is True— you both get that? If it is true, it means she didn't run away, wander off. It means a lot."

"It means the world to me." Ted seemed surprised he'd said so aloud. "You know?"

| XV |

Ted, Paul, and Patricia waved to me as I left them to board the early morning flight to Chicago. They watched me as if they'd just launched something and could only hope it would land on target. I felt that all my preparation had consisted of closing myself down emotionally. Ted and the children speculated on the possibilities as I packed a ridiculously generous assortment of clothing and went over the details of my scheduled ten-thirty meeting with Emma at the airport, which was to be followed by a meeting with the airport's head of security and a Chicago policeman by the name of Kiri Sasape.

My mother called just after the children had gone to bed Thursday night. (Though not to sleep; long after Ted and I retired to the bedroom we heard Paul and Patricia making plans for Sarah's bedroom. Ted had simply announced that they would all spend the day at home, waiting for my call. I balked at the notion, thinking it was but one more avenue to disappointment, but Ted was convinced that it was appropriate to involve the children in both the raised expectations and whatever followed.) She sounded genuinely worried about me, having heard from Carol that I was thinking about going to Chicago.

"You can't go everywhere, Anne. I mean, I wonder if you can put the kids and Ted and yourself through this without . . . You can't just go all over the place. What I am trying to say is that you have to accept your limits."

She's right, of course. "Ted thinks we have to look for her actively. It's our duty. He's right. I know it sounds ridiculous, but wouldn't you?"

Is that a dare? I am maybe going to say to my daughter, No, I wouldn't have looked for you if you were lost. "That's not my point, really."

"Mom, that is the point we're at. It's crazy, but isn't it crazier to think you can just carry on without her, just hoping the police and the national center do their part? I mean, that's madness, too."

"Well, I'm just trying to be . . . I don't know. You don't know what this woman saw, do you? I don't want to be the one who discourages you, Anne. But children—you know what I'm trying to say to you."

As always, I know what you are trying to say? "No. I honestly don't, Mom. Of course it is crazy. But we're not exactly in a position to make the rules, are we?" *Whatever that means.*

"Oh, my. I really don't know what to say to you. Oh, darling. Promise me you'll call me from Chicago? It's so . . . I do want to know how you make out. Anne? Please say you understand that I am as confused as you are. I mean it, darling. I don't want to hurt you. You'll call and let me know what this woman claims to have seen?"

"I promise, Mom. I'll be fine. I mean, it could be worse, right? I could have got a lead from Uganda, right?"

"That seems unlikely. But travel safely. My love to the kids and to Ted."

And Ted? Sentiment unbound. "Good night, Mom."

In point of fact, I did not believe that Tim Hall, Ted, I, and least of all Emma Lafayette, had any more cogent notion about why I was winging my way to the Midwest on less than four hours of sleep than did my mother.

As I walked toward the café in the terminal where I was to meet Emma, I felt the perfect fool. Somehow my contagious frenzy had gotten me back into that familiar, ridiculous position of doing something because someone had to do it.

A few young men came right up to me at the table I'd chosen and, wagging pamphlets, began to explain their political theories. They also had a globe mounted on a pole on which most of the continents were colored red. An outsized flag somewhere in the area of the North Pole carried the words, STOP THE RUSSIANS, BECAUSE THEY WON'T STOP THEMSELVES. Harvard University and *The New York Times* were somehow to blame for much of the success to date of the Russian conspiracy. I let them talk until I thought I'd spotted Emma (I was going on instinct; I had no idea what she really looked like). The woman was walking quickly. Thinking she might not see me (Tim had told her what I would be wearing, something about how I looked), I screamed, "Shut up about the Russians already."

The woman, not Emma as it turned out, quickened her pace, as did most of the nearby travelers. The two men with the globe on a stick backed off, looking at me as they left. It was a friendly retreat; we were three fanatics and we understood each other.

Emma Lafayette is a mean, crazy woman who doesn't exist except in someone's imagination. This much and more seemed clear to me by eleven-thirty. Not apparently undone, but simply facing the facts, I walked to a public telephone to call Ted.

"Don't ask, Ted. I don't know why, but she is not here. I can tell she is not coming."

Ted was trying to reason with me. I didn't even listen.

"Ted, I am in the biggest airport in the world with a bunch of men trying to talk to me about Russian soldiers and Harvard. I just want to get out of here right now. I can see the police later. I'm okay. Okay? But what I need is a place to stay and I thought maybe I should stay with that friend of Carol's in Skokie. I can use her car, maybe."

More wasted input from Ted. *It's a terrible time to lose your grip, Anne. What am I going to tell the kids?*

"Ted? Are you going to get Carol's letter? It's in the file near the door. Thanks. I'm fine, by the way. I don't know, maybe she'll show up. But I called her twice and got the machine." *Why haven't you really tried to call Emma?* "I'll call her a couple of times before I call Carol's friend. Do you have the address?"

Ted delivered the address as if he were admitting defeat. "She doesn't give a phone number here."

"I can find that." *She's probably unlisted. There are hotels in Chicago. Why go to Skokie?*

"Will you call me before you leave the airport, Anne? Tell me where you're going?" Ted had adopted his gravest tone of voice. *This is a warning of some kind.*

"I promise. I'm really all right, Ted. Maybe she just got tied up in traffic. I have to go." I hung up, immediately dialed Emma Lafayette's number. I was devastated and elated—at once—to hear her recorded voice. It was a terrible sort of vindication.

| XVI |

I sat for another hour in the café. I had decided that if Emma did not appear within an hour I would go find a hotel room for myself. Not for a moment did I suspect I was capable of managing even that simple task, however. I hoped the hour's passing would render it either unnecessary or possible. *I am lost, too, Sarah. I am completely lost.* In my refusal to allow my private chaos to speak, I shut down. I noted streams of hurrying men and women, though after a while I shut my eyes. I couldn't stand to see children holding on to their mothers' hands. And, anyway, it was unnerving—nauseating, really—to watch all the activity and hear absolutely nothing but the sound of a young child crying. Relying not on a watch or clock but, again, on instincts, I told myself an hour had elapsed. *Time to go, Anne.* The child was wailing by then. I stood.

This time it happened incrementally, as if my body was explaining to my brain what was going on. The blood simply drained from my head, trailed by a stream of cool sweat. My arms seemed to be lengthening, as if my hands would soon be resting on my feet. The joints at my knees and my hips were released.

According to a woman who was using the public telephone at the time, I had been making my odd way toward her for a while, and when I was nearly upon her I said, "Oh, for God's sake, I have to faint."

| XVII |

"Well, sister. Meet your good-luck charm." The woman who said so was standing over me. I was on a cot, covered by a woolen blanket. She was short, her red hair wound around her head rather unflatteringly. It was spectacular hair, though. Otherwise, I could see that she was wearing a plain two-piece suit that fit her like a nylon stocking. She was all smooth, rounded contours. "I'm Emma. You're Anne. You think you feel well enough to sit up?"

"Where were you? Before I was . . ."

A doctor interceded here. A young man whose face I never registered. He explained all that had gone on since I'd fainted.

He ended by saying he thought Emma and I should talk right where we were, so he could keep an eye on me for a half hour.

I was surprised and a little defensive when Emma balked at this suggestion. "She's going to be moving soon, I hope. We have a lot . . . Anne, you're closer than you know."

I know nothing. "Can you start while I'm still lying down? I mean, just in case? Oh, what a fool I am."

The doctor began to comfort me, but Emma would not tolerate his interjections. "Doctor? I think I have to talk to her right away. We've got a policeman outside and a plane to catch. May I?" She pulled a chair right to the edge of the cot. "You look like you might make it, all right. I'm so sorry about the mix-up. You were in the wrong terminal altogether, sweetie. I had you paged, I corralled a couple of stewardesses and had them looking for you. This airport is bigger than all of Chicago sometimes. Can you sit up yet?"

Would you sit up for God's sake? I'm trying to talk to you.

"They want you to speak with your husband. But he's leaving soon."

This brought me back into the fray. "He's coming out here? To get me." It seemed clear to me that Ted would do that.

"Not exactly. Listen, there is so much to get across." Emma stood up. "I'm going to dial up your husband. You think you can talk to him?" She looked at me as if I were the laziest woman she'd ever encountered. *Are you ever going to get off that cot, sister?*

"The stewardess?" I stood and only then realized my blouse was unbuttoned, my skirt unhooked.

Emma was dialing. "Nothing. Nobody who is available today, anyway. But that one stewardess could be in Hawaii, couldn't she? Anywhere. Plus, they all trade this flight for that one. It's a problem getting hold of them. Hello? This is Emma Lafayette at O'Hare International."

Who is this woman?

Emma explained to Tim Hall that I was ready to speak to Ted. Then she brought the phone toward me. Out of respect for her, I guess, I made myself walk to the little desk, waited for her to surrender her chair to me.

"Ted?"

"Hello, Anne. It's Tim Hall." *The man, not the cop, speaking.* "You bump anything?"

"Where's Ted?"

"He's at the airport by now. Anne? Jesus, this is really the good news and the bad news and its—"

"Tim? Are Paul and Patricia all right?"

"They're both right here and sending their love. They are fine, Anne. So is Ted. It's Sarah, but not bad. Good. Can you listen if I just try to tell you what is happening?"

I couldn't talk. Emma saw this and in a single gesture she took the receiver from me and hugged me. "Hang on, sister. It's going to be all right." Then, to Tim, "She's fine. Okay? I'll give her back to you."

I took the phone from Emma. "Just talk, Tim. Please."

"It was your call about the letter from Carol. Ted read it after you hung up. He called me right after that. It's the part about Friday. Your mother calling Carol on Friday to tell her Sarah was missing? Do you remember, Anne?"

I remember nothing.

"In the letter, Carol said your mother was even thinking about coming out here, to Connecticut. This was all on the Friday Sarah disappeared. But Ted is sure you didn't call your mother until after the search for Sarah. He thought it wasn't until Sunday night that you spoke with her. She was annoyed that you had waited so long to tell her? You see, Anne? Your mother just couldn't have known. Even the media didn't have the story until Saturday morning. At the earliest."

You are completely insane, Tim Hall. So is Ted.

"Anne? It doesn't mean she necessarily has Sarah. But she was involved. Or she knew of it. It has to be."

Go to hell.

"Ted is flying to Phoenix, Anne. I've spoken with the headquarters there. They have a cruiser outside the Panamerican

Complex just to be sure your mother doesn't leave with Sarah. They won't move on anything until you and Ted get there. They'll follow your lead in how to handle it all. Anne?"

I am going nowhere. You are all insane.

"Anne?"

"Listen to me, Tim. Did anyone think that Carol might have just made a mistake? What idiots. The least you could have done is call Carol. Sure, you would have to call her at the school—forget it. Honestly. I'll call her at school and get back to—"

"Ted spoke with Carol not forty minutes ago, Anne. It was the right Friday."

"Who believes Carol, anyway? She's barely capable of holding down a job. Exactly what are you saying?"

Tim Hall didn't answer. After a few seconds he said, "I'd like to speak to Emma. She's made arrangements to fly with you to meet Ted. Anne, please let me speak to Emma."

"Okay, Tim. I won't hang up the phone. I am just trying to bring in a little bit of reason here. I knew I shouldn't have come. Everybody's jumpy now. That's all. You're all jumping the gun."

"Anne? Could I please speak with Emma?"

I gave the receiver back to Emma, gave up the seat at the desk. *Of course it's impossible.*

The only words Emma spoke to Tim Hall were "That's okay" and "No problem." She hung up and turned to me.

I wanted to save her the trouble of trying to talk me into boarding a plane for Phoenix, Arizona. "I don't really know who you are, but please don't say anything that has to do with my mother. You may not understand how impossible it is, but I do. So save your breath."

"I'm not going to sell you on anything, sister."

"Please stop calling me that."

Nothing deterred this woman. She rolled herself in that chair right across the little room, to my side. "We've got a couple of hours to decide."

"I've decided. Someone has to be reasonable here." I was buttoning my blouse, annoyed that I had to appear so discombobulated in front of her.

"Listen to one thing? That husband of yours is on his way. He is on a jet airplane. Frankly, I don't know you, either. But I hear you. I hear you all right. But all I'm trying to keep in mind here is that your husband is on his way. And maybe Sarah is nowhere near Phoenix. But I spoke to a woman yesterday who was going to walk up and down a map of America until she turned up a girl named Sarah. Maybe this trip just eliminates one city. It's a beginning."

"It's a crazy place to start. Do you see this? You just don't walk into your mother's apartment in Phoenix and take a look around and walk out if you don't find what you knew wasn't there in the first place. It's not how these things are done. You make a better plan is what you do. I'm sure of that. Really, Emma. I am."

She wheeled herself still closer to me. "I don't know you, Anne Fossicker. But I like you. I won't say so again. But I see the only way out of this involving a trip to Phoenix. Don't look at me like I might be involved in something else here. I am walking out of this room. Gate nineteen. You meet me there, I'll take a free ride to Phoenix with you. You decide not to go, I'll be at home if you need a cup of coffee later on. I mean that." She stood, collected my shoes as she did. She handed me the shoes.

Don't leave me, sister. "You have children, Emma?" It was as casually spoken as I could manage.

"None. I sort of lost one husband along the way. He fell in love with Raleigh, North Carolina. We moved there to teach. Both got appointments. He also fell in love with just about every young lady on campus. Why?"

"You would be . . . a child would like it, if you were a mother. Forget it." I put on my shoes, stood up.

Maybe I could go now if Emma didn't know I was going? "I don't see any point in you staying, Emma. I don't . . . " A failure.

"I can simply leave right now. You can decide without me making it seem like you're on the spot." Emma was serious.

Even taking a few steps compromised me. I could not believe anything that had been said. I couldn't believe it had occurred, even as a mistake.

That husband of yours is on his way.

"I would need a companion. You see, Emma, it turns out that I'm one of those women who faint."

| XVIII |

When we were seated on the Phoenix-bound jet, Emma said, "I'm going to let you do any of the talking unless you want some background noise."

We traveled in silence. Both of us refused all drinks and food.

When I thought about it, it was easy to trace Ted's complete loss of control. I made no attempt to imagine how I might be able to help him. My thoughts were concentrated, compressed. The object was to say as little as possible, to get to the Pan-american Complex in a taxi, speak to the police officer, get Ted inside, try to limit the damage.

The impossible had happened. Ted was mad.

True to her word, Emma did not speak until we were in the Phoenix airport. Ted ran to us. I closed my eyes and let him hug me. *You'll be all right, Ted. I promise.*

"Emma Lafayette. You're Ted, I see. How are you?"

"I'm awfully happy to meet you, Emma. Anne and I have to leave right away."

Oh, Ted. He was intentionally not speaking to me.

Emma put both her hands to her face, then slowly shook them off. "I might, what? Should I maybe wait? Is that a good idea? I might, what? I might meet you right at that place—over there." She pointed to a bar. "Or not?"

Ted said, "We'll look for you there. It might be a long wait, yes?"

This won't take long, Ted. To warn her, I said, "If everything works out. We'll look for you. But don't wait for any other reason."

| XIX |

As a Phoenix plainclothes detective held open the door of the station wagon in which Ted and I would travel, he said, "Welcome to Arizona, Mr. and Mrs. Fossicker. It's only a ten-minute drive from here. Or so." I said nothing, feeling that the inordinate planning that had taken place in the space of a few hours made it all the more pitiful.

Once we were under way, Ted said, "Anne. I am going to tell Sarah the truth about all this. Don't you think?"

I don't really believe we'll ever have a chance to talk to Sarah again. "Oh, yes, Ted. The facts, right?" It might have been Paul I was talking to; his mind was made up, he was only pretending to solicit my opinion.

Ted was resolute in his silence. Prepared.

I pretended to take note of the local scenery—a series of monochromatic stone-and-glass buildings and tiny little oases out of which palms and strange, stumpy green plants grew. A sharp turn led us onto an almost empty eight-lane highway. As we sped by the lean landscape, the detective increased the level of the air conditioning. I thought it was excessive; for a few minutes I was actually cold. Within five minutes, with the fans blowing away, I was sweating. I couldn't believe human beings wanted to live under the sway of such heat, least of all my parents.

The Panamerican Complex was no more impressive at close range than it had been from a distance of several miles back. All in all, it resembled one of those satellite antenna dishes that collects every bad movie and rock concert ever made and brings them into your home.

Ted helped me out of the backseat into the heat. He walked imperiously to the police cruiser we'd parked behind. There was not a civilian in sight. Not one.

"It will be all right," Ted said as he took my hand.

Maybe I shouldn't make him go through with this all the way. I could go up to the apartment alone, make up some crazy lie? Mom, somehow I never got off the plane in Chicago and here I am.

But Ted was on a mission. He let go of my hand near the elevator in the tiny carpeted lobby, walked over to a RECEPTION sign. He rang a doorbell that was attached to a paneled wall.

To our surprise, the panel slid as would a glass patio door. The elderly man handed something to Ted and only then said, "You are Theodore Fossicker, I hope."

"Yes, sir. Thank you, sir.'

He's got a key? "They gave you a key to break in with? For God's sake, Ted, let's just make a quick phone call to her and see if she's at home, at least. She might be napping or eating—"

"We'll knock. Anne, would you rather not—you can wait here or with the cruiser if you think—"

"I'll make it." *He'll hurt her. He'll lose his temper when she says she doesn't know what he's talking about. He wants to do that. Even he senses this is a desperate plan.*

"Here we go."

We rode up, headed for the end of the hall. Ted knew the way. All at once he stopped. He turned to me, his face red, veins raised all along his neck. He just raised his hand way up over his head, and with that as his lead, swung himself around, flinging his palm against the thin wall. Guttural and mean, as if his voice had to be physically forced through his constricted throat, he yelled, "How could she? How could she?"

Don't hit me, Ted. Oh, God, don't let him start swinging. Protect me, Jesus. Protect my mother. She's even older.

As if in response to my prayers, the door at the end of the hall swung open. No one emerged. I could imagine an elderly tenant doing that and then hiding, hoping to scare off whoever was banging around in the hall. It worked. Ted just stared at the belt of light that was now free to spill out of the apartment.

"Look at that, Anne." Ted was in front of me, facing the light. "It's actually as if it is all right." He waited until I was at his side, then got me positioned in front of him. He directed me through the opened door. The beam of light was emanating from a spotlight that hung from the wall, under which was stuck a metal sign: MAKE SURE YOU SEE WHO IS ASKING FOR ENTRY.

Beyond the entry light, the apartment was dim. I turned to Ted. "I hope this is at least the right apartment. My mother's, I mean."

"Shh, darling. Shh. Your father is asleep." My mother was standing there, all made up, in a new white suit with a shiny yellow blouse. "Come on into the living room, dear. Hello, Ted."

Please be surprised, Mom. Think about it. Why are we here?

My mother waited for me to sit, motioned to Ted to come all the way into the living room. "I've got some coffee for you both and—"

In a normal tone of voice that sounded like bellowing in contrast to my mother's stage whispers, Ted said, "Where is she?"

"She's not here, for God's sake, Ted." I was exasperated with him and wanted my mother to be clear on this.

My mother pointed to a little suitcase, the size of a throw pillow. "That's her bag. But I thought first we should just take a minute to clear up what happens now that—"

"What? You want me to believe you have her? Who set you up, Mom? Who did you talk to? Did they tell you to humor him? No. Just tell him that you—"

Now Ted bellowed. "Where?"

My mother moved her finger, pointed toward a white door. It was slightly ajar. We all watched it swing full open. Sarah moved just beyond the threshold, stood there, happy as could be, nervous about coming forward. "Hi. Are you looking for me?"

I was lost, Sarah.

Ted literally fell to his knees. He was letting out huge breaths, sobbing. "Yes, Sarah." His voice was so soft. "We've been look-ing for you."

I was so afraid she would disappear if I even twitched. "Keep your eyes on her, Ted. Keep her here." I couldn't see, really. Hours and days and nights that had not passed, they were passing now in her presence, making me shudder as time expanded, letting me go. I finally made it to Ted, just put my hands on his head.

Sarah looked confused. *Afraid?* She shrugged her shoulders. Then she lifted her arms straight out to either side, let them fall, slapping her hands against her hips. *Like wings.* "Can you maybe just keep me from now on?" She ran to us.

What? Hours, maybe days later, Ted and I loosened our ringlike embrace, just to look at her between us.

She was crying and wagging her head. "We're happy, right?"

Ted managed to say, "Yes, ma'am."

| XX |

At some point Ted noticed that my mother had left the room. It brought us all to attention. He carried Sarah to the sofa, sat with her in his arms. "Sarah? Do you know that we didn't want you to be away from us?"

The perfect victim, she lowered her head, defeated. *Blame me.* "Gram was in the parking lot at school. Back at St. Cecilia's. She was waving when I got off the bus. I went over to her." She looked at me, then she stopped.

Blame me, Sarah. Not you. "I love you, Sarah. I want you to tell me. I know you didn't want to leave."

"I told Gram I couldn't go 'cause of the Brownies meeting. And she was real sad, too. I even went to find my Sister Clare, to ask her, but she was somewhere. So I went back to Gram since she said it was up to us what to do and she wanted me to come with her here." She had recounted this series of events hundreds of times, that much was clear.

There may be no more hellish sight than the face of a child testifying to abuse.

How do we live with our children?

Ted took her in deeper. To me, he said, "I think the rest can be put together later. She knows. Oh, Sarah. We're here."

Don't blame me, Sarah. I went to Ted and Sarah, held his head against me. "I need something more. More than facts. I'll be down in—soon. I need this."

"We can all stay." Ted was rocking Sarah.

"No we can't. I'm not giving this to her." *Save Sarah.* "I want this to die with me."

"We'll wait at the other end of the hall. There's a big window. We'll wait there." Ted stood.

Sarah had fallen asleep in his arms. She came to, looked at him, and just cried.

Courage was my proximity to him. They moved from me and I panicked.

I heard Ted say, "We won't even go to the elevator until Mom is with us. Okay?"

Save Sarah. "Ted?" I waited for him to turn to me. "Don't let go of her? And, Ted?" *You will make words of this.* "Ted? Don't let go of me?"

"I just don't know *how* . . . to let go. I don't know how."

I heard the door close behind them.

So did my mother. She walked from the room where my father was asleep. *Is he asleep? Can this be?*

My mother was carrying an overstuffed envelope. "This is your money. I was going to use it for Sarah."

"What? Did you think you could just keep her? You could pretend?" *Stop yelling.*

"It *is* your money. Or Ted's. I've never spent one dime you've sent to me." She was blank, a cipher, a parody of a mother. "You may as well take it now. I will never touch it."

What are the symptoms of Alzheimer's anyway? "For some reason, all I want to know is how." A complete lie. I hoped if she told me how, I would understand why, what she thought she was doing.

"I don't think that is necessary." She sat on the sofa.

I don't think that is necessary. I don't want you seeing boys who aren't Catholic. I don't see why you waste your time thinking about such things. I don't want these kinds of books read in my house. I don't want to discuss it. Because I said so. "You're not my mother. A mother does not take a child away from a mother. She doesn't. You are a criminal." I screamed, "I want the facts! You give them to me now or you tell them to a jury."

"Keep your voice down. Fine. Fine. You want to dwell on that, fine."

I want to bury that. All of it.

"I got on a plane on Thursday evening. You might say on the spur of the moment. An impulse. You didn't want to take care of that child. With your job this fall and all. The Brownies. Really. And day care."

You think I'm alive to you. No, lady. I'm dying as we speak. Finish the job.

"Well, that was the hardest part. Getting to your neck of the woods. You have to admit, that Connecticut airport is ridiculous. I had to fly from Phoenix to Chicago to get a flight to Connecticut. It's really the middle of nowhere. I even stayed in a hotel."

She is bragging?

"I went to the school in my rented car first thing Friday, to meet her school bus. I knew she'd be in her Brownie uniform. That poor child, with a knapsack bigger than her little back. And she got in with me—"

"She didn't want to. There are witnesses who saw her in the school building. Looking for her teacher. Crying for God's sake."

"She's never cried before?" My mother stood up, raging. "Of course, I'd have to ask Sister Clare or a day care lady. How in the world would you know? You were at work. Or you and Ted were out to some fancy dinner."

The wealthier you are the worse your nightmares. Hospitals and colleges are built because the rich get guilty as they get old. Think about how big a camel is and just how small the eye of the needle is.

She stopped pacing. Lost in thought. "I got mixed up with

all the signs for that airport of yours. I thought I was going to end up in Boston. In a rental car. It's impossible to tell around there. So I called Carol." She looked at me with utter disdain. "I know you know all this. I spoke with that police officer friend of yours at your house today. I knew something was up. Are you satisfied?"

Well, now your mother has had to go and make a fool of herself in front of the whole town of Braintree, going into that hospital emergency room in her backyard because you don't listen and you end up vomiting. Are you satisfied, young lady?

"But you loved me, Mom. You did. Why this?" I could not resurrect normal emotion. She had always done this, drained the life out of a fear or hurt. Thwarted a complaint against the world, against her.

"Please take the money when you leave. I hope you'll think twice about pressing charges." She walked away from me, to the window.

"Dad? Did he say anything?" I don't know what I expected.

"He believed me. That you were . . . I told him you were having problems, that you were sick. I said the same thing to him that I said to Sarah. He had no reason to doubt me, that you were a little . . . not up to things."

Shh, darling, your father is asleep. Your father is tired. Your father is trying to watch the ball game. Your father doesn't want you to see that boy again. Your father is asleep.

"Does Carol know?"

She turned to me. *You are a fool.* "Do you think I announced this? Be sensible. Why would I tell Carol?"

"Why not?" I'd tapped an emotion. "If it was for the best? It was just the thing to do, another impulse of yours? Why the hell not? Why not call me up and tell me I'm a goddamn failure and you can't stand by and watch me ruin the kids?" I was accelerating, finally. "Because it is not true. Say it. I am not bad. I love her. Ted is good. Do you hear me? My way of living is good. You hear me yet? My name is Anne. And my other name is Fossicker. I took a new name. I have a new name. Look at me. Anne Fossicker and Ted Fossicker and Sarah Fossicker and Patricia Fossicker and Paul Fossicker. Do you hear me?"

"Your name was Johnson first. No matter what you think."

The child is dead. Don't try to save the child. Save Anne. For Ted, for Sarah. Save Anne.

"She didn't make it."

My mother returned to the envelope. "Take this when you go. Don't blame me if it doesn't make you happy."

"I don't blame you." It had emerged from the same source as the anger. I rued it. I wanted it back. I wanted a different ending.

"Oh, don't be silly. You rant and rave—"

"I can't. That's what I hate. That I can't. Anne Johnson. I blame her. She was always hiding, hiding everything. How could you have known? What did she expect? She was so afraid."

"I didn't hurt Sarah. I took care of her like she was mine. I didn't hurt her."

"Sarah doesn't belong to anybody."

I could see her retreating into some private, tiny quarters that admitted no visitor, no one. When she spoke, it was from far away, as a child might sound when cajoled into speaking from a perch on her bed to a parent leaning on the other side of the bedroom door. "It wasn't something I planned, Anne. I can't explain it, but I just seized the opportunity. I knew it wouldn't last. I thought maybe it would make you reconsider. I know how much you love her. I thought if you could only see how easily it could all be gone . . ."

I'm sorry, Mom. I didn't mean to, Mom. I thought you liked him, Mom.

What is loved can die; it will not disappear. I could see the child now, within the boundary marked by the irregular ruins of the wall. Ever the sentinel, her back was to me. She kept watch over the strange garden she'd once believed would live, as she herself might live.

All this I could see as I looked down at my mother. Through her.

My mother ran her hand across the still-unstained flowery vines embroidered on her sofa. She walked back to the window and turned her back on me.

Like the girl in the garden. Forever I see them as I saw them at that moment. Facing away from me. But seeing what I always see in the foreground. The impossible happiness of my immortal childhood.

DOCUMENTATION

I STILL HAVEN'T found God, exactly. Emma Lafayette, the only living person to whom I've tried to explain this quest, told me that a woman looking for Him in the world (she tried but could not get me to tell her what I mean by "in the world") is something like an unmarried middle-aged man scouting around for the perfect wife. "The last thing a guy like that wants is the perfect wife."

But Emma visits two or three times a year, on her way to Yale or New York City. I may turn something up yet.

What I did turn up, three and a half years out of date, is the letter I wrote to my parents on the occasion of their retirement to Phoenix. Naturally, I was cleaning house.

The Fossickers left the house that Ted built on a hill in Fairfield County only months after they were reunited. Despite our best efforts to downplay the circumstances under which Sarah was restored to us, school friends and neighbors were anxious to talk to the television and newspaper people. The story became a morality play, a feel-good feature, a Real Life Drama. Worst of all, because our resistance was low and we didn't know any better, the whole thing became definitive.

I actually believed that it was our lot, and that we might just as well make the most of it. My idea was to have us all keep track of how we felt about things, day to day. I even began a family diary. As Patricia said, having failed to enter as much as a sentence for an entire week, "I don't know what it means, if that's what you're waiting for. It's like a lot of things that happen."

That's the problem. It is like a lot of things and yet it's as if nothing like it ever happened in the history of the world. Because it happened to me this time.

Ted suspected that our lot lay elsewhere; specifically, near the border of Greenwich, Connecticut, on which stood the block of a house that he now fondly refers to as the American Dream Palace. We moved into our new quarters on the second day of 1985.

Patricia and Paul were thrilled to be released into the public school system. In late September I'd pulled Sarah out of St. Cecilia's and enrolled her in a private day school. At St. Cecilia's she'd refused to write or read as long as Clare remained dead and unavailable for Brownie meetings. My first impulse had been to have Sarah see a school counselor or a psychiatrist. After a few introductory meetings, during which Sarah demonstrated an exemplary understanding of the facts of her recent life ("Mrs. Fossicker, do you realize that your daughter may have some reason to find it difficult to respond to the normal classroom atmosphere? We have to bear in mind that there has been some disruption in her routine."), Ted suggested that we try another school before submitting Sarah to analysis.

"It's like sending her to a graveyard every day," Ted said as if he knew this, as if he remembered daily visits to graves that could not contain ghosts.

The transfer worked, ostensibly. Sarah allowed herself to be schooled. Still, her lack of protest about being yanked out of the private school and being enrolled in the Greenwich public school system worried me. She did raise a single condition, that she not be expected to join another set of Brownies. "I only did them at St. Cecilia's 'cause of how Sister Clare was there. Sister Clare's dead."

Sister Clare dead. A grandmother kidnapper. Three schools before a semester of first grade is completed.

The facts of life. Really.

Like Paul—or, more realistically, Paul like her—Sarah first rejected and then dismissed her grandmother. My mother. Neither of them sensed an outstanding attachment to their grandfather. My father. I can see that this was the path of least resistance for them, since Ted brings to them no parents who might stir their awareness of the generation at two removes.

My mother refused to communicate with me (she went so far as to have my name stricken from the list that Carol uses for distribution of her irregular family newsletters). Since I found it impossible to express—often enough just to think about—my love for her, my need to restore her to motherhood, without conditions (*Save Sarah. Leave Anne Johnson out of this.*), I even sympathized with Sarah and Paul.

More problematic was Patricia's intention to respond to a letter she'd received from her grandmother. My mother. The short note from Phoenix arrived on the eve of Patricia's junior prom.

"Patricia, I think you need to understand that it makes me nervous, just the idea of you being in touch with your grandmother. I mean, she's made it hard on all of us to know what to do, exactly." *Give me the letter, Patricia. I want to have that letter.*

"I just want to tell her that I'm alive. Not that I think what she did was good. Maybe I forgive her." *Why can't you?*

"You forgive her? Aren't we the gracious one all of a sudden. You forgive her for what she did to Sarah? What she did to all the rest of us? Since when are you the family ambassador?" *Give me the letter.*

"She's still my grandmother."

"She's still my mother."

"She can write to me when I go to college. You won't know then. I can do what I like then." *Don't threaten me.*

Not under my roof. Not while you're living in my house. Not if I have anything to say about it, young lady. I had a store of such wisdom to unleash. *It's Patricia. It's your daughter.* "You're right. It's your choice."

"What?"

"I trust you. I don't know what you think. Maybe you can forgive her, Patricia. Maybe someone has to. I don't really think I want to know what you decide. I'm standing here looking at you and you know what I'm thinking? 'This is not coming across to her.' You know? I'm a mess on this issue, Patricia. But there is not a right or a wrong thing to do here, on its own merits. I am not daring you. I am telling you I don't know what you should do. And I wish I did."

"Like you'll be happy if I write to her? Come off it."

"I don't want you to have to think about this. But—there's the letter. You have to think about it." *I would still like to have a gander at that letter, Patricia.*

"I don't know what I should do." Patricia was embarrassed to admit this.

"You don't have to decide today. It took her a few years to get in touch. You get to think about it. But, one thing. If you want me to be part of the decision, you have to know that I start out against it. It may not be fair. Just a fact. I hate to say this, but I mean it. I don't need to know what you decide. It's your decision."

Patricia eyed me suspiciously, then smiled. "She didn't say anything in the letter except she thinks about me. And how people make mistakes." *You've made mistakes, haven't you?*

"Even people who love you make them." *Mistakes! It was an accident?*

"Anyway, I don't know what I want to do."

"If you want to talk about it I can only say I'll try to be calm. No promises. Okay?" *Go ahead, show me the letter.*

"Thanks." *Other kids see their grandparents twice a year and get Christmas gifts.*

Other kids are not the Fossickers.

It was a beginning. Patricia was willing not to say it. I was willing not to say it. Somehow we'd both learned that it was not enough to be what we'd learned to be. We'd both had handicapped teachers. We were learning how not to hurt each other in spite of how we'd learn to love each other.

I don't know what she finally did about the letter, or with the letter itself. Preliminary searches of the downstairs (*Maybe she wants me to find it.*) turned up nothing—nothing but a desire to control a daughter who doesn't need controlling and to pretend, if only for the minute of the reading, that my mother needed me. *Use facts. And spare your daughter.* I called off the search.

But one of the facts is that it didn't happen to Patricia. It didn't happen to me, much as I am haunted and encompassed by the shadow it casts. Week after week I remind myself, or Ted reminds me, that it happened to Sarah. *Save Sarah.*

Sadly enough, it is not the circumstance or even the event that Sarah savors as she might a strangely sour candy, enthralled by its strangeness even as she rejects it. Foremost in her memory of the day she was abducted (*Sarah was abducted by my mother.*) is that she could not find Sister Clare and, failing that, made the wrong decision. Sarah chose to climb aboard that rental car. Sarah made the Big Mistake.

Decisions aren't what they used to be. A school bake sale might generate a week of interviews with every family member and several friends before an unsatisfactory choice is dictated by the late hour. Conversely, no barrage of ready answers to the hypothetical problems she poses will assuage a simple concern like, "Will I get up in time to make the bus tomorrow morning?" I've had forty-five-minute discussions with her, during which I assert that it is unlikely that I will oversleep, my alarm will fail to ring, Ted will have to rush to work and will forget to wake me, Paul will shut off his alarm and fall back to sleep, Patricia will leave the house in a hurry to catch a ride with a newly licensed friend, and Sarah herself will simply not hear her alarm; more unlikely still that all of this will happen on a single morning. And I've listened as she gets herself out of bed, runs across her dark bedroom above the kitchen six or seven times to check the alarm button on her clock radio.

And then I hear my mother say, "I didn't hurt her."

And then I remind myself that each of my three children has a store of remembered punishments, misunderstandings, and simple loneliness to raise above my nightly assertion: "I love you."

So I try to live by Ted, next to him, and according to my love for him, which is less assuming, less didactic than the love a mother has to offer. Even Ted isn't perfect, and neither is my love for him, of course. Which explains the God business. Having dashed hope as a way of being, and seeing that I am still incapable of loving selflessly, perfectly, I suspect that I've overlooked an intermediary step that is somewhere in the world but not seen. Somewhere above hope but beneath love? It's as if I would use that step and not need it. Something about this God in the world would be like stepping out of myself so I could simply love. I mean love simply, without conditions, without mistakes.

As Emma said, "If you manage that one, sister, then it will all be true. Anne will evaporate and Ted will have found the perfect wife."

I dont' mind the evaporation part so much; but imagine being born again as the perfect wife.

In the meantime, I have found a nearly perfect boss. Determined to understand the fact that working was not the Big Mistake, and having given up most of what I thought it was to be a Mother, working descended to its proper level, as a component part of a life. Editing the bimonthly *Where in the World?* for the local museum association has made me think again, and interact, and it excuses the condition of the kitchen floor. And it's not full time, though my schedule is often cramped. And if I am not a woman of this world, what can I ask of my daughters? And, and, and . . . But I have this boss, who isn't bothered when I call to say I want to work at home, who was confused when I asked permission to have Sarah do her homework in our single, huge office when I stay after three o'clock—confused that I should ask at all. The boss's name is Mary Ann.

I was an imperfect witness by myself. I also had to see through Ted's eyes; I didn't see Sarah by myself. So Ted shouldn't be the sole witness to the world beyond. I must look. I must see, too.

Because the witness is witnessed. Sarah will not look and see only that I have kept the fondest things in my heart. She will see that those things belong in the world beyond the garden wall. In real soil seeds give way to plants that thrive, others that die. She may feel, as I have felt, that a seedling is a tender, lovely thing. But she will also see that she has work to do. In real soil, only the dullest, hardiest plants will thrive without cultivation. And even after months and years of labor she will see that some lovely fragile flowers die. But they will die. She won't forget them all but they will not be seen.

We are not only witnesses, any of us. We're meant to watch and bring to bear what we have learned.

Of course, I haven't exactly got a green thumb. And presently I have a task ahead of me. I have to lock the door and walk away from the house that Ted built.

For two years we rented the house on a hill to a brilliant young engineer who'd come to Fairfield County to redesign the computer software for a local aeronautics company. And, as Janet Ameron tells it, to sleep with as many neighboring wives as time permitted. She claims that it was only because among the furniture we'd left for the tenant were our master bedroom pieces that she remained on the familiar side of fidelity. "His nickname is the Programmer. And the Digital Don Juan."

Seeing that everything—dishes, linens, beds—was exactly as we'd left it, I wished we'd sold the house immediately.

What did I expect?

Mirrors on the ceilings, maybe. A heap of broken plates.

Renting instead of selling had been a concession to me. I thought it ought to mean something to Ted, his first home in America. He said he'd built a hundred others like it, in a hundred other undistinguished towns.

But Sarah had come back to us here. Patricia, Paul, and Sarah had been born to us here. Ted could only say, "That wasn't exactly what I was thinking about when I built it."

But I had come here. *As if to Eden.*

"We have a couple of choices, Anne." Ted was sitting with Patricia at our dining room table, filling out a financial-aid questionnaire. "Patricia can go to the University of Chicago and we sell the house, or Patricia can go be a maid for whatever tenant you find for the old house."

The old house.

I've spent three days here, waiting for something, wandering from empty room to empty room. All but the kitchen chairs and table was dragged away for resale. Beneath the stack of linens in a built-in closet in the upstairs hall I found the letter to my parents.

Mom and Dad—

How your love does shine on me. How time past and present comes together now.

Enough.

For more than fifteen years I'd struggled to tell the same story and get the happy ending. It was a lovely story, I'd heard it told a million times. In some way, with this letter, I was on the very last page: I'd figured out the happy ending. I could tell the story to my children. And they could pass it on.

Like committing the perfect crime. That's what Ted said years ago when I wagged the letter to my parents and told him that the only reason I could imagine having written such outright lies was to prove that I could do it.

What I didn't know then is that anyone can do it. Even a child.

AN
AMENDED
ARTICLE OF
FAITH

I STILL THINK that introspection is a kind of expressway to unhappiness, but it may be the only alternative to sitting around and committing the perfect crime, accidentally or not. I may never really give up this business of looking into myself: I am only determined to carry it on in the world. Without walls. That way, Ted and the kids can see me. And so can anyone else who might be out here.

About the Author

Michael Downing was born in Pittsfield, Massachusetts. The youngest of nine children, he was graduated from Harvard College in 1980. He has worked as a staff editor and contributor at *Harvard Magazine, Oceanus,* and *FMR.* He lives in Cambridge, Massachusetts.

VINTAGE
CONTEMPORARIES

"Today's novels for the readers of today." — VANITY FAIR

"Real literature—originals and important reprints—in attractive, inexpensive paperbacks." — THE LOS ANGELES TIMES

"Prestigious." — THE CHICAGO TRIBUNE

"A very fine collection." — THE CHRISTIAN SCIENCE MONITOR

"Adventurous and worthy." — SATURDAY REVIEW

"If you want to know what's on the cutting edge of American fiction, then these are the books you should be reading."
— UNITED PRESS INTERNATIONAL

On sale at bookstores everywhere, but if otherwise unavailable, may be ordered from us. You can use this coupon, or phone (800) 638-6460.

Please send me the Vintage Contemporaries books I have checked on the reverse. I am enclosing $ _____ (add $1.00 per copy to cover postage and handling). Send check or money order—no cash or CODs, please. Prices are subject to change without notice.

NAME _____

ADDRESS _____

CITY _____ STATE _____ ZIP _____

Send coupons to:
RANDOM HOUSE, INC., 400 Hahn Road, Westminster, MD 21157
ATTN: ORDER ENTRY DEPARTMENT
Allow at least 4 weeks for delivery.

VINTAGE
CONTEMPORARIES

___ **Love Always** by Ann Beattie	$5.95	74418-7
___ **First Love and Other Sorrows** by Harold Brodkey	$5.95	72970-6
___ **The Debut** by Anita Brookner	$5.95	72856-4
___ **Cathedral** by Raymond Carver	$4.95	71281-1
___ **Bop** by Maxine Chernoff	$5.95	75522-7
___ **Dancing Bear** by James Crumley	$5.95	72576-X
___ **One to Count Cadence** by James Crumley	$5.95	73559-5
___ **The Wrong Case** by James Crumley	$5.95	73558-7
___ **The Last Election** by Pete Davies	$6.95	74702-X
___ **A Narrow Time** by Michael Downing	$6.95	75568-5
___ **Days Between Stations** by Steve Erickson	$6.95	74685-6
___ **Rubicon Beach** by Steve Erickson	$6.95	75513-8
___ **A Fan's Notes** by Frederick Exley	$7.95	72915-3
___ **A Piece of My Heart** by Richard Ford	$5.95	72914-5
___ **The Sportswriter** by Richard Ford	$6.95	74325-3
___ **The Ultimate Good Luck** by Richard Ford	$5.95	75089-6
___ **Fat City** by Leonard Gardner	$5.95	74316-4
___ **Within Normal Limits** by Todd Grimson	$5.95	74617-1
___ **Airships** by Barry Hannah	$5.95	72913-7
___ **Dancing in the Dark** by Janet Hobhouse	$5.95	72588-3
___ **November** by Janet Hobhouse	$6.95	74665-1
___ **Fiskadoro** by Denis Johnson	$5.95	74367-9
___ **The Stars at Noon** by Denis Johnson	$5.95	75427-1
___ **Asa, as I Knew Him** by Susanna Kaysen	$4.95	74985-5
___ **A Handbook for Visitors From Outer Space** by Kathryn Kramer	$5.95	72989-7
___ **The Chosen Place, the Timeless People** by Paule Marshall	$6.95	72633-2
___ **Suttree** by Cormac McCarthy	$6.95	74145-5
___ **The Bushwhacked Piano** by Thomas McGuane	$5.95	72642-1
___ **Nobody's Angel** by Thomas McGuane	$6.95	74738-0
___ **Something to Be Desired** by Thomas McGuane	$4.95	73156-5
___ **To Skin a Cat** by Thomas McGuane	$5.95	75521-9
___ **Bright Lights, Big City** by Jay McInerney	$5.95	72641-3
___ **Ransom** by Jay McInerney	$5.95	74118-8
___ **River Dogs** by Robert Olmstead	$6.95	74684-8
___ **Norwood** by Charles Portis	$5.95	72931-5
___ **Clea & Zeus Divorce** by Emily Prager	$6.95	75591-X
___ **A Visit From the Footbinder** by Emily Prager	$6.95	75592-8
___ **Mohawk** by Richard Russo	$6.95	74409-8
___ **Anywhere But Here** by Mona Simpson	$6.95	75559-6
___ **Carnival for the Gods** by Gladys Swan	$6.95	74330-X
___ **Myra Breckinridge and Myron** by Gore Vidal	$8.95	75444-1
___ **The Car Thief** by Theodore Weesner	$6.95	74097-1
___ **Taking Care** by Joy Williams	$5.95	72912-9